HARM

HARM

HUGH FRASER

URBANE
Publications

urbanepublications.com

First published in Great Britain in 2015 by Urbane Publications Ltd
Suite 3, Brown Europe House, 33/34 Gleamingwood Drive,
Chatham, Kent ME5 8RZ
Copyright © Hugh Fraser, 2015

A CIP catalogue record for this book is available from the British Library.

ISBN 978-1-910692-73-8

Design and Typeset by Daniel Goldsmith Associates, Cheshire
and Julie Martin
Cover by Oliver Bennet at Daniel Goldsmith Associates and Julie Martin
Printed and bound by CPI Group (UK) Ltd, Croydon, CR0 4YY

urbanepublications.com

The publisher supports the Forest Stewardship Council® (FSC®), the leading international forest-certification
organisation. This book is made from acid-free paper from an FSC®-certified provider. FSC is the only
forest-certification scheme supported by the leading environmental organisations, including Greenpeace.

1

MEXICO, 1974

The armoured glass revolving door twitches into motion as I enter its orbit and sweeps me firmly into the foyer of the Acapulco Flamingo Resort Hotel. In its vast atrium, towering coconut palms glower malevolently, as if resenting the brilliantly coloured birds that flit busily between them. Glass lifts waft silently up and down, flaunting their superiority over nature. A diminutive busboy approaches me with intent upon my suitcase and my local currency. I ignore him, inhale a lungful of conditioned air and walk towards the reception desk, passing five mutations of the species cocktail bar, deployed around a sunken aquarium, offering infinite varieties of alcoholic fruit salad. In the ethnic version, a gypsy quartet, wearing overlarge sombreros and a collective rictus grin, sing four-part harmony with depressing jollity. Jaded waiters lurk beside pillars, embalmed in contempt for the guests, who they irritate with their unnecessary presence.

The receptionist greets me with vacuous enthusiasm and runs through the checking-in procedure. I obtain a key, repel the busboy and head for the lifts. The foyer dwindles below as I glide to the fifth floor and step out into a long curving corridor that gradually relieves me of my sense of direction as I move along it. The room offers a minimal array of comforts with its functional layout and moulded surfaces, but I note the sizeable mini bar beneath the TV and the pristine bathroom. After putting down my suitcase, unplugging the telephone and closing the velour curtains on the view of the atrium, I lie on the bed. Shrinking gratefully into myself, I vacate my personality and drift into sleep.

A knock wakes me. It could be hours later. I arrived in the early afternoon and now there is no light edging the curtains as I switch on the bedside lamp and move to the door. I look through the spy hole. It is Randall, suitably distorted by the lens, unless some effect of altitude or cabin pressure during the flight has caused his face to bulge hideously. I contemplate with some pleasure the catastrophic effect this would have on this narcissist, with whom it is my misfortune to share responsibilities, for the immediate future. He knocks again and a ripple of irritation corrugates his distended features. I am tempted to ignore him and prolong my solitary confinement but I open the door and smile.

'Hey,' he says.

Randall is a manner masquerading as a person. He has exchanged any individuality he might have possessed for a repertoire of gestures, physical and verbal, stolen from people who he perceives as having 'made it', and he's beginning to resemble a ventriloquist's dummy.

'Looking good,' he says.

Randall wants to sleep with me. All men, apart from

homosexuals, paedophiles and the very old, want to sleep with me. I am not a classic beauty by any means but I have 'it'. 'It' is what makes a woman sexually attractive to men. When a woman has 'it' she will dedicate herself to her conquest with Napoleonic determination, devoting years to the project if necessary. I have spent a large proportion of my life since the age of thirteen enduring the overtures of men with designs on my body, whose seduction techniques have run the gamut from acquainting me with Kierkegaardian philosophy in candle-lit private dining rooms to bellowing "Fancy a fuck?" across a pub car park.

'Eight-thirty?' says Randall.

'What?'

'Meeting?'

Inflecting everything as a question is Randall's way of implying that he is reminding you of something you have been stupid enough to forget, even though he is giving you information you could not possibly have obtained.

'Where?' I ask.

'Martin's suite?'

'What number?'

'Pick you up ...?'

'What number?' I repeat.

'Six nineteen?'

'Right.'

'Drink first?

'No, I have ... er ...'

I gesture vaguely back into the room and dismiss him with a smile which will leave him wondering if he should try his luck again later. I really ought to tell him I'm a lesbian living with a black cab driver, then he can spend a few weeks trying to figure out whether I meant the cab or the driver and give me some peace.

I shut the door and check the shower. Moderate pressure. When I turn on the TV, Richard Nixon bangs on about the war on drugs. I open my suitcase, shove some clothes into the wardrobe and take out my gun, wondering idly why I always wrap it in underwear when I travel. It sits heavily in my hand. I pop the magazine, fill it with ten rounds from the toe of a shoe and slide it back in with a little more force than necessary.

I ponder the odds of staying alive beyond the weekend. I like the simplicity of crime, it has pure lines, a sharp silhouette and a great buzz. A corporation plunges an entire country into poverty for a spike in the share price. A government murders tens of thousands for some bullshit ideology dreamt up by stupid old men. Crime between consenting adults is clean, and fair-minded.

I take a shower and select a light suit for the meeting. I have been hired by Martin and Randall to take care of a drug dealer called Rodolfo Cortez who has failed to honour an agreement. We're posing as property developers looking to buy land for development in a nearby town called San Marcos, a cover that legitimises our presence here and allows us to move around while we find Rodolfo Cortez, exact revenge, and consolidate Martin's reputation, here and in London. We know where Cortez is based, but not his exact location. I walk along the curved corridor. Two

American teenaged girls in wet bikinis slouch along ahead of me, mumbling everyday discontent. I reach Martin's suite and knock. Randall opens the door. 'Hey.'

In the living room, Martin, a powerful six-footer with a shaved head, broad shoulders and a bull neck, stands with his back to the Pacific Ocean conjuring millions of dollars into the space between him and three Mexican estate agents, who are sitting together on a long leather sofa. The estate agents are under the impression that they are being commissioned to negotiate the purchase of the land in San Marcos and handle the sale of the development once it is built. They are young and well-dressed in light linen suits. One, tall and languid with a thin moustache, appears to be trying to maintain a distance from a short, plump little man who sits next to him and fidgets with a pad on his knee. Their colleague at the other end of the sofa is thin and wiry with a mop of dark curly hair and a preoccupied look.

Martin introduces me and I sit in an armchair, taking a sheaf of brochures, architects' drawings of the proposed resort development and various flow charts from my briefcase and laying them on the coffee table as Martin blathers on about projects we have supposedly completed in Portugal and Greece and our desire to meet with the relevant government officials for planning consents and allocation of services. I must say he does all this rather well, his Essex twang giving him a certain rough diamond credibility. Randall has apparently been instructed to keep his mouth shut and it only remains for me to slip in a few remarks in my posh p.a. voice and cross and uncross my legs a couple of times. I put a note in the diary for a trip to San Marcos the following afternoon as Martin wraps things up. The estate agents gather up the brochures, assure us of their enthusiasm and support for our exciting project, wish us a happy stay in their wonderful country and leave.

'Cool?' says Randall.

Martin ignores him and sits beside me on the sofa. 'Hello, doll.'

I ignore the insult, pour myself a Tequila, and cross to the window to take in the magnificent subtropical coastline resting below me. I tune out whatever aspect of the obvious Randall is busy pointing out and consider that one of the advantages enjoyed by the career criminal is the freedom to behave among colleagues exactly as he, or she, cares to. Executives in other fields of business are constrained to put others at ease with gentle wit and pleasant conversation. Among criminals, a repulsive personality is a distinct advantage and can often instil essential fear and respect without the necessity for precursory violence. Friendship is dangerous, it encourages trust, the prerequisite of betrayal; almost always the cause of things coming unstuck.

Martin comes to stand beside me at the window. 'Went OK?' he asks.

'So we've got access. Now what?' I reply.

'Since we're here, we might as well have a look at a couple of other opportunities.'

'What about Rodolfo?'

'I thought you might find out where he is and shoot him in the head.'

'While you open a gift shop on the prom?'

'Something like that, yeah.'

Martin is a pit bull. He is good but impulsive. He's clearly entertaining fantasies of hijacking the Mexican drug trade and ought to be disabused of them before he gets himself killed. Since I'm merely associated with him for the matter in hand, my only interest is to get the job done and return to London.

I look him in the eye and say, 'The deal was that you find him and I do him. If you're going to fuck about, I'll get on a plane tomorrow.'

He gives me a hard stare while he considers whether to let a woman tell him what to do, then he glances at Randall and smiles.

'All right, Rina, no need to get your knickers in a twist,' he says.

I give him a look of utter loathing as we arrange to meet in the foyer the next morning, rent a car, and go in search of Cortez.

I leave Martin and Randall deciding where they are going to begin their survey of Acapulco's night life, and return to my room.

I stand at the window watching people come and go across the foyer. The lifts abseil silently up and down. A man seated at a table in one of the bars glances up in my direction before summoning a waiter. I close the curtain, undress and get into bed with Erica Jong.

• • •

I am woken by the Sombrero band murdering La Bamba in the foyer. I open my eyes and turn to look at the time. Martin's severed head is staring at me from the bedside table.

I try to move but can't. It takes me a moment to gain control of the fear, then my body unfreezes and I take the gun from between my legs, look under the bed and move to the corner of the room. I check the wardrobe and walk slowly to the bathroom. Randall's head is leaking blood in the basin. I pull on jeans and a T-shirt, slip into a pair of trainers and pocket passport and money. I am fitting the silencer to my gun, and wondering why I haven't been killed as well, when I hear a key slide into the door. I hold the gun behind my back. The door opens and I recognise the curly-haired estate agent from last night, coming towards me with an AK 47. As he opens his mouth to speak, I jump at him and kick the gun out of his hands. He gets a lucky hold on my weapon and wrenches it away from me. I twist my arm around his neck, grab a ballpoint pen off the dressing table, and jam the sharp end into his ear. He screams and hits the floor. I kneel on top of him, reach for one of my stiletto shoes, and stab the pointed heel into his neck just below his Adam's apple. Blood spurts from the hole and he goes limp.

I hear people approaching along the corridor. I open the window, step onto a ledge below and make my way slowly along it, clinging to a line of raised brickwork at arm's-length above me. In the crowded foyer, people point up at me and security men talk into radios. I look back to see if I am being watched from the room but see no one. As I move along the ledge, something is being shouted in Spanish through a loud hailer. I reach a vertical steel beam. As I climb round it, it starts to hum and vibrate. I look up and see a lift plunging towards me. I pull back onto the ledge as it slices past me and stops a few metres below. I put my arms round the steel beam, slide down it and land on the roof of the lift. The crowd that has gathered below gives something between a gasp and a cheer.

I lie flat as the lift drops to the ground floor, then climb down the side of the cage, put my head down, dive into the crowd and force my way through the press of bodies before the security men can see which direction I go in. I break free of the crowd and sprint for the main doors. Two men run after me but I am through the exit, down the steps and wrenching open the door of a taxi before they hit the fresh air. Breathing hard, I wave my gun at the terrified driver and drag him out. I jump in, start the engine and screech out of the access road onto the main drag.

Cutting through the traffic, bringing the blaring horns to a hysterical crescendo, I see that I am being followed by a black Mercedes. With no idea where I'm going, I swing a U-turn and head for an entry ramp signed to Highway 95D. The Mercedes follows me onto the crowded two-lane highway and settles in behind me. We climb from sea to mountains. When I see a toll booth ahead, I swerve right into the slow lane and brake hard, narrowly avoiding being rear-ended by a truck. The Mercedes overtakes in a cacophony of horns and barges into the inside lane in front of me. I pull the taxi onto the hard shoulder and skid to a halt. I jump the crash barrier and scramble up a steep sandy bank into trees and thick undergrowth which claws at my legs, preventing any serious headway on such a gradient. I turn and see two men, one short and one tall, coming up after me. I recognise the other two estate agents from last night. Two others are aiming rifles at me from the bottom of the bank. I know I am done. I turn towards them, and raise my arms.

They surround me and take me to the Mercedes, making no attempt to hide their weapons from the traffic streaming past. The tall one searches me and takes my passport and money. He opens the rear door and gestures me into the back of the car. The short one opens the door on the other side and sits next to me.

The tall one gets in on my right. As the car moves onto the highway, he turns to me and smiles.

'Cigarette?' he asks.

I shake my head and turn away.

At the toll booth, we are waved through without payment and the car surges into the fast lane. Shorty studies my breasts and begins fondling the left one. I pull away from him. The tall one barks at him in Spanish, leans across me and swings his fist into his face. Shorty yelps as blood explodes from his nose. The man in front raises his rifle, shouts at them and they fall silent.

Since it seems that my life is not immediately in danger, there is little to do but wait to see what my captors want from me. I sit back and take in the rugged scenery as dense vegetation and palm trees give way to emaciated pine trees and scorched scrubland. After a while, we leave the highway and climb up a twisting two-lane road with a sheer drop to the right. I consider diving over the front seat, wrenching the wheel and plunging the car over the edge, but conclude that, even if I survived, I would probably still be outnumbered.

After a few more bends we stop at a pair of iron gates beneath a wrought-iron arch. A high stone wall curves away on each flank. Armed guards open the gates and we continue along a curved, tree- lined driveway. As we emerge from the trees, I am confronted with the most vulgar building I have ever seen. A vast squashed hacienda style wedding cake, oozing arches and porticoes from a bulbous central tower, crawled over by malign-looking creepers and climbers bent on strangling its buttresses and lacerating the dirty white stucco grimly adhering to its ageing shanks. In the precariously balanced bell tower the rusted incumbent hangs limp and impotent, as if embarrassed to toll for this obese monstrosity.

Guards in military-style fatigues, toting AK 47 assault rifles, appear from a pink gazebo beside a kidney-shaped swimming pool as we approach. The car stops in front of the main entrance and I am escorted through the metal studded front door. Inside, the vulgarity continues. A yellow marble staircase with a gold bannister rail curves upwards and becomes a gallery encircling the wide entrance hall. My trainers squeak faintly as we cross the purple marble floor. A door opens at the top of the stairs and an elegant figure in a black silk suit walks slowly down the staircase. The armed guards back away. I hold my ground as he approaches and says, 'Señorita Walker.'

I shake his outstretched hand. His grip is too firm and his dark, hooded eyes contain a warning. He is middle aged, neither short nor tall, and whipcord thin, with smooth serpentine skin drawn over a fine bone structure.

'Please to come this way.'

He ushers me towards double doors, which are opened by my erstwhile captors. We enter a large, high-ceilinged reception room with cut glass chandeliers and fake regency red plush furniture trimmed with gold leaf. Old masters peer glumly at us as if uncomfortable on the pink brocade wallpaper. I expect the Ugly Sisters to flounce in at any moment and order me to sweep the floor. 'I am Manuel. Please to sit. You will have drink? Your usual Scotch whisky?'

I nod, noting his familiarity with my drinking habits. He waves Shorty to the drinks table, and I check that he pours both drinks from the same bottle.

'I am sorry for the necessity of dealing with your friends in this way.'

'They're not my friends.'

'That is good. They serve purpose and now are gone.'

'What purpose?' I ask, as Shorty hands me my drink.

'To bring you here to me, Señorita Walker.'

'You didn't need to cut their heads off to get to me.'

'They cut heads?'

'They cut heads.'

Manuel grabs Shorty's wrist as he sets down his drink and asks him a question. Shorty's answer unleashes a volley of Spanish invective and several vicious blows to the head. Shorty almost falls off his platform shoes as he totters to his position by the door.

'I apologise for my operatives. They were not supposed to cut head, only to kill.'

I begin to get an idea of what could be going on here. They didn't kill me with the others because the cobra here has heard about me from somewhere and wants to use me. My guess is that he somehow arranged for Martin and Randall to be ripped off by Rodolfo so that they would come over here to sort him out, bringing me with them. There's only one way they could be sure Martin would hire me for the job.

'You got to Randall?' I ask.

'Yes.'

The stupid idiot. They will have got the rip-off together with him, on the promise of a big pay day and a career in the drug trade if he convinced Martin to hire me for the trip. I get into Mexico with cover and anonymity and he gets wasted along with Martin.

'I know you will not come for simple invitation.' He got that right.

'What do you want with me?'

'There is a man I wish you to kill.'

'Why?'

'That need not concern you.'

'Why me?' I gesture at the guards. 'You seem to have plenty of local talent.'

'This man is well protected and difficult to get to. He likes beautiful blonde women from the North. You are such a one, and you have the skills required.'

'Who is he?'

'His name is Enrico Gonzales.'

'Is he in the drug business?'

'He is Minister of Justice.'

2

LONDON, 1956

I wake up and nudge Georgie to get out of bed. It's her turn to go and get milk. She groans and turns away, pulling the blanket off me. I stare at the mould on the ceiling and feel the cold on my legs. I get up on one elbow and look at little Jack sleeping on the other side of her, wondering how he always starts off lying between us and ends up next to the wall. Sleep on, Jack, there's not much to wake up for. I get out of bed and put on my skirt, blouse and coat. I take the pot from under the bed and go through the kitchen, past Mum snoring on her mattress on the floor. I unlock the door onto the landing and go down the stairs to the back yard and into the privy with the stinking broken toilet that the nasty Polish landlord won't fix. As I empty the pot, something skitters past my feet and down a hole in the floor. The toilet's nearly overflowing so I poke down into the foul mess with a bent stick we keep there that reaches some way round the bend. A deep groaning comes from somewhere down below and the level in the bowl lowers itself a couple of inches. I straddle it and pee.

I take the pot back upstairs, and then go out the front door and into the street. No one's about this early. The dirty old tenement houses on each side glower down at me, cold and hard. Curtains of old blankets and bits of tattered cloth are closed behind dirty windows.

I pull my coat round me as a bitter wind whips my bare legs and head round the corner and along Golborne Road towards Ladbroke Grove. If I can get to Jean's Café before the milk's delivered I should be able to … I stop dead and duck into an entry as a gang of Teddy Boys come round the corner in front of me, laughing and jostling each other. I know a couple of them from our street and I can see they've been on an all-nighter in some shebeen. They're drunk, pilled up and trouble and I don't feel like being grabbed and felt up this morning, thank you. They see a West Indian bloke on the other side of the street and jeer at him. One of them chucks a stone at the man as he hurries on his way and they move on without seeing me.

I reach the corner of Ladbroke Grove and weave round an old tramp lurching along the pavement snarling some nonsense. I'm in luck. The milk cart is almost at the café. As I get there, I see Jean's boy inside wiping tables. The cart draws up and I go and stroke the horse's head. The milkman's a scrawny old boy with a red face. He gets down and dumps a full crate outside the door of the café. While his back is turned, I slip round the rear of the cart, lift a bottle, put it under my coat and walk slowly back up Ladbroke Grove.

Back in our street, a small, worried-looking man clutching a brown paper bag hurries past me on his way to some job he hates. An old woman in curlers opens a first floor window, shakes some bedding out and leaves it hanging over the windowsill. A toddler in a filthy pullover and no trousers is crying on a front step, banging his fist weakly on the door. He looks appealingly at me but I don't go to him. He's there for a reason and you never interfere. A football bounces towards me as I reach our house. I kick it back to a couple of kids playing in the road and go inside.

The hall isn't much warmer than the street outside. In the kitchen Mum is still snoring. I put the milk on the table and fill the kettle before waking Georgie. She gets out of bed and shuffles through to the kitchen. Jack has wet the bed again and I lift him up and put him on a chair at the kitchen table. I take the wet blanket off the bed, let down the drying rack in the kitchen, hang the blanket on it and hoist it up out of the way, hoping it doesn't drip.

The kettle's boiled and I fill the teapot and put the frying pan on the stove. I pour a glass of milk for Jack and Georgie and cut bread. The dripping in the frying pan melts and I dip slices of bread in it, fold them over and give them one each. Jack doesn't like milk but I've always made him drink it because they say it will stop him getting rickets like some of the other kids in the street.

I put a cup of tea beside Mum and dump the gin bottle in the bin, hoping she doesn't wake up before I take them to school. I put some newspaper and wood bits on the fire, light it and tell Georgie to take Jack to the privy and then get ready for school. She opens the door to the landing and Elvis tells us not to step on his blue suede shoes from upstairs. Lizzie must be up early for once and out of the bed she earns her living in. Her door shuts and a man in a

smart overcoat clatters down the stairs. Georgie pulls Jack
back into the kitchen as the man hurries past, holding his
hat over his face. Georgie looks back at me.

'Go on, you're all right,' I say, as the front door closes.

I coax some coal onto the fire and sit and watch as it
catches and ekes some meagre heat into the room. I look at
Dad's picture in his uniform on the mantlepiece. I wonder
where the old sod is now. I'm glad he left us even though
it's hard without him, with Mum being on the drink and
everything. But I don't miss his shouting and his hitting
and his hands all over me. He left us a wad of money from
some robbery and went on the trot with a young'un. So
we got chucked out of the house in Kensal Green and
moved to these two rooms with a few bits and pieces on a
horse and cart. Now Mum's drinking the money and I'm
stealing food to put on the table and wondering how the
rent will be paid when it runs out, which it will soon.

I put the rusty metal fireguard in place and look for
the kids' coats, which should be hanging behind the door.
Mum has put them over her feet and I take them off her
and shake them out. Georgie and Jack come in and I wet
a cloth under the tap, wipe their faces and hands and put
them into their coats. At least they get a free meal at school
and maybe a chance to get a decent job when they leave.
I left on my fourteenth birthday last year when Dad did
a runner. I never listened or paid attention in the lessons
so I can just about read and write and add up, but not too
well. Barlby Road Primary was rebuilt after the war and
the new classrooms were all fresh paint and clean floors,

but I never knew what the teachers were on about most of the time, so I just messed about with Claire from our street in the back row and got hit with a ruler or cuffed round the ear. We bunked off most days and went up Whiteleys in Queensway until we got chucked out, or over the park until it was time to go home. The school inspector came to our house once but he soon went away again after Dad knocked him out. Dad put me on his knee and we had a laugh about it then, but I want Georgie and Jack to learn things and pass exams and that.

On the way to school Georgie asks me if she can go to her friend Mary's house after. I say she can, although I know I've got to nick some eggs or something for her to take with her. She's had her tea there a few times now and I've got to give them something.

When I drop them at school, Jack won't let go of my hand at the gate. I know he's being bullied because of his clothes getting ripped and messed up and I've told him he's got to stand up for himself. I know who's doing it and I could take care of it myself but he's got to learn to fight and it might as well be now. I push him through the gate, walk up the Grove to the bridge and back along the canal. I get to our street and along to the basement where my mate Claire lives.

Johnny Preston is leaning on the railing combing back his black brylcreemed hair, with a couple of his heavies standing near him, all wearing the drape and the Crombie coats. He's a big man with a reputation for being cruel and vicious. I knew him as one of Dad's mates and I'd heard he was in prison, but he's out now and looking at me. As I go towards the stairs to the basement he moves in front of me.

'Hello, Rina.'

'All right, Johnny?'

'How's your mum these days?'

'She's all right, thanks.'

'Maybe I'll come round and see her.'

'If you want.'

'You're going there now, aren't you?'

'If you like.'

As I turn, I see Claire's scared face at the basement window. It's only a few yards to our house. Johnny follows me up the steps and in through the front door, leaving his two thugs loitering on the pavement. The Irish woman on the ground floor is shouting at her kids as we pass her door.

We go up the stairs and into our kitchen. Mum is sitting at the table with a cup of tea in front of her and a glass of gin raised to her lips.

'Oh my God!' she says, dropping the glass.

'It's all right, Mum,' I say, although I know it isn't. Johnny is looking at Mum and half smiling.

'Now, there's no need to get bothered, Alice.'

'What do you want?' says Mum.

'How about a nice cuppa tea?'

Mum looks at me and I go to the pot by the stove and pour him one. Johnny looks around the kitchen and wanders into the back room. Mum looks at me anxiously and pours herself another gin with a shaking hand.

Johnny comes back in.

'Is this how he left you?' he asks.

Mum looks down at the table, saying nothing. 'You and three kids in two lousy rooms?'

He sits down opposite her.

'Can't be easy. Eh, Alice? After that nice house up Kensal Green?' I put the tea in front of him. He looks up at me.

'Sit down, Rina,' he says.

I sit between the two of them. Johnny unbuttons his coat and leans forward.

'Isn't anyone helping you, Alice?' Mum shakes her head. 'We'll have to see about that.'

Mum looks at him. He takes her hand. 'You know he got shot last night?'

I feel my stomach lurch up into my throat. I think I'm going to be sick.

Mum stares at Johnny. He nods slowly. 'Oh fuck,' she says.

'I'm sorry, Alice. I told him he had to pay them, but he wouldn't do it.' He takes a drink of tea. 'Typical of old Harry, always thinking he could get away with it.'

Mum looks up and says, 'Where was it?

'Bermondsey.'

'Who …?'

'Alice, you know I can't.'

Mum nods and looks down at the table again, breathing heavily. I stand up and get a glass of water from the tap. I feel scared but I don't know why. I don't care about Dad, he was a right bastard and he probably deserved it, but Johnny's up to something and it doesn't take long to find out what.

I turn and lean on the sink as he says, 'So, Alice. That means you and me have a bit of business.'

Mum doesn't look up. 'What business?' she says.

'Where did he put it?'

Mum looks at him. 'Put what?'

'Come on, darling, you know what I mean.'

'What?'

'All that lovely money he stole from them rich people.'

'I don't know about any money.'

'Well, I know you do, Alice.'

'On my life, Johnny, I don't.'

'Now, Alice, there's no need for any aggravation about this …'

'He give us a few quid when he left and that's it.'

'Harry told me, as I sit here, that he told you where he'd hidden it …'

'He never …'

'And if you've got any sense, you're going to tell me where it is.'

'If I knew, we wouldn't be living in a shit hole like this.'

'And if you're very nice to Johnny, he might just see you all right.'

'I swear I don't know.'

'Yes, you fucking do!'

Johnny stands and kicks a chair against the wall.

'I did three years for that bastard and he fucking owes me!'

'Johnny, I don't know …'

'Right, you stupid fucking cow!' Johnny goes to the window and tears back the curtain. He opens the window and whistles to his mates to come in. He takes off his coat, folds it, puts it over a chair and opens the door. The two men enter and stand each side of Johnny. I see that one of them is his runty little brother, Dave, who's a mean little sod.

'Come here, Rina,' he says. I don't move.

Johnny takes a cut-throat razor out of his inside pocket and opens it slowly.

I go round the kitchen table towards him and he grabs my arms, turns me round to face Mum and holds me against him with the razor at my throat.

'She's turned out a nice bit of stuff, hasn't she, boys?' Dave and the other one laugh.

'Who'd a thought an old dog like you and a pig like Harry could make a nice bit of skirt like this, eh?' His hand's on my tits, then it's moving down.

'Johnny …'

Mum starts to get up, but Dave goes behind her and pushes her back into the chair.

'Where the fuck is it?'

'I don't fucking know!'

'Don't fucking know? Don't fucking know?'

Johnny spins me round and throws me onto the table. I feel the gin glass break under my shoulder blade. My legs are wrenched apart and my arms are pinned down. Johnny opens his flies and I scream with pain as his cock gouges into me. A hand's clamped over my mouth. I rip my teeth into it and taste blood. The hand lifts. I scream again. Then a fist hits me and it goes dark.

3

I swallow the rest of my whisky slowly and meet Manuel's eyes. 'So where do I find this Minister of Justice?'

He smiles. I expect a forked tongue to appear. 'What they say of you is true. The professional.' He gets to his feet and beckons the tall one over. 'Roberto, show Señorita Walker to her rooms.'

Turning to me he says, 'We talk later of details. Please now to relax. Perhaps to swim or walk in gardens or what you wish. Adios, Señorita Walker.'

Shorty opens the doors and Manuel leaves. Roberto smiles and indicates the French doors at the far end of the room. He still wears his estate agent's linen suit, and I follow his tall, elegant figure onto the terrace reflecting that, if you are going to be abducted, it may as well be by people with good manners.

He leads me to a bungalow with a flat roof and a tiara of cornice work, one of several beyond the swimming pool. The accommodation within is predictably opulent and completely inappropriate for the sweltering midday heat. Too many ornate tables and chairs of various sizes are dotted about in inconvenient locations. In the large master bedroom, suede leather drapes are tied back to reveal a four-poster bed bearing a gold silk bedspread that Louis the Fourteenth might have coveted. The suede theme continues, via the bloated sofa and armchairs, to the bathroom walls and toilet seat. The pale beige colour lends it a distinct resemblance to human skin. As Roberto bows and turns to leave, a woman in a maid's uniform enters and stands inside the door with her hands folded in front of her. She's about thirty-five years old, petite and pretty with dark hair tied back, and a slim compact figure.

Roberto turns back. 'This Juanita,' he says. She smiles and nods.

I return her smile. 'Hello, Juanita.'

Roberto leaves. A guard with an AK slouches past the window, glancing in as he passes. Juanita and I smile at each other again. Her face has a fine bone structure and her clear brown eyes have a watchful look. She hesitates before indicating the wall of fitted wardrobes. I give her the nod of assent she seems to require and she opens the first one to reveal a rail of dresses and various garments above rows of expensive shoes. She takes out a black silk trouser suit and a silver evening dress and offers them to me. I take the suit and note the Sonya Rykeil label. The dress is by Valentino, and they are both in my size. I put them back on the rail. Fiorucci jeans hang next to Calvin Klein. I am clearly to be dressed in some style for the Minister of Justice. Juanita goes to the dressing table and shows me rows of expensive cosmetics by Dior, Clinique, Chanel, and drawers of underwear and bikinis. The bathroom is similarly well equipped with all a modern girl could need.

Juanita returns to the bedroom and shows me a bell

pull beside the mantelpiece. She tugs at it and says, 'I come. OK?'

'OK,' I say.

Juanita nods and leaves. The guard with the AK glances in again on his return journey.

I sit on the bed and breathe deeply. I am alive, at least for the moment. Even though the job Manuel has for me is well within my area of expertise, I have no intention of doing it. As soon as it is completed, I will be killed so as to preclude any possibility of the murder being traced back to him. I have to escape as soon as possible and leave the country. In the meantime, I have to appear to accept the commission and build Manuel's confidence as far as I can in the hope that he will relax his security sufficiently for me to find an opportunity to make my exit.

The heat bears down on me and I cross to the window. The ultramarine pool glistens outside. I change into a white bikini, walk slowly across the hot tiles of the terrace, ignoring the attention of the several guards deployed around, and dive into the pool.

The water feels like silk, soothing and cooling my skin as I swim around the curves of the pool. I turn over and float on my back, the sky impossibly blue above me, fringed with palms craning inquisitively to inspect their pale-skinned visitor. After a few languid lengths, I paddle to the side, climb the steps, stretch out on a wicker lounger and let the sun ease some of the tension from my body.

Minutes later I hear footsteps. A tall white male stands beside the lounger.

'You wanna cold one?'

I rise onto one elbow, shade my eyes and take the beer he is offering. He sounds American and looks about thirty-five years old, with fine blond hair to his shoulders, high cheekbones and crystal blue eyes. His skin has that flawless Nordic sheen and a light, even tan. He's over six feet tall and looks in good shape.

'Thanks,' I say.

'May I join you?'

'Please.'

He smiles, sits on the lounger next to me and cracks open his beer. I sit up, turn towards him and ask, 'And you are ...?'

'Your husband.'

'What?'

'For the hit.'

I sip beer.

'I'm a US Army envoy advising about Nixon's war on drugs.'

'With that haircut?'

He laughs. 'It'll be gone.'

'Pity.'

'Not really, in this heat.'

'And I'm your English wife?'

'Right.'

'So why are you ...?'

'Same as you, I guess. I was here trying to settle some business and got taken.'

'Drug business?'

'Yeah.'

'So you're about as keen to do this as me.'

'I'd say so.'

'How long have you been here?'

'Two days. There's no way to get out. They have it tighter than a fish's ass.'

A guard approaches, glancing at us as he passes. 'What do you know about the job?' I ask.

'You want me to brief you?'

'Why not?'

'We're going to a government reception at the Palacio Nacional in Mexico City. The US Federal Reserve just lent The Bank of Mexico three hundred sixty million bucks, so they figure they owe us a party. Also, they just discovered a couple oil fields in Chiapas so they want to do deals on crude. We meet the minister there. He's a sex predator who likes northern tail and watching his wife getting fucked. If we make the right noises, the money's on him asking us back to his place for a private party. We play around a little and then kill them.'

'How do we get in?'

'With fake ID. They have someone inside who cooked the invite.'

'When is it?'

'Tonight.'

'What did the Minister do?' I ask.

'He had the army burn Manuel's marijuana fields even though he was paying him off. Some other drug boss will have offered him a couple million more to put Manuel out of business. Once that happens, Manuel has no choice but to cut off the head.'

I see Roberto come out of the house and talk to one of the guards.

The American sees him and lowers his voice. 'Roberto's the good cop. The little guy's a psycho.'

'Thanks for the warning. What's his name?'

'Guido.'

Roberto approaches us and smiles.

'Manuel wonders if you join him for lunch in one half hour?' he says.

The American looks at me. 'Cool?'

'Why not,' I say.

Roberto nods and goes back to the house. The American stands.

The sun forms a halo round his head. 'My name's Lee.'

'I'm Rina. I suppose I should put some clothes on,' I say, rising from the lounger.

'Me too.'

'Where have they put you?'

'I'm over in back. Shall I pick you up in a half hour?'

'Please do.'

Lee walks round the corner of the bungalow. I go inside and find that Juanita has turned down the bed and lowered the mosquito netting around it, lending the room the air of a private intensive care ward. I take off the bikini and step into the powerful shower. I let the water pummel my neck and back for a while, then I shampoo my hair and soap my skin.

The bathroom door opens. Through the shower curtain

I can see the blurred outline of a short figure that isn't Juanita. I turn off the shower as it approaches. The curtain is ripped back and the midget Guido is there with a gun in his hand, grinning like an idiot, his face still bruised from the beatings he's already taken today. He leers at me and says something in Spanish. As he lunges for me, I plunge a straight finger into his eye. He reels back and I knee him in the balls. He hits the marble floor hard and lies screaming, one hand covering his bleeding eye socket, the other holding his crotch. He twists his stunted body from side to side in a vain effort to get to his feet.

I decide not to kill him. Stepping over the sobbing mess on the floor, I stash the gun in the cistern, wash the blood and slime from my finger in the sink and wrap myself in a towel, as the front door crashes open. Guards enter and surround the writhing figure. He looks up at them with his good eye and whimpers pleadingly. Two guards shoulder arms, pick him up and carry him out onto the terrace. The other two guards search the room. One of them finds the gun in the cistern. They look at me for a moment and then leave.

I go into the bedroom, dry off and put on fresh underwear, the Valentino number I looked at earlier, and carefully make up my face. I select one of the several whiskies available from the mirrored cocktail cabinet, pour myself a stiff one, turn on a table fan and relax on a sofa. Lee was right. Getting out of here is going to be difficult. The guards' response was almost instant.

There is a knock at the door. 'Señorita?'

'Come in.'

Juanita hurries in, bristling with indignation. She puts down the mop and bucket she is carrying and takes my hand in hers.

'So sorry, so sorry ... Animalejo! ... Animalejo!' she says.

Taking this as a comment on Guido's personality, I smile and say, 'It's OK.' I wish I had the Spanish to tell her that on the Richter scale of violent attempts on my virtue, this one barely registered.

'You strong. You teach him lesson. Is good. You sure you are OK?'

'I am OK.'

Seeming satisfied that I am unharmed and undimmed, Juanita goes to the bathroom and begins mopping the blood from the floor.

Lee arrives as I am draining my whisky glass. 'Hey, you look great.'

'Thanks. You want a drink?'

'I think maybe we should go over.'

He opens the door for me and we walk across the terrace. The slouching guards straighten up as we pass. Lee is wearing a light blue silk shirt, white trousers and Gucci loafers. His hair is brushed back and tied in a neat pony tail, revealing a strong jawline and a fine profile.

As we approach the house, Roberto appears.

'Manuel sends you many apologies for that he is detained by some business for a short while. He say please to wait and have drink and he will come soon.'

Roberto shows us to a table beside the pool.

'Señorita?'

'Whisky, straight.'

He turns to Lee. 'Gimme a beer.'

Roberto goes inside. A light breeze wrinkles the surface of the pool and whispers through the palm trees. Lee sits back and closes his eyes. I look at his strong, elegant frame and wonder if I can trust him.

'Where are you from?' I ask.

'Originally, Chicago.'

'And now?'

'Beverly Hills.'

Roberto arrives with our drinks.

'How long have you known Manuel?' I ask once he has gone.

'A while. I met him at Woodstock. We were both selling grass and his Acapulco Gold made mine look like lawn clippings, so we got into moving gold over the border around Tijuana and up into LA and Hollywood. Then coke happened, business exploded and things got rough between drug bosses down here.'

'So why would he kidnap a business partner?'

'There are no rules here. I fit the bill, is all. Most of his US dealers are Mexican. I'm the only white guy and I was in the Marines, so I can pass for military and bullshit about the war on drugs.'

'When did you leave the Marines?'

'A few years ago. I got captured in Nam. Got out, returned to the US with a combat pack full of smack, got into the drug business and never looked back. How did you get started in your line of work?'

'It was in the family.'

I am spared any further interrogation as Roberto appears from the house.

'Please to come now.'

Roberto escorts us to the front door of the house. We go in, cross the hall and are shown into a large, dimly lit dining room. My eye is immediately drawn to a life-sized skeleton, in a purple hooded robe trimmed with gold, standing on a plinth beneath an arch at the far end of the room. The skull leers at me from beneath a wig of silver hair. The ashen bones of its right hand grip a long handled scythe while the left hand holds a globe with the land masses and oceans of the earth in yellow and blue. The whole apparition, lit from within, exudes a ghostly orange radiance. The eye sockets of the white skull seem to follow me as I walk towards a round table in the centre of the room where Manuel sits, flanked by a semicircle of white-coated waiters holding silver trays. An identical miniature version of the skeleton, about a foot tall and complete with scythe and globe, glows eerily in the centre of the table.

Manuel rises and says, 'Please to come, sit and have champagne.'

Three waiters come forward and pour from three bottles. Manuel raises his glass.

'To a successful operation.'

We toast. Three more waiters advance and place plates

of delicately presented hors d'oeuvres before us. I taste a coconut shrimp and realise how hungry I am.

Manuel toys with a scallop. He looks up at me and says, 'Lee has told you what is to be done, yes?'

'Yes,' I say.

'All is clear?'

'There is one detail ...'

'Yes?'

'How do we get out after the killing?'

'Señorita Walker, you are the expert in this, as you showed us at the hotel this morning. Lee too has escaped from Viet Cong and after that from US Marine Corp, so for you this will be no great difficulty, I think.'

'And if we do get out?'

Manuel takes a folder from beside his chair and opens it. 'Here is your passport and first class open ticket.'

I see that the passport is mine. The ticket looks genuine.

'After kill, you go to Benito Juárez Airport. At information desk, you ask for Pedro Álvarez. You say who you are and he gives these to you. You leave immediately on next flight.'

Waiters replace the hors d'oeuvres with some sort of small roasted bird surrounded with even smaller birds. I reckon my chances of getting out of here to be about as good as the birds' were. They'll probably get me at the airport. The glowing skeleton on the table seems to agree with me. Manuel sees me looking at it.

'This is Santa Muerte, the White Girl who protects us from death. She has looked upon you now and so you will be safe in your business this evening in Mexico City.'

Keeping his eyes on me, Manuel's smile doesn't waver as he picks up a bird and slowly tears it apart.

4

Georgie and Jack are asleep next to me. Jack whimpers in his sleep and then sighs and turns over. He sounds a bit chesty again. No wonder, sleeping in a damp room with the plaster flaking off the walls. I'll take him to the doctor soon. They thought it might be diphtheria the last time, but it was just the flu. He's not that strong, though.

I stare at the stripe of light on the ceiling and listen to the faint sound of the music coming from some drinker that's started up in a basement or a living room somewhere near. A radiogram and a few crates of nicked booze is all it takes. It won't be long before it gets smashed up by some gang that wants the protection.

I wonder if I'll sleep tonight. I close my eyes and turn on my side. I'm thinking of the sea, like it was when Dad took us to Southend when I was little, before Georgie. I'm sitting on the sand between him and Mum, looking at that enormous sea. Dad and Mum are talking and I just look at the sea and think how big it is and …

He's unlocking the front door. My stomach turns. I only hope he's alone. It sounds like it. I slip out of bed and I can see him against the light of the street lamp coming through the window. He puts a bottle on the kitchen table, moves to the sink and I hear him pissing. He takes his coat off and puts it on the back of a chair. I go to the doorway and he sees me.

'There's my little girlfriend.'

He walks towards me and presses me up against the door frame. He leans against me and squeezes my tits. I feel his hardness against my stomach where the sickness is rising in me. He tries to kiss me and I turn my face away. He takes my head in his hands, turns my face to him, puts his mouth on mine and forces his tongue inside. I'm going to be sick. I try to pull him down onto the floor so he won't do it in the bed next to Georgie and Jack, but he puts his arm round underneath me, picks me up and lays me on the bed.

The weight of him knocks the air out of me when he pins me down on the towel that I've put there to catch the blood. His stinking breath and the pain when he shoves his big vile self into me. Georgie wakes up and sees him. She turns away and tries to cover Jack's eyes with the sheet, as if the poor little kid hasn't seen it before, the great foul beast who comes in the night and lies on top of his big sister and heaves and snorts and farts and stinks and leaves a filthy trail of slime, then lumbers off to sleep in the armchair or on the floor and is there in the morning like a dead thing that no one speaks about.

He grinds on into me until he's spewed his foul load, then he heaves himself off me and into the armchair with the one arm. Soon he's snoring like a pig. I reach out and hold Georgie's hand.

'Shhhhh … It's all right … Off to sleep now.'

Jack hasn't woken up properly this time. Georgie settles and then her breathing tells me she's going to sleep.

I take the rag from under the pillow, put my hand down and wipe myself. I take the towel out from under me and put it under the bed. I don't think I've bled tonight. I look at his dark shape in the chair. I lean over the side of the bed and reach underneath for the pot. I pull it out and retch over it, but nothing comes up. I hear a sound in the kitchen. Mum is getting up off her mattress, coughing. I hear her open the bottle he put on the table and pour a drink. She's been awake the whole time. I lie still and look up at my stripe of light on the ceiling. The tears are making it wavy.

• • •

I'm filling the kettle next morning when he comes in the kitchen and stands by the table. I can feel him looking at me but I don't turn round. The rag and bone man's shout echoes down the street as his cart clatters past.

'Here,' he says.

I look round. He's peeling a couple of quid off a roll of notes and putting them on the table. I turn back to the sink and he comes and stands behind me, put his arms round me and presses his lips into my ear.

'You know you like it, you dirty little girl.'

Mum turns over in her sleep. The gin bottle's half empty beside her. He walks over to Mum and stands looking down at her.

I turn back to the stove and light the gas under the kettle. I feel the warmth of the gas on my stomach. Why is he just standing there? I'm feeling sick again. I'm going to fall down. Go, you bastard. Get out! I put my finger by the gas flame. I push it nearer the flame and I feel the lovely burn and I'm not in the kitchen at all, it's just me and the burn and I'm strong as the burn and I'm climbing up and up … and the door slams and he's gone.

I go to the sink, put my finger under the tap and turn it on. The water runs over the burn and it throbs nicely for a bit.

Mum turns over, opens her eyes and says, 'Turn that fucking tap off!'

'I've got to get their breakfast, haven't I?'

She throws a pillow at me. 'Shut up and get out, the fucking lot of you!'

'All right, Mum, it's all right.'

'Fucking load of cunts!'

She turns to the wall and pulls the blanket over her head. She can be like that in the morning if she wakes up in the night and has a drink. She won't remember. She doesn't remember much of anything these days. I put the money in my knickers, fill the teapot and go through to wake Georgie and Jack. I make sure they're getting dressed and take the pot downstairs and empty it in the privy.

When I get back, they're dressed and sitting at the table. I pour tea for myself and give them both a glass of milk and a slice of bread and margarine with a bit of sugar inside. I decide I'm going to spend some of his lousy two quid on some meat and potatoes for tonight. I sit at the table with them. Georgie looks at me as if she's accusing me of something.

I say, 'Come on now, you don't want to be late.' I get their coats.

Jack holds up his bread and says, 'I haven't finished.'

'Take it with you,' I say.

'What if it's nicked?'

'Come on, you.'

I put them into their coats and open the door. They file past me and we go down the stairs and along the hall. The Irish woman's door opens and she shoos her two boys out, throwing a tennis ball after them. She gives me a quick smile and a shake of the head and goes back into her room. She hasn't been in the house long, so I don't really know her. I haven't seen her husband for a bit. I open the front door and the boys tumble into the street in front of us and start kicking and heading the ball between them. I take our Jack's hand and we dodge past them towards Golborne, and off to school.

• • •

When I get back to our street, the sun's shining. The tall tenements cast a big shadow so the street's only sunny for a bit in the middle of the day. I don't want to go home and I've got some money, so I go down the steps to Claire's and knock on her door. The curtain on the basement window is pulled back and her mum peers out. She sees it's me and smiles and nods. I hear her call for Claire and I wait beside the big old pram they keep down there for fetching coal. Claire opens the door. She's in her nightdress with the ripped hem and looks half asleep and even thinner than usual.

'Hiya,' she says, yawning and stretching an arm up above her head. Her dark hair, normally back-combed and lacquered into a bouffant, is flattened down and limp. Her brown eyes are puffy and half closed. She swings the door open and I follow her to the kitchen where her mother's pouring tea into a flask.

'You all right, Rina love?' she says.

'Not bad, thanks.'

'I've forgotten to put his flask in this morning. I'll have to take it to him or he'll go mad when he sees he hasn't got it.'

Claire's dad works at the brewery in Bramley Road when they need casuals. He's all right, but he's got a temper on him and I know he knocks her mum about sometimes when he's drunk. She's a kind woman. Always cleaning and trying to keep things nice.

'Is your mum all right?' she asks.

'Not too bad,' I say.

She looks at me as if she knows how bad it really is. She's minded Georgie and Jack sometimes, and given us bits of food and helped us a lot in different ways. She gets on a chair and wipes off some damp that's running down the wall behind the stove.

'We'll drown in this basement one of these days.'

I laugh and she gets down and says, 'Do you want a nice cup of tea, Rina love?'

'Not at the moment, Mrs Welch, thanks very much.'

Claire comes in from the bedroom. She's rebuilt her hair and put on a pair of tartan slacks and a faded, lemon-coloured blouse. I feel shabby next to her in my worn-out grey skirt and my dirty old jacket.

Her mother screws the top on the flask and says, 'I'd better get this round to him. You off out, you two?'

'Yeah,' says Claire.

'Tara, then.'

'Tara, Mum.'

'Bye, Mrs Welch.'

The front door shuts and Claire says, 'Fancy going up the Two Bare Feet?'

'Yeah, go on then.'

• • •

The Italian bloke heaves the lever down on the coffee machine and a thin squirt of black liquid oozes out of the pipes into the glass cup underneath. He holds the milk jug up to the steam pipe and it gurgles and fizzes. I give him half a crown and get one and six change. We take our cups and sit at a table by the wall under a picture of Johnny Ray singing his heart out. A couple of girls sitting on stools by the counter turn round and glance at us.

Claire looks at me for a moment. 'He's been back, hasn't he?' she says. I nod. 'You've got to do something, Reen.'

The door opens and a group of teenage boys walk in. One or two wear the drape and the others are in cheap moth-eaten jackets and drainpipes with the brylcreem and the quiff. One of them is Sammy, Claire's boyfriend. He's quite good looking with his swept back black hair and his sideburns.

He stops at our table. 'All right, girls?' Claire ignores him.

He walks on.

I look at Claire and say, 'What's up?'

'We got chucked out of Whiteleys yesterday.'

'What happened?'

'Doorman stops us. "We don't want no slum kids in here," he says.'

'Flippin' cheek.'

'And he does nothing.'

'Sammy?'

'Nothing. Just walks away.'

'What did you do?'

'Called him a cunt and went after Sammy and called him a cunt as well, and he says the geezer's connected and it's not worth it, and that.'

'He's all right though, Sammy.'

'Can't have that though, can you?'

'I suppose not.'

'Slum kids. Fucking insult.'

The boys are standing round the juke box looking at the song titles. *Singin' the Blues* rocks gently forth.

Sammy walks to our table and says to Claire, 'Fancy a dance?'

Claire ignores him, and he stands looking a bit embarrassed, with his mates watching, so I get up and do a slow jive with him. Sammy's quite good and it feels nice to have a dance and have people watching. I slip under his arm and do a reverse turn.

As we come together he says, 'She's got the hump all right.'

I smile at him. 'You'll be OK.'

The record ends and we go back to the table. I sit opposite Claire and Sammy pulls a chair up to the end of the table and sits down just as the driving beat of *Rock Around the Clock* powers out of the speaker. Sammy gets up again and I do too, then Claire jumps up between us and pushes me out of the way. I sit down and watch them twist and twirl and show us what great jivers they are together. The boys start clapping and whooping and whistling, and I reckon they're all right again.

I have a couple of dances with one of Sammy's mates, but when he asks if he can see me again, I pretend I didn't hear him and tell Claire I've got some shopping to do. Sammy's got his arm round her now, and she gives me a wave as I step out into Westbourne Grove.

I decide to give Whiteleys a miss and head for the posh butcher at the corner of Garway Road. I buy two pounds of stewing steak and slip a couple of eggs into my pocket while he's reaching into the window for the meat. I walk along Westbourne Grove to Portobello Market, making my way through the stalls and the old junk and rubbish that's piled up in between them. I say hello to one of the stallholders who lives in our street and buy potatoes from him. He gives me a couple of carrots, a twisted looking turnip and a wink, and I go on up the hill, past the old clothes and the china and cutlery stalls, along Golborne

Road and into our street. Someone's playing the piano in the Earl of Warwick on the corner.

The pavement's quite full with people out in the sun now. A bookie's runner hurries past me with his leather bag under his arm. There are boys playing football in the road and aproned women talking and gossiping in groups around front steps, and little kids running about and chasing each other in and out of the legs of Teddy Boys, who've managed to get hold of the thirty guineas for the drape suits and the brothel creepers, lounging around and smoking and ignoring the girls, who are busy ignoring them in return. An African woman wearing a big turban and a long skirt with a sort of a shawl wrapped round her waist gets some looks from people as she walks along the edge of the pavement, staring straight ahead of her.

There are four black men with suitcases standing outside our house. They look like railwaymen or labourers. I go up the steps. I can hear a woman shouting and a dog barking. I open the door and see the landlord's rent collector standing at the foot of the stairs. He's a tall man in an expensive suit with a walking stick in one hand and the leash of an Alsatian dog in the other. The dog strains forward, slathering and snarling at the Irish woman, who is standing in the doorway of her room with her sons clinging to her legs on each side of her. The dog barks at her and the woman starts screaming. The man in the suit wrenches the dog away, smacks his stick against the rotten wood panelling on the side of the staircase and shatters it. The Irish woman stops screaming.

He fixes her with a stare. 'You were told.'

A man appears behind the woman and forces his way past her, carrying an old suitcase and a pile of clothes. I move out of the way as he goes out of the door, down the steps, and dumps the stuff on the pavement. The Irish woman is crying now. Another man comes out of her room with a basket of linen and another battered suitcase and throws it down beside her other possessions. She starts to plead with the man in the suit to let her stay. He ignores her, turns to me and nods towards the staircase. When I don't move he twitches the dog's lead. It gives a low growl and moves towards me. I look at the Irish woman to try to show that I feel sorry for her and go upstairs. On the landing, I stop and look over the bannister. She has hold of her boys' hands and they're walking slowly out through the front door. The man with the dog beckons to someone I can't see. The four black men who were standing on the pavement come in through the front door and go into the Irish woman's room.

• • •

I walk into our kitchen and Mum's at the window. I put the meat and the vegetables by the sink, stand beside Mum and watch the Irish woman and her kids picking up their stuff and moving off down the street.

Mum says, 'Good riddance to her.'

'What if we're next?' I say.

'We'll be all right.'

'How do you know?'

'Johnny's told him.'

'Told who?'

'Bielsky, the landlord.'

'Are you sure?'

'He won't get himself on the wrong side of the Prestons.'

I know she's right. They're one of the hardest families on the manor, with a lot of connections, and they were here long before the Polish landlords came to town.

'I'm going up to see Lizzie,' I say.

'All right, love.'

I go upstairs and knock on Lizzie's door. I wait a bit and then I hear her come to the other side of the door.

'Who is it?' she says.

'It's me, Rina.'

She slips the chain and opens the door. 'Come in, love.'

Her pink nylon dressing gown falls open to reveal her black lace bra and pants as she reaches for her cigarettes on the kitchen table. 'Sit down, love,' she says as she lights a cigarette and picks up the kettle.

'Cup of tea?'

'Yeah, thanks.'

She fills the kettle and turns on the gas, tries to light it and fails. 'Fucking meter's run out.'

She rummages in her handbag for her purse and opens it. 'Never a shilling when you need one, dammit.'

'Here,' I say.

I feel among the change in my pocket for a piece of old

lino I've cut out into the size of a shilling, and hand it to her.

'Ta, love.' She looks at it and laughs. 'I ain't used one of these in a while.'

She goes out to the landing and puts it in the meter, then she comes back and lights the gas.

'Lovely.'

She sits down at the table.

'Did you know her downstairs got thrown out?' she says.

'I saw it.'

'Poor cow. Two kids. First her husband fucks off and now this.'

'Why did they get rid of her?'

'More rent off four Jamaicans in them two rooms.'

'I suppose.'

'They'll probably put four more of them in there next week.'

'What do think she'll do?'

'What can she do? If she's got no one to go to, she'll probably ask them for another place and they'll offer her something if she'll go on the game.'

'They're horrible.'

'Don't I know it.'

There's a knock at the door.

Lizzie stands and says, 'You'll have to go, love. Come and have your tea another time. OK?'

'OK.'

Lizzie opens the door and gestures me to leave. I walk

through the door and past the man with the dog waiting outside. He goes inside and the door shuts.

Something makes me wait on the landing.

There are mumbled voices and then Lizzie shouts: 'No!' There's a slap and a short bark and the sound of someone falling down.

I go down the stairs. The kids will be home soon.

5

The car surges down the drive, raising dust. We're followed by another Mercedes containing six of Manuel's goons, suited up to look like security men. Guards open the iron gates and we turn onto the two lane road that leads down to the highway. As we lurch round a sharp bend, our driver suddenly brakes hard, slews the car sideways and hits the rear end of a donkey cart, sending a cascade of melons into the valley below. The driver clings desperately to the cart as it sways dangerously over the abyss for a moment until the bellowing donkey wrenches it back onto the road. The driver falls off the cart, gets to his feet cursing loudly and turns to confront whoever has almost killed him. Roberto steps out of the car. The cart driver sees him, bows his head in submission and steps aside to let us pass. Roberto gets back into the car and we continue down the winding road in silence.

Lee is seated next to me, looking convincing with his military haircut and immaculate US Army General's uniform. I see him take in the deep red Diane Von Furstenberg wrap dress I selected, to give me an elegant but liberated look. He reaches out and takes my hand in his.

'You look beautiful,' he says.

I withdraw my hand, turn and look out of the window.

'Just rehearsing,' he says, as he leans back and closes his

eyes. We join the highway and a sign tells me that we are on the Autopista del Sol, two hundred and fifty kilometres from Mexico City. We stop at a toll booth. The driver pays and exchanges a few remarks with Roberto as we pull away. The road twists and turns through valleys and hills shimmering under the dazzling sun.

I consider the evening ahead and feel a tingle of excitement. I put my hands between my knees and check the mechanism of the bracelet on my right wrist that releases razor sharp teeth, long enough to pierce the cervical segment of the carotid artery when twisted in a certain way. I made it in a jewellery class some years ago, during one of my attempts to embrace a slightly more conventional means of making a living. As ever, I soon traded the cloying relationships and creeping stupefaction of ordinary work for the electrifying excitement of murder, and adapted the bracelet accordingly. Nothing comes close to the purity and simplicity of the contest. It is either him or me.

I settle back in my seat and let mile after mile of beautiful mountain scenery soothe my soul. We cross an elegant white suspension bridge spanning a broad peaceful river glistening far below. The highway curves on through the parched hills beyond.

Lee opens his eyes and turns to me. 'You OK?'

'Yes.'

He looks nervous. I hope he's going to perform his role adequately and not land us in a Mexican jail. His story sounded far too neat and well prepared. Vietnam,

Woodstock, running drugs into California; a bust here and there would have made it more plausible. I take the ID I have been given out of my evening bag and study it. I am Caroline Johansen from Rockville, Maryland.

They've copied the photograph from my British passport and created an American one with considerable skill.

I turn to Lee. 'What's your first name, General Johansen?'

'Would you believe Spencer?'

'Tell me about Rockville.'

'Small city about twelve miles out of DC. I'd say we moved there with our two children around ten years ago, after we met while I was attached to the US Embassy in London.'

'Names?'

'Sally and Jim, seven and ten. We're staying at the Four Seasons.'

I nod. Lee looks at me as if expecting more. He's scared and wants to talk. I ignore him and close my eyes.

It seems like moments later when Lee wakes me and I look out of the window at the Mexico City skyline. The high-velocity calm of the highway gives way to the fractious skirmishing of urban traffic as we're caught in the sticky web of the city. A hysterical chorus of horns blares around us as we twist and heave through the broiling mess of metal and flesh, our long black car with its gold-braided occupant giving us some small purchase in the struggle.

We eventually enter a large open square. An outsize

Mexican flag billows self-importantly from a tall mast in the centre. A smaller version waves back at it from the top of the central tower of a solid, official-looking, four-storey building that occupies one side of the square. Along its full length, bright red shutters, standing proud of its second-floor windows, add a brash confidence to its imposing façade. We join a line of cars approaching the entrance.

'Here we go, dear,' says Lee, putting on his hat.

We draw level with a uniformed soldier who opens the rear door of the car. We step out onto a red carpet. Our security team exits the car behind and gathers discreetly around us. At the entrance to the Palace, we are asked to present our ID and then escorted across a hall, towards the foot of twin staircases that curve away from each other and meet again on the floor above, in front of an enormous mural triptych of incredible detail, depicting what I take to be the history of Mexico.

We climb the stairs to a large open landing, surrounded by baroque arches, with a view onto the square beyond. Further murals of extraordinary richness and colour line the walls. A uniformed official ushers us into a large stateroom where the ornate arched ceiling echoes a cacophony of premeditated cordiality and mutual congratulation exchanged by a large gathering of older men in military uniforms and evening wear. Expensively dressed women decorate the crowd, some young and fresh, others old and grotesque, with that embalmed look that comes from spending too much time and money trying to look less decrepit.

Roberto and his team deploy themselves near the door. Waiters bearing trays of champagne weave skillfully among the crowd. Lee takes my elbow and pilots me towards a group near the centre, which appears to be gathered around a tall, distinguished, silver haired figure, about sixty years old, standing next to an extremely beautiful dark-haired woman of about my age. They listen politely to a corpulent, red-faced man who appears to be delivering an impassioned plea for something or other. During a slight pause in his peroration, Lee takes my hand, approaches the silver-haired man and speaks to him in confident Spanish. The silver-haired man turns abruptly away from his interlocutor and smiles warmly at us, extending his hand first to Lee and then to me.

'I am Enrico Gonzales,' he says.

Lee shakes his hand and replies, 'Spencer Johansen. This is my wife, Caroline.'

'What a great pleasure to meet you both. I hope you will enjoy our little party. May I introduce my wife, Adelina?'

Adelina has the deepest dark brown eyes and skin so creamy that I have trouble letting go of her hand after we shake. Her silver sheath dress contains a luxurious body that appears to be making a subtle attempt to escape from it. She envelops me in a radiant smile.

'How do you do?'

Her voice is a mellifluous purr that sends a ripple of pure pleasure direct to my pelvic floor. She senses my reaction and offers me another, slightly more knowing smile before turning to greet Lee. I find myself beginning to look forward to whatever entertainment might be available later and move a little closer to Gonzales, who compliments me on my dress, while staring at my cleavage.

We exchange pleasantries until a bell chimes and a gold-braided military man mounts a podium and addresses the audience. Gonzales excuses himself, goes to the podium and delivers a short speech, which is received with enthusiastic applause.

Returning to our group, he engages Lee in conversation while glancing at me occasionally and completely ignoring various important looking men who seem to be waiting to speak to him. I stand as close to Adelina as I dare and inhale her sensuous perfume. There is a round of applause as the speeches come to an end and a string quartet begins to play. A uniformed man dripping with gold braid asks if I speak English, and when I say I do he offers to show me round the palace. I decline politely, whereupon he begins a detailed biography of the glum-looking figure whose portrait hangs above us; an Emperor of Mexico from a couple of hundred years ago who, although completely bald, would have carried off first prize in any side whiskers competition.

Just as I am becoming paralysed with boredom, Adelina sees that I need rescuing and joins us. She says something apologetic in Spanish to the historian and tells me of some dignitary who wishes to meet me.

As she steers me away she says, 'It is time to freshen up, I think.'

As we move through the crowd towards the exit, I see

Roberto nodding to a couple of his team near the door. They follow us across the hallway. We go through a door at the head of a corridor on the other side, leaving the guards lurking outside. The ladies room has a pink and black marble floor. White basins and gold taps are sunk into a red marble slab beneath a long mirror.

Adelina moves to the mirror, and as she catches the light from above she seems to blush a little as her silken skin reflects the colour of the marble. She looks at me for a moment, as I wait by the door, and then lowers her eyes. I move to her side and feel a shiver of excitement as our shoulders touch. I find her eyes with mine and we share a cautious smile and turn slowly towards each other. I feel her breathing quicken as I take her hand and stroke her fingers. We hold each other's gaze for a moment then move closer. As our lips touch and I begin to lose myself in her delicious softness, the door opens.

We separate hurriedly as Lee says, 'Oh. Hey … I'm sorry, I thought this was the men's room.'

Adelina turns away and says, 'The next door, I think.' She reaches into her bag and takes out a lipstick.

'OK, cool. Sorry.'

Lee looks at me for a moment and leaves.

I look at my smeared lipstick in the mirror and make repairs. Adelina says, 'We should get back.'

She turns towards the door and I hold her arm.

'It is OK,' she says as she opens the door and sweeps past the guards and across the hall towards the reception.

I make a final check of my makeup, straighten my dress

and follow her. Lee appears beside me.

'What the fuck was that?'

'Just rehearsing,' I reply.

'Don't expect me to go down on Gonzales.'

'How's it looking?'

'Not so good since you took off with Señora. I need you to do some work here.'

Some people are leaving as we enter the state room. I pick up a glass of champagne as we approach Gonzales. Adelina is standing beside him, laughing and smiling as he tells some story to a couple of tough-looking middle-aged men in very shiny suits. As he shakes hands with them and turns away, Adelina takes his arm and whispers something to him.

He turns to me and Lee.

'Have you managed to see much of our country during your visit, Mrs Johansen?'

'Not as much as I would like to.'

'We must see if we can arrange to show you some of our sights while you are here.'

Gonzales pulls his wife towards him, rather as though she is one of the sights he is referring to, and says, 'I think perhaps it is time to leave now. May we invite you to dinner at our house, General and Mrs Johansen?'

I look briefly at Lee and say, 'That would be delightful.'

'You will come in our car, of course.'

'With pleasure,' says Lee.

'You may tell your driver to follow.'

Adelina smiles at me and Gonzales shakes various

hands as we make our way out of the room, down the stairs and out onto the red carpet. Roberto and his men follow at a distance and then head for our cars, parked some way along the square, as a very long black limousine glides to a halt beside us. A uniformed chauffeur gets out and opens the door. Gonzales indicates the back seat and smiles warmly as he settles in beside me. Lee and Adelina sit opposite us. As the car moves off, Gonzales takes a bottle of champagne from a compartment beside him, pours four glasses, and we toast Mexican/US relations. Lee produces a silver snuff box from his pocket and we relax into a haze of champagne, cocaine and Aretha Franklin.

As we purr through the sub-tropical night, Gonzales stretches back and casually puts his arm around me. I move closer and he pulls me to him, kissing my neck and squeezing various parts of my body. I undulate dutifully in response while taking as much pleasure as I can from glimpses of Lee fondling Adelina's sumptuous breasts and then sliding his hand between her thighs. Gonzales becomes increasingly enthusiastic, but just as I am wondering how much further he can get his tongue down my throat before I throw up, there is a loud bang from behind us and a blaze of headlights through the back window.

A pick-up truck lurches alongside us with two machine guns mounted on the back. I dive to the floor and heave Gonzales on top of me. Bullets thump into his back and head as the guns drill their load into us. We are tossed around in a tornado of bullets, bodies and shattered glass. The car careers off the road, bounces through the undergrowth and smashes into a tree. I lose consciousness to the sound of squawking birds and machine gun fire receding into the distance.

6

I'm sitting in the armchair with one arm, with Jack curled up on my lap, and I'm trying to follow what Jeremy Fisher's up to, now he's decided to go fishing and set off with enormous hops to the place where he keeps his lily pad boat, but he's losing me. I'm wishing I'd learnt to read properly at school instead of bunking off all the time so I could at least read him a story without stumbling and bumbling over the words, but I think Jack's falling asleep anyway after his stewed steak and carrots. I reckon the first decent meal we've had for weeks has left us all a bit groggy with shock. Georgie's sitting at the kitchen table bent over her exercise book writing something and Mum's back on her mattress sipping gin and looking at an old Woman magazine.

The growly blues music from downstairs is throbbing through the floor. At least they're off early in the morning to shovel shit, or whatever they do, so it goes off later. They're quite friendly when you see them, so I don't mind them really, although I know they get a lot of trouble going about.

Jack's out cold so I pick a few lice out of his hair and crush them between my thumbnails, then I lift him onto the bed and take his trousers and his pullover off him. I put him next to the wall and cover him with the blanket. I go into the kitchen to tell Georgie it's time for bed.

There's a shout in the street and I look down and see a young Jamaican running fast along the pavement. Two men run after him and catch him as he reaches the corner. They throw him on the ground and lay into him with fists and feet, then walk away laughing and leave him lying in the gutter. I watch him for a bit and I see him crawl onto the pavement and lie against the railings.

I'm thinking about whether to go and help him when a policeman comes round the corner and goes over to him. The copper says something to him and then steps over him and walks away. He's bleeding from his face and I watch him pull himself up on the railings and hobble off round the corner. I turn and see that Georgie's still writing in her book. I tell her she can finish it in the morning, and she goes into the bedroom and gets undressed.

I look at Mum on her mattress. The magazine's slid onto the floor, her eyes are shut and she's snuffling and wheezing. I take the glass out of her hand and look at the wreck she's become with the drink, not knowing who she is half the time. I think of the glamour girl who used to say goodnight to me when she and Dad left me at Grandad and Grandma's and went up west in the Daimler for a night out. She curses in her sleep and kicks her legs out at some enemy she's dreaming about. I put her blanket back on her and go into the bedroom.

Georgie's sitting on the side of the bed in her vest and pants. She looks at her little brother and says, 'He's really getting it at school, you know.'

She lifts the blanket and pulls up his vest. There are

bruises on his back and up one side. This has happened since I took him for a bath last week or I'd have seen it. He hasn't said anything to me about it in case I complain to his teachers, which will make the bullying worse. If I go after the kids and give them a smack, it will start off all kinds of trouble with the families, ending up in God knows what kind of warfare. He's got to learn how to look after himself. Make an example of one of them. I wish Grandad was still here to teach him a few tricks, like he taught me. He was a fighting man. Five-foot-tall, thin as a rake and muscles like whipcord. He worked in the Notting Dale brickworks and fought anyone in the street or in the ring until he was feared by everyone. He liked a laugh and a joke and I loved him. He coughed his lungs up one night in the pub from the Woodbines and the brick dust and died on the floor. Grandma went a couple of months later in her grief at losing him.

I look at Jack snuggled up and decide to have a talk with him in the morning. Georgie's in bed now and asleep. I pick up the Jeremy Fisher book, look at the pictures of the silly frog and try to think if I know anyone who's good at reading who I could learn it from. Georgie's better at it than me, but it doesn't seem right to ask her. I get out the mending kit and try to sew up a rip in Georgie's skirt. I've only got black cotton and the skirt's grey but it'll have to do. I make a decent job of it and put the skirt on the back of a chair for the morning. The slow, pulsing beat of the blues from downstairs is making me drowsy and I take off my blouse and skirt and slip in beside Georgie.

• • •

The boat's rocking. I hold onto the side of it and reach out to stop Jack falling into the sea. The waves are getting bigger. I can see Mum and Dad on the beach waving at us. I'm scared and I wave back and try to shout to them to come and get us, but I can't make a sound and the boat's tipping up and down and Jack falls over the side and I'm holding on to his collar and I'm being dragged off the boat into the sea and I keep waving to Mum and Dad, but they're dancing together on the beach and not looking at me, and Jack's gone into the water and a big hand comes out of the sea and pulls me down under the waves and the water's crushing me and …

His hand's over my mouth and he says, 'What are you crying about, you silly girl?'

I struggle underneath him, then I go limp and he takes his hand away, kisses my neck and says, 'Bad dream?'

He lifts the blanket off me and puts his hand between my legs. I hate him. If I try to stop him, he'll hit me and do it anyway, only more violently. I lie still. He sits up on the edge of the bed and pushes his fingers into me. Georgie wakes up and turns over and away from us. She lies against Jack and puts the blanket over him so that he won't see us.

Johnny looks at her bare legs. He reaches over, takes hold of her ankle and pulls her into the middle of the bed. He climbs over me and turns her onto her back. She screams. He rips her knickers off and stuffs them in her mouth. He pulls her legs open, kneels between them and takes his cock out. Jack's awake. His eyes are wide and he's holding the blanket to his face and pressing himself against the wall. I slip off the bed and creep into the kitchen. I grab the carving knife off the draining board and tiptoe back into the bedroom. He's on top of her, trying to get himself inside. I kneel on the bed behind him and rub my hand between his legs and round his balls.

'Oooh yes,' he says.

I get on top of him and ram the knife into the back of his neck. He shouts and snaps his head back. I pull the knife out, grab a handful of his hair, lift him up against me and slice the blade across his throat. His blood spurts out against the wall. Georgie scrambles out from underneath us, grabs hold of Jack and runs into the kitchen. Mum shouts something. His body goes limp and I let him fall forward onto the bed. Mum comes to the doorway.

'Fuck me, Rina.'

I look down at him and I know he's dead. I've stopped him.

• • •

Mum's taking the knife out of my hand.

'Come on, love.'

She helps me off the bed, puts her arm round me and tries to sit me down. I don't want to sit down. I'm not tired. I feel good. I'm all calm inside. I look at the bleeding mound of guts on the bed and I'm glad I've done it. I can do anything.

Mum's pulling the furniture off the old carpet. What's

got into her? I haven't seen her move further than the kitchen table for months. Jack's crying. Mum's calling for Georgie and telling her to go and get Lizzie from upstairs. She rolls Johnny to the edge of the bed and takes hold of his shoulders.

'Help me get him onto the carpet,' she says.

I take his ankles. We lift him off the bed and put him down in the middle of the carpet. He's still bleeding. Mum takes her old cardigan off and wraps it tight round his neck. She searches through his pockets and finds a packet of fags, a lighter and a roll of fivers and some change. She pockets the fags and the lighter, hands me the money and says, 'Put that somewhere.'

I go over and stuff it into the back of the armchair. Mum goes to the bed, picks up the sopping blankets and puts them next to the body. She wipes the handle of the knife and stuffs it in among the bedclothes. She lifts the edge of the carpet and folds it over him. Lizzie comes in with her eyes wide and stands looking at me. She's naked under her coat and I want to go to her.

'Help me roll him over,' Mum says.

'What about the kids?' I ask.

'Leave them.'

Me and Lizzie get on the floor with her and roll him over until the carpet's wrapped right round him.

Mum says, 'We've got to get this out of here now.'

'Where to?' asks Lizzie.

'Basement?' says Mum.

'It's boarded up.'

'I know.'

'We'd need a crowbar to get in and there's four foot of water in there.'

'Well, what then?' says Mum.

'Bury him,' says Lizzie.

'Them Jamaicans keep their shovels out the back,' I say.

'Hang on, let me think,' says Mum.

Lizzie puts her arm round me and says, 'It's OK, love.'

I lean my head on her shoulder and feel the soft skin of her neck against my cheek. I press myself into her.

Mum stands up and says, 'Rina, get the kids round to Claire's. Tell Maureen to mind them and bring Claire back here.'

I've never seen her like this. I put on my skirt and blouse, grab the kids' clothes and go in the kitchen. They're sitting at the table. Georgie's crying now and holding onto Jack.

'It's all right, you're just going round to stay with Maureen for a bit,' I say.

I notice Johnny's coat over the chair and pick it up. There's something heavy in the pocket. I turn away from the kids, put my hand it the pocket and take out a gun. I slip the gun into the oven, take the coat into the bedroom and hand it to Lizzie. I go back in the kitchen, wet a cloth under the tap and wipe the blood off Georgie's face and hands, then I dress her and Jack and take them downstairs into the street.

The moon's out and the street's empty and dead quiet. The clubs have shut and no one's up yet. We go along to

Claire's and down the steps. I tap on the window and wait. Georgie's shivering and I pull her to me. The curtain's pulled back and Claire's there. She sees the kids and disappears. The door opens and we go into the hall. Her mother's standing behind her.

I say, 'I'm sorry, Mrs Welch.'

'What's up, love?' she says.

'Mum's not well. She's being sick and I've got to take her to the hospital and I wondered if you could look after them until …'

'Of course, love.'

She puts her hands out to the kids.

'Come here, my lovelies, let's go in the kitchen and see what we can find.'

They go in the kitchen. I turn to Claire. 'I've done him.'

'You haven't.'

I nod and she looks at me and sees that I have. 'Fuck me, Rina.'

'Can you come and help us?'

'Get rid?'

'Yeah.'

'Fucking right!'

She takes her coat from behind the door, puts on a pair of slip-ons and follows me up the steps and back to our place.

Mum and Lizzie have got their coats on. They've tied some bits of old rope round the body and they're dragging it through the door onto the landing.

Mum says, 'Two at each end.'

We each get hold of a corner and I say, 'Where are we taking him?' The three of us look at Mum.

'The dump down Talbot Grove,' she says.

'Serves the cunt right,' says Claire.

'Come on. And keep it quiet.'

We half carry him and half slide him down the stairs into the hall. Mum says, 'Rina, get them shovels.'

I go out the back and find three shovels. I pick them up and when I get back they've got him down the front steps and on the pavement. I put the shovels on top of him and we lift him up. He's bloody heavy and the shovels fall off and clatter onto the pavement.

'Hang on a bit,' Claire says.

She runs along and goes down her steps. A moment later, she's up again and pulling the old pram behind her. She wheels it along to us.

'Good girl.' says mum.

We hump him up into the pram; the wheels splay outwards under the weight but it just about holds up.

'Good job it's for twins,' Claire says.

We wheel it to the end of the street, stop beside the derelict shop near the corner and I nip ahead and have a look. There's no one about except an old bloke slumped in a doorway. I beckon the others and we roll the pram along Golborne Road. We're about half way along when I see a pair of headlights swing out of Ladbroke Grove and come towards us. A Ford Zephyr slows down as it approaches us.

'Don't look. Keep going,' Mum says.

The car stops a few yards away. The front doors open and two blokes in dark suits get out and stand in our way.

'What you got there, girls?' one of them says.

Mum walks up to him and throws a punch at his head. He's on the floor before I know what's happened and Mum's pushed the other one up against the car and chopped him in the throat. While he's choking and sliding down the car she swings a kick at the one on the floor and grabs the handle of the pram.

'Come on you lot,' she says.

We go on down Golborne. Lizzie's laughing.

'I think your old man would have been proud of that one.'

'It's easy when they're pissed,' says Mum.

We swing the pram round into Portobello and down the hill. We pass a couple of odd stragglers who don't pay us much attention, and then we turn off to the right and get to the dump on the corner of St Mark's Road. It smells to high heaven. We go round to the back of the dump and shift a filthy old mattress and a rusty bed frame, making a passageway through the sacks of rubbish and broken bottles.

We clear a space near the middle, and me, Lizzie and Claire start digging while Mum keeps watch. The ground's soft from all the rotting muck that's laying on it so it's easy to dig up, and by the time it's starting to get light we've made a good-sized hole. We get the body off the pram and drag it beside the hole, then we roll him out of the carpet and drop him in.

Mum comes to where we are and leans over the hole. She picks up a shovel, turns his head sideways with her foot, raises the shovel up, drives it down blade first and slices his face off. Lizzie clutches her stomach and turns away.

'Let them find him now, eh?' says Mum.

I take a last look at him and dump a shovel full of wet muck on what's left of his head. We fill the hole and stamp the soil down and then we pile some old junk and rubbish on it. We take the carpet and the bed clothes and drop them in different places round the other side of the dump.

We get back to where Mum's waiting with the pram and she says, 'If they can't find the body, they can't prove a fucking thing. Back to bed now, and well done. You two come and see me tonight and I'll have something for you. Now off you go. Different ways back now.'

Lizzie and Claire nod and go off in different directions.

Mum says, 'You take the pram and the shovels and put them back where you found them. I'll see you at home.'

She walks off up Talbot Grove and I wait a minute, and then follow her. I take a different route back to the Grove and then cut through to Golborne. I get to our street in full daylight and put the pram back in the basement by Claire's front door. I go into our house, put the shovels back and run upstairs. I really want to talk to Mum but when I go in the kitchen she's passed out on the mattress with a half-empty bottle beside her on the floor.

I take the gun out of the oven and weigh it in my hand.

It looks the same as the one of Dad's that I found once, and I remember how to open it, by pushing the little lever on the side. The barrel tips forward and I see it's full of bullets. I close the gun, pick up a kitchen knife and go into the bedroom. The floorboards are rotten all along the back wall and when I prise one up with the knife, it falls apart in my hands. I find a more solid one in the corner and hide the gun underneath.

I wash, make a cup of tea and sit at the kitchen table. I should feel tired but I don't. I feel like dancing on the table. I look at Mum and I feel proud of her. I fold my arms on the table in front of me and rest my head.

In the half-light a man in a hood is banging on an iron bell with a shovel. I jerk upright. The old clock with the cracked glass above the fire place is dinging its little tune.

It's time to take the kids to school.

7

I open my eyes and try to move. It's pitch dark and I'm trapped under a great weight. I try to free my right arm and a searing pain shoots into my shoulder. I'm pinned underneath something solid but I am just able to breathe. My arms are trapped, but I can move my left leg. I raise my left knee and push against a solid edge which shifts a little. I keep pushing until I am able to free my left arm and slowly pull myself out. I get to a sitting position and lean back against something solid. I try to move against the pain and nothing seems to be broken. I look around me and make out shapes which mean nothing, until I remember that I am in the wreckage of a car that has been strafed with machine gun fire. I reach out a hand and encounter a face. The hair tells me it is male and the skin feels like it belongs to Gonzales. I explore in another direction and discover a high heeled shoe that I don't want to find the owner of.

I grope around to try to find a way out of the wreck and discover a cavity where a window used to be that is just big enough for me to squeeze through. Progress is agonisingly slow as I negotiate jagged metal and shattered glass, but I finally make it out onto flat ground, lie on my back and pass out again. When I come round, the moon emerges from cloud above me and I can see the wrecked car more clearly. The one which contained our guards is lying on its roof some distance away.

After a while I am able to get to my feet. I walk to the rear of the car and try to open the trunk. It seems jammed solid but after a few attempts I am able to wrench it open. I find a tire lever and a torch in the tool compartment, prise open a rear door of the car and shine the torch on Gonzales. He lies on his back as if asleep. His dark blue suit is soaked to a rich crimson. Adelina's shattered body lies next to him, contorted by the impact. Her face has been exploded by a fusillade of lead and one of her arms is twisted impossibly around her neck as if she is trying to pull her head off her shoulders. Her beautiful body is cratered with bullet holes.

It takes a moment before I realise Lee is missing. I check the front of the car but only find the driver, bowed over the steering wheel in an attitude of devotion, as if protecting it from the evil bullets that have ripped into his flesh. I search the area around the car in case Lee has been thrown clear and find nothing. I go to the back-up car. Roberto and his colleagues are tangled together inside, in a grotesque collage of death.

I locate my shoes, which are wedged under Gonzales's legs, and start climbing down the steep hillside away from the wreckage while considering what to do next. I have no money, no identification and I look as if I have just escaped from a massacre. The passport identifying me as Caroline Johansen is in Lee's pocket, wherever he is, and Manuel's promise of my own passport and ticket home at the airport, in the care of Pedro Álvarez at the information desk, is clearly a trap.

I clamber down the slope until I come to a dry river bed. Sirens wail in the distance as I walk along the hard cracked surface. I need to get to a place where I can steal money and transport, and then get lost in Mexico City until I can buy some ID and a plane ticket. A lizard whips across the river bed in front of me. I turn to look at the flashing lights now assembling at the scene of the shooting. A helicopter is beating its wings a long way off and I can just make out its winking lights emerging from the glow above Mexico City. I continue along the river bed, hoping that I'll find a road that will lead me to people and cars.

I reflect on the past twenty-four hours, and wish I had listened to my reservations about working abroad when Martin first approached me with the job. I never liked the drug business. Too many amateurs and too many foreigners, but the profits were big and the risks small, with HM Customs full of disgruntled men and women willing to look the other way for a wad of cash. Villains had elbowed the hippies aside, piled into this new expanding business and started to make a lot of money. Martin had put a lot of work my way and paid well. Things were quiet and I reckoned that, as a freelance, it made no sense to turn work down.

The roar of the helicopter interrupts my thoughts as it sweeps over the hilltop and flies straight over the crime scene towards me. I am blinded by a searchlight and buffeted in its downdraft as it hovers directly above me. I run to the river bank and dive into the undergrowth. The helicopter lands on the river bed and the searchlight follows me as I run up the bank. I hear thrashing in the vegetation behind me.

Hands grip my arms and push me forwards onto the ground. I am handcuffed and carried down to where the helicopter stands on the river bed, its blades whoomfing the air. Arms reach out from the cabin, pull me up the ladder, force me into a seat in the rear, take off my cuffs, and snap a seat belt shut around my waist. My captors scramble up the ladder, the door is closed and we accelerate into the sky.

As Mexico dwindles below us I try to identify the men surrounding me. They look military but are not in uniform. A man in front of me turns suddenly.

Lee.

'So, how about that?' he says.

'Just as it was going so well,' I reply.

'Are you OK?'

'Yes. How did you get out?'

'Bullet-proof vest.'

'You knew?'

'No way. It was precautionary. That kind of shit happens down here.'

'Who was it?'

'I have no idea.'

'How did you find me?'

'You have a tracking device in your shoe.'

'You put it there?' I ask.

'Yes.'

'Why?

'In case you skipped at the reception.'

'And the chopper?'

'We were planning to fly you out from the mansion as soon as we got there. When I rolled out of the car, I got to a phone and called the bird over.'

'What's going on, Lee?'

'We're taking you to Texas.'

'Why?'

Lee indicates his fellow passengers. 'We'll talk when we get there.'

'How far is it?'

'Ten, maybe eleven hours.'

He reaches into a compartment in front of him, takes out a small package and offers it to me.

'Pastrami on rye?'

As he turns away from me, I see the Drug Enforcement Agency acronym on the back of his overalls.

While I'm wondering what Lee can want from me, and considering whether I'd rather kill him quickly or just maim him for life, the helicopter hits turbulence and weaves crazily for several seconds before the pilot regains control.

I can do nothing until we land and so I settle back in my seat, eat my first American sandwich and go to sleep.

• • •

I wake up shivering and aching all over. The helicopter has landed. Dawn has broken and I can see an airport control tower through the window.

'Where are we?' I ask.

'We're refuelling,' replies Lee.

I make out the words 'San Antonio Airport Authority' on the side of a truck on the runway.

'Where are we going?'

'You'll see,' says Lee.

His tone is hard. Perhaps we've left laconic Lee in Mexico. The helicopter engine erupts into life again and we take off. It's clear they're not going to give me a passport and put me on a flight home. The tracking device tells me that they planned to abduct me either before or after the hit. Which means they either knew Manuel was going to capture me or decided they could use me when Lee found out who I was. I wonder if they were responsible for the shooting. It seems unlikely they would risk my life as well as Lee's, and shooting a government minister and his wife probably goes beyond the DEA's remit.

A couple of hours later, the helicopter keels over into a dive and starts to descend steeply towards an airport below. I find a passing comfort in the drawling monotone of the pilot as he talks into his microphone before lowering the machine gently onto the tarmac. The door is opened and the ladder swings down. The agent next to me handcuffs me and releases my seat belt. I follow him onto the runway and he leads me to a jeep a couple of hundred yards away. After a short journey through the suburbs of some city we arrive at a long, white, bunker-like building with rows of slit windows and a tall wire fence.

As we stop in front of the gatehouse, Lee turns to me and says, 'There are a couple of things we have to do with you here. Just stay cool and I'll explain later.'

I am taken from the jeep to a fortified steel door. Lee says something into an intercom and the door slides open. We pass through and it clangs shut behind us. Two more doors are opened by guards and we enter a reception area. I am taken to a side room by two female guards and put through an admission procedure which includes photographs from various angles, fingerprints and a body search conducted by another female guard with an advanced case of obesity and a very long index finger. I am given a white prison overall and trainers in exchange for my blood stained Diane Von Furstenberg and my earrings and bracelet and shown to a cubicle where I change.

Another female prison guard, thin and wiry with a ratty face, escorts me along a wide corridor to a bare room with a table and two chairs. Ratface slams the metal door shut and stands beside it, staring vacantly into space. I sit at the table. After a short while a guard enters and places a tray bearing a cup of coffee and a bowl of what looks like pulled teeth with a small brown nipple at one end covered in some kind of syrup. I ask her what is in the bowl.

'Hominy grits,' she says, as she leaves. I taste a tooth and find it slimy and unpleasant. The coffee is reasonable and most welcome. Minutes later a man in a dark suit enters. He looks about fifty, tall, tanned and well-groomed with penetrating pale blue eyes beneath greying hair. He sits opposite me, takes a file from a briefcase and opens it.

He looks at the file, and then at me. 'You are Miss Rina Walker?'

'Yes,' I reply.

'The State Attorney's Office is in possession of evidence that you are an illegal alien who entered this country as a fugitive. It also has access to witness statements from members of the Drug Enforcement Agency to the effect that you committed a murder while in Mexico and subsequently entered the United States illegally. You are liable to be charged as such and may receive a considerable prison sentence if found guilty. You will be kept here at Gatesville Women's Correctional Facility where you will be held until a decision is made regarding the nature of the charges to be brought against you. You will then be formally charged and brought before a court.'

He sees that I am about to speak and immediately closes the file, replaces it in the briefcase and walks out of the room, slamming the door behind him. I'm wondering how Lee got to know about the killing at the hotel when Ratface opens the door again, steps forward and says, 'OK, come on.'

I drink the last of the coffee and follow her. We walk to the end of a long corridor and turn a corner. A guard unlocks a steel door and we step into the main hall of the prison. The angry buzz of several hundred incarcerated women presses in on me. Three tiers of cells line the walls, iron walkways at each level are accessed by stairways at each end of the hall. Prisoners come to the doors of their cells to see who has arrived. We climb to the first floor to a crescendo of howls, wolf whistles and the rattle of prison bars. Guards shout orders and clatter the bars with their nightsticks to quieten the noise, but to little effect. On the walkway, Ratface steers me past leering invitations, catcalls and vacant stares to a cell at the far end of the block. She unlocks the door and I am relieved to find I am alone in a two-berth cell. The din outside quietens.

I look around the cell in search of any evidence of a cellmate but find none. As I lie down on the lower bunk and wonder what happened to Lee, I hear a voice that seems to be coming from nearby.

'Hey, honey.'

I decide not to reply.

'You OK in there?'

I recall a wistful face at the bars of the cell next door as I passed. 'Yes, I'm OK,' I reply.

'It can be rough when you first come in.'

'I'm OK, thank you.'

'You ain't from around here, are you?'

'No, I'm not.'

'Where you from, honey?'

'England.'

'Well, ain't you a long way from home?'

Although I routinely resist sentimentality, I feel the truth of her remark.

'Good lookin' pussy like you gonna need protection in here, honey.'

'I'll be all right.'

'You got exercise period in ten minutes and you gonna find out different, out in that yard.'

'I'll be OK, thanks.'

'I can help you, honey.'

'No, thanks.'

'They all stupid like you over in England?'

I close my eyes and try to block out the voice of my neighbour and the racket of the prison.

'Oh boy, you one dumb bitch.'

She hits the bars with something metal and a guard shouts down the landing to keep it quiet.

Moments later, a siren wails. Through the bars I can see guards positioning themselves at intervals along the walkway, mostly leaning on the rail. At a shout from one of them, the cell doors slide open in unison and prisoners emerge and move towards the staircases. I linger in my cell until a guard comes to the door.

'Exercise. Go!'

I follow my neighbour, who turns and scowls at me as we descend the stairs. She is a young, slender Hispanic woman whose cold- hearted stare belies the soft tone of her voice. We turn into a dimly lit passageway and, as we file through a gate into the prison yard, I see her talking to an older, thick-set Caucasian woman with a shaved head and tattooed arms.

As I make my way towards the side wall, I am jostled into a corner of the yard and surrounded by a group of five or six prisoners, including my neighbour, who ignore the guards' instructions to keep moving and stare accusingly at me. One of them steps forward and punches me in the stomach. I lunge for her neck with both hands, but two of them pull me off her and throw me against the wall.

The circle parts to admit the shaven-headed one, who looks me up and down and says, in a deep rasping voice, 'OK, fish. Now you find out who runs this joint.'

'Fuck you,' I reply.

She slams a fist into my groin. I kick out at her but she has moved back and stands grinning at me.

'You a tough gal, English? I like that, but you too nice a cunt to get damaged. So you just calm down a little and we work something out here.'

I stare at her as she approaches me again.

'OK, cunt, this is how it works. You belong to me and these guys. You do what you're told and don't fuck with us and you be OK.' She thrusts her face close to mine, flicks my hair and licks my cheek. 'First thing you gonna do is carry a little stash in your pussy and another one up your ass.'

She beckons my neighbour and puts her arm round her.

'You get yourself to the can straight after chow tonight, and Pixie here gonna shove it up you good and hard, and you gonna take it, or we throw you in the shower and take turns making a whole lot more room up there.'

Her entourage snigger and leer. She takes her eyes off me for a second and I twist sideways, smash the heel of my right hand into her larynx and drop kick the woman beside her under her chin. I swing round and a blade glints in the sunlight as it slices towards me. I get a lucky kick at the hand that holds it and it clatters to the ground. I land beside it as a maelstrom of punches and kicks rain down on me and hands close round my throat. A hooter blasts insistently, my attackers are pulled off me and I am picked up, thrown up against the wall and handcuffed. The tattooed bear dyke lies on the floor beside me, clutching her throat and trying to breathe.

Two guards drag me back into the building, across the main hall, along a dark corridor and down a flight of concrete steps. I am pushed into a dimly lit cell with no windows. The door slams shut behind me. I crawl to the bed and collapse.

8

I'm standing outside the school gate with Georgie, waiting for Jack to come out. She hasn't said a word about last night, or anything else, come to that. She's staring in front of her as if she's in a dream.

'You all right?' I say.

She looks at me and goes, 'Mmm.'

She looks away into the distance again. I say, 'Last night ...'

'It's all right.'

Something about the way she cuts me off makes me go quiet. Maybe it's best to leave her alone. I see Jack come out of the boys' entrance and walk towards the gate. There're a couple of boys a little way behind him, laughing. One of them flicks something at him. Jack sees us and walks faster towards us. The two boys also see us and stop laughing.

When they get to the gate, I go over to them and say, 'Hello, boys.' One of them mumbles something and the other one giggles. 'Have you met our Jack's brother?' I ask.

'No,' says one. The other one shakes his head.

'He's looking forward to meeting you two. He's just come out of the Scrubs.'

One of them goes pale. The other one goes to say something but his mate grabs his wrist.

'Come on,' he mutters.

They walk slowly away and I go back to Georgie and Jack.

'Who's for an ice cream?' I say.

That puts a spring in Jack's step and it feels good to buy them a treat on the way back with *his* money. It was still stuffed into the armchair when I looked for it. Thirty-five quid and a few bob in change, which will last us a good long time, as long as I'm careful. Mum buys her own gin out of the money Dad left and pays the rent. She won't tell me how much she's got left but it can't be much, so I don't know how long we can hang on. I've told her to go to the National Assistance for money but she won't. She says Dad taught her to never get your name down on any forms or official things, so they can never find you that way.

It's warm and sunny when we get back to the street and I sit on the steps and watch Jack join in with a football game in the road. I see a couple of Georgie's friends with a skipping rope and a hula hoop on the other side, and I tell her to go over and join them, but she shakes her head and sits down on the pavement. She starts tracing something in the dirt with her finger. I try to see what it is but I can't make it out.

A gang of Teds are leaning on the railings outside Claire's, smoking fags and combing their hair. One of them's got a portable radio and he's trying to get it working, holding it by his ear and twisting a knob. He finally gets it to give out some tinny rock and roll and hangs it on the railings by its handle. He starts moving to it and Claire comes up the basement steps. He takes her hand and twirls her round but she's not in the mood and breaks away from him. His mates laugh at him as she walks away.

She comes and sits next to me on the steps and speaks quietly. 'Anything happened?'

'No.'

'No one's missed him yet, I suppose.'

'They will.'

'Yeah. That family, you don't mess with the Prestons.'

'I know.'

The window opens above us and Mum calls to us to come up. We go upstairs and into the kitchen. Mum's sitting at the table with Lizzie, who's in her fluffy pink dressing gown, black lace undies and high heels. I feel a tingle as I sit down beside her and get a waft of her perfume. She puts her arm through mine and it feels nice. Claire sits down next to me and I notice there's no gin bottle on the table for once.

Mum says, 'Right. We all know what's gone on so there's no point talking about it. You did well last night and I've got something for you both.'

She takes two sheafs of notes out of her pocket and puts one in front of Claire, the other in front of Lizzie.

'There's a bullseye each for last night.' Claire's looking shocked.

Lizzie picks up the notes and says, 'Cheers, Alice.'

'There'll be another one for you both in a bit, if all's well.'

'Lovely,' says Lizzie.

'I don't even need to say that no one knows except us,' says Mum. She looks directly at each of them. They both nod.

'We don't even talk about it between ourselves. One of us says something in a pub and someone hears it and that's how it all comes apart. It never happened. All right?'

'Understood,' says Lizzie.

'Claire?'

'I've got you, Mrs Walker.'

I'm thinking of how long it's been since I've seen Mum like this.

'Do you think it's all right where it is?' asks Lizzie.

'If they ever get round to clearing that dump, he'll be nothing but old bones and they won't stand a chance of identifying him.'

I hear heavy footsteps on the stairs.

Lizzie stands up and says, 'Back to work. Thanks, Alice.'

She gives Mum a hug and follows the footsteps upstairs. I can hear her greeting someone on the landing.

Claire's looking at the money as if she's never seen fifty quid before. Maybe she hasn't.

Mum says, 'Off you go now, love.'

Claire gets up, puts the money in her pocket and says, 'Thanks, Mrs Walker.'

'Take care, love.'

'You coming out later, Reen?'

'Maybe,' I say.

'See you then.'

'Yeah.'

She stands by the door for a moment as if she wants to say something, then she opens it and leaves.

I turn to Mum.

'Where did you get that money?'

Mum's reaching into the cupboard under the sink with her back to me. She turns round holding a bottle of gin. She takes a glass off the draining board, fills it and drains it in one. She sits down heavily at the table and refills the glass, takes another drink and looks at me. Her eyes are narrowed and hard with hatred.

'The fucking Prestons. How could you be so fucking stupid?' she says.

I feel a coldness in my stomach. I lean back as she swings her fist across the table at me. The gin bottle goes over and she lunges for it and rights it. She drains her glass again and fills it.

I stand up. 'Where did you get that money?'

'What fucking money?'

'What you just gave them.'

'Who?'

'Lizzie and Claire, who'd you think?'

'I don't fucking know.'

'Yes, you do.'

'You do, I do, you do, I …'

She's slurring now and going into one of her turns. She stands bolt upright, points her finger at me and starts yelling.

'I'll tell your dad on you and he'll fucking have you,

you silly fucking …!'

Her body jerks suddenly. She slumps back into the chair and falls sideways off it and onto the floor. She lies on her back, dribbling and making long moaning sounds. She rolls onto her side and tries to get up onto all fours. She can't find the strength so she sinks back down onto the floorboards and lies still. Her mouth's opening and closing and her eyes are searching about as if she's looking for something she recognises.

I'd normally help her to her mattress now, but I don't. I go to the metal box she has by the mattress and look in it. I know Johnny was right. She knows where Dad's money's hidden and she's used it to pay off Lizzie and Claire. She could have stopped him doing that to me and she didn't. I know she's going off her head, but when she's got her mind straight, like she had last night and when he came round and asked her, she knows just what she's doing.

There's nothing in the box but some of her old clothes, a couple of photos of her and Dad and us kids in the old days, and one of her and Dad getting married. A good-looking, happy young couple. I look at the pictures and I feel that cold feeling again.

I rip them into shreds and fling them in the fire. I rip up her clothes and they go in too. I get some newspaper from the pile beside the fireplace, ball it up, shove it underneath and light it. I pick up another paper and fan the flames until the whole lot's burning up. I could set fire to the whole kitchen and burn it all and her along with it. I think of her sitting there while he did that to me, knowing where the money is and saying nothing.

I go and stand over her. She's out cold. For two pins, I'd stick that carving knife into her like I did with him. Instead I pick it up and press the blade into the palm of my hand. The blood starts oozing and I'm going off into the pain and I'm not me anymore and all I feel is …

The door opens and Georgie says, 'We're hungry. Can we have our tea?'

I put the knife behind my back. I look at the two of them standing in the doorway and feel tears coming. I take a big breath and say, 'Of course you can. Just help me get Mum into bed and I'll make you a nice spam supper.'

• • •

I'm in the street with Claire and Sammy a couple of evenings later when I see Johnny's brother Dave and two of his mates coming along the pavement. I turn to go indoors, but Claire holds my arm and stops me. People move a bit out of their way to show they know they're from the Preston firm. They walk past us and stop to talk to a group of Teds a bit further up the street. After a bit, Dave leaves them and walks back towards us.

He stands looking at me for a bit too long, and then he smiles in a twisted sort of a way.

'Fancy a drink, Rina?' he says.

'I can't, Dave. I've got the kids indoors.'

Claire nudges me and says, 'You go on. I'll keep an eye.'

I look at her. She's telling me to act normal and I know she's right. 'All right, yeah, cheers, Dave,' I say.

'See you down the Elgin in half an hour?'

I nod and he walks away. His mates follow him along the street. Sammy says, 'What does that swanky git want?'

'I'll soon find out,' I say.

'He's the runt of the litter, isn't he?' says Claire.

Sammy laughs and says, 'He tried to slash Bobby Teague and Bobby threw him in the canal.'

'Yeah, then brother Johnny got hold of Bobby and smashed his knees,' says Claire.

'Yeah.'

Sammy laughs and Claire says, 'Go and get us ten Weights from the pub.'

'Give us the money then.'

She takes half a crown from her pocket and gives it to him. He walks off towards the Earl of Warwick.

Claire says, 'You've got to go.'

'I know.'

'You going to be all right?'

'Yeah.'

'He might be nothing, but his Dad and his uncles aren't.'

'It'll be all right.'

'Do you want me to come with you?'

'No, but you can lend me a decent skirt and blouse.'

• • •

As I come down Westbourne Park Road to the Elgin on the

corner of the Grove, I can hear the singer crooning out a Frank Sinatra song. There's a couple of Teds outside the pub arguing about something. There's no one on the door so I go in. The bar's full and noisy. The singer's on a raised platform in the corner with some old girl on the piano and a bloke on the drums. He finishes his song and a couple of people clap. I can't see Dave so I sneak through the crowd and get to the bar. The barman sees me and says something to an older man standing near him. The older one finishes serving someone and comes over. He folds his arms on the top of the pump handles and looks down at me.

He says, 'You're joking, right?'

'What do you mean?' I say.

'I mean you're not eighteen, now piss off.'

Someone behind me puts his hands on my shoulders. The barman looks past me and says, 'Oh. Sorry, guv.'

Dave comes beside me. Without taking his eyes off the barman, he says, 'What you having, love?'

'I'll have a whisky.'

Dave leans on the bar and says, 'We'll have a bottle.'

The barman gets a bottle of whisky and two glasses from under the counter and puts them on the bar.

Dave picks them up and turns away without paying. 'Let's find a quiet corner, eh?' he says.

I follow him past the singer, who's well away with his Al Jolson bit now, and we get a table against the wall at the back of the pub behind the piano. Dave sits close to me. He's looking round and checking who's in the pub. He turns to me but he doesn't speak.

I say, 'Free drinks?'

'We've got this place,' he says.

I know he means his family have got the protection.

He pours us both a whisky, turns towards me and says, 'I'm not going to fuck about, so you listen to me, all right?'

I nod.

He leans closer and says, 'I know what you've done.'

'What are you on about?'

'I was with him when he went into yours and I know what you and them slags did with him.'

I reach for my glass and take a drink. I should feel scared but I don't. I feel myself relaxing. It's like I'm watching myself and him from somewhere else.

He refills his glass and says, 'I'll get his body off the dump and show it to the filth if you want.'

I'm worried now for Lizzie and Claire, but I don't speak. He looks at me and says, 'Why don't you say something?'

I can't work out what his game is. He knows I did it and now he's got to get his revenge and kill me to save his face. Those are the rules. So why is he buying me whisky and giving me enough warning to go on the trot and get away with it? He sighs and puts his glass down. The piano stops and the song ends. A few people clap. He's still waiting for me to speak.

After a bit, he looks down at his drink and says, 'Johnny was an evil bastard and I don't blame you for what you did.'

I say nothing.

'He's done that to a few.'

'Yeah?'

'And worse.'

'He started on Georgie.'

'What is she, ten?'

'Nine.'

'Fuck.'

I can't believe I'm hearing this. The Prestons are one of the hardest families with a top firm. The father, George Preston, is the most feared man on the manor, and I've got his second eldest son telling me I've done right by killing his brother.

He says, 'It's not right to do that to kids.'

'You stood there watching the first time he did it to me.'

'I had to, didn't I?'

'Oh yeah?'

'If I hadn't, he'd have beaten me half to death.'

The old girl starts playing the piano again and the singer gets his teeth into another old song. There's a shout from the other end of the bar and a scuffle breaks out. More yelling, and then the door slams as someone gets kicked out.

Dave looks at me steadily and says, 'If I tell my Dad what's happened, you're dead. You know that, don't you?'

I nod.

'There's a way out of this for you.'

'Go on.'

'Do you know a bloke called Nick Bailey?'

'Everyone does.'

'Yeah.'

'What about him?'

'Johnny moved in on two of his clubs and he nicked some snide gear he had hidden as well. They've had a row going since way back and now Nick's threatened to do him.'

A glass smashes somewhere nearby. There are beads of sweat on Dave's forehead as he pours himself another drink.

'If I put it about that Nick done Johnny he won't deny it, because it'll make him look good.'

He takes another look round the pub as if he could be overheard, even though he couldn't be if he stood on the bar and shouted.

He looks into my eyes and says, 'But you'll have to kill him.'

'Why don't you do it?'

'Cos I've got you.'

9

I count the dead insects sticking to the metal cowling around the solitary ceiling light. Its amber glow barely penetrates the gloom of the dank cell. The pain is intense. I focus on it and cling to it as it rolls through my body like a brute force, hugging me and claiming me as its own. I drop from the bunk onto the hard floor to intensify it, rolling on my bruises and grazed flesh and crying out as the floor pushes into me, making me solid and strong. I disappear into the pain and lie still against a wall.

I hear distant voices and a lock turning. The cell door opens and I am picked up and laid on the bunk. Lee and a guard are looking down at me.

Lee leans close to me and says, 'You OK?'

I lift myself up slowly and sit against the wall. 'Mmm,' I reply.

'You did a little damage out there.'

'Good,' I say.

Lee tells the guard to get him a chair and hands me a cup of coffee. I take a sip and press my back into the cold wall, but the pain only hurts now. The guard places a chair by the bunk and Lee gestures to her to leave.

He sits down and says, 'I didn't mean for this to happen.'

'Really, how considerate.'

'You were supposed to be put in solitary. They screwed up. I'm sorry.'

'I decided to put myself there.'

'Right.'

'What is this, Lee?'

'We want you to do something for us.'

'What?'

'Help us bust Manuel.'

'Or else I get convicted and spend a good few years getting to know those ladies out there.'

'Yes.'

'And if I do?'

'You get your passport and we deport you without notifying the British authorities.'

'How do I know you'll keep your word?'

'You don't. But you do bad things, Rina, and you know too much about us. We won't want you around once your cover's blown.'

'Why me?'

'Because you're good and he'll trust you.'

'Do I have a choice?'

'No.'

'How does it work?'

'You go see Manuel and tell him you want to buy a million dollars' worth of cocaine.'

'Why would he believe I have a million dollars?' I say. I'm curious to see how he's going to work this.

'You tell him your old boss Martin left a million bucks and change across the border in El Paso for a deal he was planning, and you know how to get it.'

'Why don't you just go in and bust him?'

'We have no jurisdiction there.'

'So get the Mexican police to do it.'

'He's paying them off already and I want the collar.'

'So set him up yourself.'

'He knows I'm DEA.'

'How come?' I ask.

'We needed to explain how I escaped the shooting, so we arranged for him to find out.'

'Why wouldn't he think I was DEA as well?'

'Because you killed an agent in Acapulco.'

'What?'

'In your hotel room.'

'He was DEA?'

'We busted a couple of Manuel's Mexican guys in LA a while ago, turned them around, put them on the payroll and sent them back to work for Manuel. They were both on the detail that Manuel sent to pick you up from the hotel in Acapulco. Guido, the little guy, was one, and you killed the other. After our little mishap on the road last night, Guido conveniently found evidence I'd left behind at the house that I and the agent you killed are with the DEA and gave it to Manuel. He went ape-shit, and Guido was able to convince him that you and I never got in the car with Gonzales.'

'So why would he trust me now?'

'You tell him I pulled you out after the reception, took you to the US, had you charged with the murder of the agent and you escaped.'

'He'll never buy it,' I say.

'Yes, he will.'

'You're crazy.'

'Because that's what you're going to do.'

'What?'

'Escape.'

'From here?'

'Yes.'

'You mean you'll let me out.'

'No. You have to be seen to escape and Manuel needs to get to hear about it from his Mexican friends in here.'

'And how the hell do I escape?'

'We'll talk about that.'

'There's no way I'd go back to Manuel's,' I say.

'What else would you do?' asks Lee. 'You're out and alone and it's a long way to Canada, you have no passport, no contacts and you're wanted by the police, so it makes sense that you'd get yourself back to Mexico to avoid being recaptured here. Once you're there it also makes sense that you'd want to take over Martin's deal and sell the drugs yourself.'

'It also makes sense that you've set me up to do it.'

'Maybe so, but he's running that risk every time he sells a pile of drugs. In this case, a million makes it worth it.'

'How am I supposed to have travelled a thousand or so miles and got over the border with no money and no ID?'

'You stole a car, drove to El Paso, picked up a little walking around money and bribed the border guards. It happens all the time.'

Lee looks at me as if he's expecting an answer. 'I have no choice,' I say.

'Right. You hungry?'

'Yes.'

Lee goes to the cell door, opens the hatch and speaks to the guard. He returns to his seat and says, 'You tell Manuel that you'll go to El Paso to get the money by yourself, and arrange to meet him at the border at a time and a place that we'll advise you of through Guido. You say you'll only deal with him alone. If he brings anyone else, you won't play.'

'What if he tells me to bring the money from El Paso and buy the coke from him at the house?'

'You say you want to sell it in the US, but you have no way of getting it over the border and you know that he does it all the time.'

'Will he do it?'

'For a million? Sure.'

The door opens and the guard enters with a tray of food, which she hands to me. I take the cover off a foil dish which has various compartments containing some kind of bean stew, vegetables, potatoes and a slice of bread. I taste it tentatively and find it surprisingly good.

Lee watches me as I eat.

'Those bruises will add authenticity. You should get out there before they fade. How soon can you make it?'

'I'll have to look at my diary,' I reply. Lee laughs.

'You're about as cool as they come, Rina.'

I know I have to do what he says. If I stay in jail either the sisters will kill me or I'll end up on death row on a multiple murder charge. I reckon I stand a better chance of getting home from Mexico than the US.

As if reading my thoughts, Lee says, 'Guido'll meet you at the border and he'll kill you if you try to run.'

'What's in this for him?'

'If we get Manuel, he gets US citizenship.'

I finish eating and Lee calls the guard to take the tray. He offers me a cigarette.

I refuse and ask him, 'You were never a dealer, never in the Marines?'

'Oh, all that is true.'

'So?'

'I got busted in LA like those Mexican guys, got recruited and the career path took a swerve. The DEA need guys with professional experience, not degrees from Princeton.'

'So why didn't you set Manuel up when you were dealing with him before?

'I was just about to when he hauled me in. It screwed up months of planning, so we had to improvise a little. Lucky for me you were there too, huh?'

Lee moves to the door and knocks on it.

'I have a report to write. Get some rest and I'll check in with you later. Be ready to go in six hours.'

The guard enters. As she leans close to pick up the tray I briefly consider killing her and Lee, locking them in the cell and taking my chances. Although I'd probably get shot before I got fifty yards down the corridor. They leave and the cell door clangs shut.

I lie on the bunk and breathe deeply. The pain is dull now and no use to me. I'm tempted to hurt myself but I know I need to be present and clear to find a way out of this mess. He's right about getting back to Mexico. If I skip on this side of the border, every cop in Texas will be looking for me. I need to go along with the plan as far as Mexico and wait for an opportunity to take control.

I slide into sleep and dream of insects surrounding me and chattering hysterically in American accents. As I try to run away from them on leaden legs, the cell door opens.

The guard enters and says, 'Get up.'

I follow her down a corridor to a shower room and am given soap, shampoo and a towel. The guard steps into the room with me, locks the door behind her, leans her considerable bulk against the wall and watches me take off my overall and step into the shower. She stares at me with cold eyes, her mean lips pursed, while I enjoy the feel of the soapy water on my tired body. I turn the temperature to its hottest and feel the burn of the scalding water on my bruised flesh.

I am alone for a few blessed moments until the guard shouts, 'That's enough now. Come on out of there.'

I turn off the water and dry myself. The door opens and two guards enter with a woman in a light blue nylon overall carrying a small tin box. She puts the box on the table, takes out latex gloves and puts them on.

'Vaccination,' she says.

The guards take hold of me and bend me over the table. I try to struggle free, but can't move. I feel a burning pain between my shoulder blades. I am held down for a few seconds more and then released. I stand against the wall feeling the pain recede.

The woman in blue puts the syringe in the box along with the latex gloves, snaps the box shut and leaves, followed by the two guards. The remaining guard hands me my overall and I put it on.

She unlocks the door and says, 'Out.'

She follows me back to the cell. Lee is waiting outside. 'I'm taking the prisoner for interrogation,' he tells her.

The guard takes a clipboard down from a shelf beside the door and gives it to Lee, who signs it and returns it to her. I follow Lee along the dark corridor and we climb stairs to a brightly lit ground floor passageway. We enter an office with a view of the perimeter fence and I see that it is dark outside.

'What the fuck was that?' I ask.

'Radio frequency identification device, injected subcutaneously.'

'What?'

'You're tagged. We know where you are at any time. If you decide to go off route we report the passport, driver's license and the car as stolen and send the cavalry after you. I wouldn't try to dig out the chip, it's right next to your spinal cord. We'll get it out safely after the job's over.'

He indicates a canvas bag on the table.

'There are some clothes. Put them on and I'll be right back.'

He leaves the room. I try to reach the place between my shoulder blades where I was injected and can't. I open a bag on the table and find a pair of bell bottom jeans, a tie-dyed T-shirt, a leather jacket, a pair of All Stars and assorted underwear. I shed my overall and put on the clothes. I look at my reflection in the window and see an ageing hippy looking back at me. I frizz my hair up and then drag my fingers through it to complete the effect.

Lee enters and says, 'Hey, didn't I see you at Altamont?'

'Is this the best you could do?'

'You look cool. Nobody takes a hippy for a serial killer.'

'Not yet.'

'Right.'

Lee sits down, takes a blade with a taped handle from his pocket, and places it on the table in front of me.

'This is how it goes,' he says. 'I call the guard and say I need to go to the john. She stays with you and you make your move. The service entrance to the building is through the second door down the passageway to the right. There are two doors after that one, straight ahead of you, with one guard at each.'

He reaches into a pocket.

'This is the key to a green Chevrolet Impala parked along the street outside to the left. There's a map under the dashboard. You follow signs to Gatesville, then head for Austin, then San Antonio and you cross the border at Nuevo Laredo.'

'What do I use for a passport?'

Lee takes a wallet from his pocket and lays an American

passport, a driving licence and a sheaf of dollars on the table.

'Remember Caroline?' He taps the passport. 'This will get you in and out of Mexico, but if you try to fly home with it, you'll get arrested.'

'You've really covered all the angles.'

'It's what we do.'

He pushes the money towards me and says, 'This is enough for gas, food and a night in a motel.'

'How far is it to Manuel's?'

'About eleven hundred miles, so it should take two nine or ten-hour days. Can you handle that?'

'We'll see, won't we?'

'I guess so.'

'Why don't you just take me back in a helicopter?'

'He needs to believe you escaped. We can make sure he finds that out from his Mexican friends in here, but you need to be able to tell him how you got there. Also, he has all kinds of contacts with border guards and police and he can probably check that you crossed the border.'

I put the passport, licence and money in various pockets and put the prison overall back on. I peel some tape off the handle of the blade and stick it to the underside of the table. I need to get out of this building before I use it to do some serious damage to the smooth-talking bastard sitting opposite me.

'What time is it?' I ask.

'Three-thirty a.m. Good to go?'

'Yes,' I say.

He knocks on the door and the guard enters. She is about my height and weight with cropped dark hair and an angular, acne-scarred face, deep set eyes, a prominent nose and thin lips. She directs Lee to the men's' room, locks the door after he leaves, stares at me briefly, sits on a chair by the door and chews at a fingernail.

I get to my feet slowly and clutch at my stomach. I let out a gurgling moan and reel forward onto the table. The guard crosses to me, says something I don't hear and puts a hand on my back. I grab the near edge of the table, wrench it off the floor, pin her against the wall with the table top and ram my forehead into the bridge of her nose. Bone crunches and she goes limp and slides to the floor. I put down the table, pull her into the middle of the room and remove her weapon belt, shoes, trousers and shirt. I see that she's wearing my bracelet and I unclip it and put it on my wrist.

I take off the overall, leather jacket and jeans and put on her uniform, noticing that she's wearing split-crotch panties, which I decide to leave with her. I put the hippy kit back in the bag, sling it over my shoulder and strap on the weapon belt which contains a Smith and Wesson .38 snubnose, pepper spray, baton and hand cuffs. I check the gun is loaded, unclip the handcuffs, roll the guard onto her back and cuff her wrists. She stirs into consciousness. I help her up, sit her in a chair, stand in front of her and point the gun at her head. It seems a long time since I had power.

'What's your name?' I ask.

'Delores,' she says, swallowing blood.

'Listen to me, Delores.'

'Fuck you.'

I hit her in the face with the gun butt. She passes out again and I realise that I don't have time for conversation. I unlock the door, move behind Delores and pull her to her feet. As she comes round, I lock my arm around her neck and hold her with her back against me.

I press the gun barrel into her temple.

'We're walking out of here now and if you make one sound, or one move, I will blow your fucking brains out.'

As we leave the room I notice the blade, still taped to the upturned table, and decide to leave it.

I push the guard along the corridor to the second door on the right and put her against the wall beside the door. I take the key ring from my belt and show it to her.

'Which one?'

She points to a key. I put it into the lock and make her stand in front of me with the gun at the back of her head. I reach around her, turn the key and remove it from the lock.

'Open it,' I say.

She turns the handle. I kick the door open and take her along an empty corridor to a door at the end. As we approach it, I hear voices on the other side. I turn Delores round to face me and force the gun barrel into her mouth.

'When I knock on that door, you tell them who you are and then you tell them to open it.'

She nods and I turn her round to face the door, get a

grip of her neck with one hand and kick the door.

Delores says, 'One four nine seven. Open up.'

The lock turns and the door swings open. Two guards reach for their guns. I shoot one in the leg before she can draw and she goes down. I put the gun to Delores's head and the other guard backs off.

'Gun and belt over here,' I say.

She unclips her belt, throws it to my feet and lays her gun beside it. I tighten my grip on Delores's neck and point my gun at the unarmed guard.

'Cuff yourself to her,' I say, pointing to the guard on the floor who is cursing and trying to apply pressure to her thigh to stop the bleeding. As the cuffs lock, I push Delores towards the two of them.

'Now her,' I say.

The unarmed guard handcuffs Delores to the wounded guard and all three are locked together on the floor. I take the wounded guard's gun, put it in the corner out of their reach, and put the gun from the belt on the floor into my back pocket. I unclip the handcuffs from the belt I am wearing and cuff Delores to the bars on the inside of the door we entered by. I try various keys in the lock of the external door until one of them turns. It occurs to me that I won't get through the gate wearing a weapon belt so I take it off and toss it out of reach of the guards. As a parting gift I empty a pepper spray into each of their faces, and leave.

The balmy Texas air wraps itself round me like a warm blanket as I walk along the perimeter wire towards the main gate. I hear a distant scream from somewhere above and a maniacal laugh echoing after it. I find an ID card in my shirt pocket and see that I am Delores Skepski. I memorise her number as I approach the gate, but the solitary male guard slouching outside the guardhouse merely nods at me, releases a lever on a side door and swings it open. I nod back at him as I walk through the door and across a grass area to the road. The green Chevrolet is parked a short distance away. I unlock it, get in and relax at the wheel for a moment. I put the gun in the glove compartment, check the map is there, turn on the ignition and gun the engine.

10

I've left Dave in the pub. He's seen some mates come in and gone over to them, and I've slipped out the back door. I'm walking up Westbourne Park Road, looking at the new moon in the starry sky and thinking about what Dave's said. The air's still warm and the pubs haven't chucked out yet, so the street's fairly quiet. A car slows down and crawls along beside me. I cross the pavement and walk beside the railings. The driver's an old baldy with horn rimmed specs. He decides I'm not a brass and accelerates away. He'll be lucky to get home with his wallet tonight.

Dave's said he'll grass me for Johnny if I don't do Nick Bailey. I doubt if he would because it would cost him his reputation if it was known, unless he can get the police to keep his name out of it. I reckon he's decided to make me take care of Nick because he's scared of doing it himself but he wants the credit. If I refuse, he'll either grass me or tell his Dad, and then I'm either dead or inside for a long time. I can't disappear because of the kids. I'd leave Mum behind no trouble, but where could I take the kids with no money? I know I'll have to do it. I've done it once and I can do it again. I don't care about Nick Bailey, it'll only be one less nasty violent bastard on the manor. I just need to make sure I'm not caught.

I get back to our street. Claire will still be at ours and she'll ask me what he's said. I don't want her involved. No one must know, except Dave, and I can handle him later.

When I get indoors, Mum's passed out on the mattress and Claire's at the table holding a glass of gin.

'They're all tucked up, good as gold,' she says.

'Asleep?'

'I think so. Jack's been coughing a bit.'

In the bedroom, I can see Georgie lying on her back, staring at the ceiling. She doesn't look at me.

I say, 'You all right?'

She nods a bit without taking her eyes off the ceiling. I watch her staring for a moment. She's hardly said a word since that night and I don't know what to do for the best. I can't take her to the doctor or anything. "Hello doctor, have you got something for a nine-year-old girl who's had a man stabbed to death on top of her while he was in the middle of raping her?" I just hope she'll come round and be her bright lovely self again. At least Jack's all right. He thinks it was a bad dream and we've told him it was.

I go back to the kitchen.

Claire says, 'Well, what did he say?'

'Wanted to know if I'd seen him.'

'Do you reckon he knows anything?'

'I don't think so.'

'Did he ever come round here with him, after that first time?'

'No.'

'Did he say he was missing?'

'No.'

'I suppose he wouldn't.'

'I think we're all right. If he knew anything, he would have said.'

'Yeah.'

I yawn and say, 'Thanks for minding them.'

'No bother. Your mum was more trouble.'

'Eh?'

'Kept calling me Doreen and telling me I was out of order and she was going to tell Maurice on me.'

'That's her sister. Got killed in the war. She had an affair with an American airman while her old man Maurice was off on the Ark Royal, then she got killed by a bomb. She's always on about it.'

'She ain't right, is she?'

'No.'

'I'll get off then.'

Claire goes to the door. She opens it and says, 'Sammy reckons he's a poof.'

'Dave?'

'Yeah. Goes to some secret club in Rotherhithe, he says.'

'Oh yeah?'

'See you tomorrow.'

Claire goes and I make a cup of tea and sit at the table for a bit. I look over at Mum snoring and I wonder where she's put Dad's money. I look at the dishes she's left dumped up in the sink after I've left it all tidy. I look at the mess everywhere, the grey dirty walls and rotten window frames and the smell of the damp and I think how it would be to live somewhere nice and clean and comfy.

Jack starts coughing and I go in to him and pick him up. 'There, there now, you're all right,' I tell him.

I take him into the kitchen where it's a bit warmer and get the cough mixture from under the sink. I put him on my knee at the table and give him a spoonful. He keeps on coughing for a bit and then he settles and leans against me. I stroke his hair and rub his back and I can feel how hot he is, even though it's a cold night. I feel him going back to sleep. I'll get him to the doctor's straight after school tomorrow.

I take him back to bed and lie him down. He snuggles up to Georgie and I look at them both and I'm thinking how I can get hold of enough money to get us out of here and into somewhere decent where a little boy won't be coughing his lungs up.

I go back to the kitchen. The stink tells me Mum's shat herself. I sit at the table, and I look over at that mean selfish woman lying in her own filth, and I know what I'm going to do.

I put my coat on again and take a kitchen knife off the draining board. I go into the bedroom, prise up the floorboard and take out Johnny's gun. The cold metal feels good in my hand. I thumb the catch, spin the cylinder and check it's full. I close it and check the safety. I put it in my coat pocket, go out onto the landing and lock the door behind me. I put the key behind a loose bit of skirting board, go upstairs to Lizzie's and knock on her door.

She opens it and says, 'You all right, love?'

'Yeah, but I've got to go out for a bit. They're asleep.

Can you look in, make sure they're all right for me?'

'Key in the usual place?'

'Yeah.'

'Go on, you're all right.'

'Thanks, Lizzie.'

As I get to the stairs she says, 'You heard anything?'

'No. You?'

'No.'

I go down the stairs and into the street. I'm hoping he's still in the Elgin. It's getting near closing time and I walk fast past the Warwick, onto Golborne and down to the Grove. I get to the Elgin and go in. It's packed now and I push through the press of bodies and try to spot Dave. Someone's grabbing my arse and I twist away from him and see Dave sitting at a table with some of his firm grouped round him. He sees me and gets up. I turn and make my way back through the crowd to the door. I look round to make sure he's following me and I go out through the door and walk a few yards up the street. He comes out of the pub and sees me. I walk a bit further and turn into an entry. Dave follows me in and leans on the wall opposite me.

'I'll do it,' I say.

'Yeah?'

'I want to do it quickly.'

'All right.'

'When?'

'I've got to get the word out that he's done Johnny first.'

'I never knew you were stupid as well as weak.'

He comes towards me clenching his fist. 'You fucking watch it, you little cunt.'

I whip the gun out and point it at his face. 'Recognise this?' I say.

He stands back against the wall and says, 'Hang on now, Rina.'

'You tell people Nick's done it *after* I've killed him.'

'Eh?'

'Or he'll be tooled up and waiting for you, won't he?'

He thinks for a bit, then says, 'Yeah, I suppose.'

'This way we surprise him. Get it?'

'Yeah.'

'And I want a monkey for it.'

'Fuck off.'

I press the gun barrel against the middle of his forehead and pull back the hammer.

'You're a fucking worthless cunt like your brother, and I'll drop you right here if you don't stop mucking me about.'

He's shaking now, inside his sharp coat.

'All right,' he says.

'Two hundred at my house, five o'clock tomorrow, the other three when it's done. And I want to know where he goes of a night and what he does. All right?'

'Yeah.'

I can hear voices and laughter back in the street. The pub's closing. I put the gun away and walk back to the street. Dave's behind me. His mates are standing outside the pub. They see us coming out of the entry and I pull

Dave to me and kiss him and say goodnight. His mates whoop and laugh. One of them gives a wolf whistle. I walk away up the hill, spit out the taste of beer and fags, and I'm feeling good, like I'm finding my strength. As I turn the corner, I can see Dave laughing with the others.

• • •

As I go up the stairs, I can see our door's wide open and I can hear Jack coughing. I run into the bedroom and he's lying naked on the bed. Georgie's got a bowl of water and Lizzie's holding a wet cloth on his forehead.

Lizzie says, 'He's ever so hot, Reen, and he's been coughing his little heart out.'

I can see the cough mixture on the table. I pick him up and cradle him. I can feel how hot he is and the way he's trembling.

I say, 'I'm taking him to the hospital.'

'How are you going to get him there?' asks Lizzie.

'I'll have to carry him.'

I hear footsteps on the stairs and I realise I've left the door open. Lizzie says, 'Oh fuck. That'll be a trick. Hang on.'

She goes into the hall and I can hear her talking to someone.

Georgie says, 'I want to come.'

'You stay here and get some sleep,' I say.

'I'm coming.'

'No, Georgie.'

She goes into the kitchen, gets her coat from the back

of the door and puts it on. I get the gun out of my pocket and put it back under the floorboard just as Lizzie comes back into the bedroom.

'The trick's got a car,' she says. 'He's going to drive us to the hospital.'

'How come?' I say.

'Don't worry about it.'

'But …'

'Come on.'

Lizzie picks up the old shawl off the bed and puts it round Jack, and then she pushes me out the door and on to the landing. There's an old boy in a black hat and overcoat with a white moustache and round glasses standing on the landing. He looks nervous when he sees us and scurries down the stairs in front of us. His car's parked outside. He opens the door and me and Jack and Georgie get in the back. I smell the leather and sink into the soft seat. Jack's still hot and trembling in my arms. He coughs some phlegm into the shawl and I can see blood in it. Lizzie and the old man get in the front.

He starts the engine and Lizzie says, 'Paddington General, Harrow Road. Do you know it, Bernard?'

'Not really,' says Bernard.

'Opposite Marylands Road. Go to the end and turn left.'

Bernard drives the car through the back streets to Harrow Road and we pull up in front of the hospital.

Lizzie says, 'You go in and get him seen to and we'll wait for you just round that corner.'

She points to a turning just beyond the hospital.

Bernard says, 'I can't be waiting.'

'Shall we go and see your wife then?'

'Oh, well ...' he says.

Lizzie puts her hand on his leg and says, 'I think you'll be happy enough waiting, you old dog.'

I get out of the car with Jack. Georgie follows me to the main door of the hospital. Just as I'm going in, Georgie points to a sign by the door.

'Emergency. It's over there,' she says.

We walk to another door further along the building and go in. There's noise coming from a room off the corridor on the right and I look into a dimly lit room with rows of benches with people sitting and lying on them. Some are asleep and some look pretty bashed up and drunk with it. There's an old geezer shouting at the far side of the room, and people are telling him to shut up. A nurse is going along the front row of seats. She's talking to people and writing in a book she's carrying. There's a young Indian bloke in a white coat leaning against the wall behind her, yawning.

Jack starts coughing and I go up to the nurse and say, 'Can you help him, please?'

'Take a seat.'

'He's really bad.'

I show Jack to her, but she just looks down at her book and says, 'Take a seat.'

I turn to the bloke in the white coat and say, 'He's really bad.'

'You'll have to see the nurse,' he says.

Jack's coughing really badly now. I go right up to him and hold Jack up.

'Please, will you have a look at him. Please!'

Jack gives a big cough and then a rasping sort of noise when he breathes in. The Indian bloke looks down at Jack and feels his forehead. He takes a tube thing from round his neck, sticks the ends of it in his ears and puts another end on Jack's chest. He moves the thing around on his chest for a bit.

'How long has he been like this?'

'He's been coughing for a couple of weeks, I suppose.'

'The fever?'

'Just tonight. Couple of hours maybe.'

'Longer,' says Georgie.

He puts the tube thing back round his neck, takes Jack off me and says, 'Come with me.'

He strides off towards a door at the back and we follow him. The nurse calls out, 'What on earth do you think you're doing, doctor?'

'Emergency,' he says, over his shoulder.

'They're all …'

The door slams shut on her words and we follow him down a long corridor to a door at the end.

He stops and says, 'He's very ill. I'm taking him in for treatment. Wait here and someone will come and take the details.'

'Will he be all right?'

'I can't say. Wait here.'

He takes Jack through the door and I can see bright

lights and the end of a bed with a black metal frame as the door swings shut. We sit down on a bench and I'm kicking myself for going out and not being there when he got feverish. Georgie's sitting next to me staring straight ahead of her.

I say, 'Go and tell Lizzie to take you back with her.' She shakes her head.

'Do as I tell you.'

'No.'

I take her arm, turn her towards me and say, 'I'm telling you to ...'

The door opens and a West Indian nurse appears. She looks at me clutching Georgie's arm and says, 'Everything all right here?'

'Yes,' I say.

The nurse comes and stands in front of us. She's tall and fat and I can feel her white apron brushing against my knees. She smells all clean. She takes a pen out of her top pocket and raises up a board she's holding.

'Patient's name?' she asks.

I give her Jack's name and address and his age and that and she asks where his parents are. I tell her his Dad's away in the army and his mother works nights, and she looks at me a bit strange and writes something down.

I say, 'When will he be out?'

'He's been admitted for treatment. You come back at midday tomorrow and go by main entrance, ask for the children's ward and the nurse or the doctor will see you.'

'Will he be all right?'

'You go now. You come tomorrow and you bring your mother.'

She opens the door, and turns and looks at us for a moment and then leaves. The door swings shut with a hissing sound.

I stand up and say, 'Come on then.' Georgie doesn't move.

'We can't stay here all night,' I say.

'You go. I'm staying.'

'You can't.'

'Go.'

I'm standing there wondering what to do. It's all official in here and I saw the way that nurse was wondering why there was no grown-up with us. If they send someone round and see the state of Mum they could take Georgie and Jack away and put them in a kids' home. I grab Georgie's arm and pull her along the corridor. She starts wailing and biting my wrist, but I just keep dragging her along and luckily no-one sees us. When we get into the emergency room, there's so much noise and kerfuffle with people shouting and waving their arms about, no-one notices us passing through.

Once I get her onto the street, she calms down and goes silent and sullen. We walk round the corner and I can see the car parked a little way up the street. As we get nearer, I can hear someone whimpering. Bernard's in the back seat and his head's bobbing back and forward. I hold Georgie back and pull her into a doorway. Bernard lets out a juddering sort of a sigh and slumps forward. Lizzie sits up beside him. I give it a moment and then we go to the car.

Lizzie sees us, gets out of the back door and says, 'Where is he?'

'Keeping him in.'

'What did they say?'

'They're giving him treatment, they said.'

'That's good.'

She opens the back door. Bernard is pulling his trousers up.

She says, 'Come on, look lively, you old trout. Time to get off back to the missus.'

He scrambles out of the back and gets behind the wheel of the car. 'Most irregular,' he mumbles.

'You've saved yourself thirty bob, so stop moaning.' We get into the car and the old boy drives off.

When we get back to ours, Georgie goes to bed and me and Lizzie have a cup of tea. We don't say much, and when she goes upstairs, I go through to the bedroom and get undressed. Georgie's reading so I make her put the book away and try to go to sleep. When I get in beside her I can see her tears coming as she stares at the ceiling.

11

I search frantically for the Chevrolet's clutch pedal and nearly wrench the gear lever off the steering column until I remember that the car is American and equipped with an automatic gearbox. I move the gear lever into drive and ease the car towards the lights of Gatesville. As I reach the end of the street and turn onto a main road, I hear sirens wailing. There is a sudden flare in the rear view mirror as every light in the prison is switched on. Moments later, I am blinded by headlights as three police cars race past me towards the prison.

On the outskirts of Gatesville, I pull into a parking lot behind a warehouse and consult the map. I need to go south on Highway 36 to Temple and then pick up Interstate 35 to San Antonio and Nuevo Laredo. I drive on into town. A sign tells me I am on East Main Street and I reach an intersection with a sign to Temple. I turn onto Highway 36, wind the Chevrolet up to seventy miles an hour, roll down the window and let the warm wind blow the prison stink out of my hair.

After a few miles I pull over at a truck stop, find the ladies room and change into the jeans, T-shirt and All Stars. I tear Delores's uniform to shreds, stuff it into the used sanitary towel bin and dump her shoes in the cistern. I steer the car back onto the highway and put my foot down.

Dawn breaks and the sun rises over distant rolling hills. I turn on the radio. Tammy Wynette tells me to stand by my man and the disc jockey forecasts another hot one. The Chevrolet rolls along, bouncing and sashaying sensuously when it meets a bump on the road. I relax back into the soft leather bench seat, savouring the sense of speed and solitude, and consider possible moves. Lee's assurance that I'll end up back at Heathrow with no problems after helping him to capture Manuel is about as reliable as any of his other promises. He'll either throw me back in jail or hand me over to the Mexican police as soon as he's got Manuel. If I dump the car and the clothes and somehow get free of the tracking device, it puts me on the run from the Texas police with a stolen passport and a murder charge. Once over the border, I am out of US jurisdiction, but still under the one eye of Guido. I reckon my best chance of getting home and out of this whole mess is to drive on to Manuel's and try and work something out when I get there.

At Temple, I join the interstate and ride south through the gathering heat, with the flat expanse of Texas farmland on each side of me. I cross the Colorado River at Austin, and a couple of hours later the highway is scything through the urban sprawl of San Antonio. By midday I am parched and hungry. At a sign for Love's Truck Stop, a few miles north of Laredo, I take the exit ramp and park between a white Cadillac spattered with mud and a Volkswagen Beetle. I walk past a line of very tall trucks with chrome chimneys rising proudly above their cabs like cheerleaders' batons. I enter the diner and take a booth by the window. A couple of heavy-looking truck drivers at the far end of the counter turn and take in my hippy weeds. I study the menu and hope they haven't seen Easy Rider.

A pretty, raven-haired waitress, about my age, with a fulsome figure and a broad smile, comes to the table, pours coffee and asks what she can get me. I order a hamburger and appreciate her rear view as she wiggles away on high heels and relays the order through a hatch behind the counter. A couple more drivers enter and mount stools at the counter, adding their cowboy boots to the row resting on the foot rail. The waitress greets them, pours coffee and takes orders. One of the drivers at the far end is still staring at me. He says something to the one next to him and they laugh. The other one turns, grins at me and runs his tongue obscenely over his upper lip. I give him a cold look and stare out of the window.

The waitress arrives with my hamburger and says, 'Don't you pay that mean bastard no mind, honey.'

I smile and shake my head.

'He just some sad old trucker, ain't got it up in years.'

'Goes to bed with his gearstick.'

We laugh. The trucker turns away, snarling some remark to his friend. I pay attention to my hamburger and ignore the occasional glance from the counter where the truckers are discussing whether AM or FM is the best CB radio. An older woman with a stooped figure comes in and goes behind the counter and into the kitchen. As I finish the last of my hamburger, the waitress comes to the table and leans her hip against it.

'You want some pie?' she says.

'Just the check, thank you,' I reply.

She takes a pad from her shirt pocket, scribbles some figures on it, tears off the page and places it on the table. I give her a five-dollar bill and she gets change from a purse under her apron. She hands it to me with a broad smile.

'You have a good trip now,' she says.

• • •

A blast of afternoon heat hits me as I walk through the door and cross to the car. I get in and open all the windows. A truck is blocking my way forward, so I reverse out and then drive round the back of the diner. I brake as two figures come out of the back door of the diner and cross in front of the car. As they walk towards a grey van belonging to Texas Beef Incorporated, I recognise the two guys who stared at me from the counter. One of them sees me as they open the doors of the van and says something to the other one. They shut the doors, walk back towards the car and stand in front of it. One is short, bald and broad-shouldered with a large beer gut. The other is medium height, dark and lean, with a couple of days stubble on his lantern jaw.

I lean forward, as if I'm trying to get a look at them, and take the gun from the glove compartment. I slide it into the back of my waistband and step out of the car.

The bald one folds his arms, cocks his head and says, 'You wanna suck on my dick, sweetheart?'

His friend finds this remark amusing and adds, 'Or are you one of them lesbeens?'

Just as I'm deciding to pull out my gun and nip this sparkling repartee in the bud, the waitress comes out of the back door of the diner. She takes in what is happening and hurries towards us.

'Carl, Duane, you get on out of here right now,' she snaps.

'Fuck you, Charlene, we gonna teach this here hippy bitch a lesson.'

'You just get back in your old meat wagon and get going before I get Frank and Charlie out here.'

As she speaks, a large truck sputters into life somewhere nearby and hoots its horn as it grinds past the front of the diner.

Baldy looks at it and says, 'Well now. Wouldn't you know it? They just left. Who you gonna get now? Old mother Jackson and that spic midget you got in the kitchen?'

Charlene glares at him but says nothing as the lean one takes a hunting knife from behind his back. I grip my gun and contemplate shooting him, but I don't want to land Charlene in trouble.

'Hey look!' I shout, pointing at the door of the diner.

As Baldy turns his head, I swing the butt of the gun at his jaw and knock him out. He falls heavily onto the gravel. Charlene is trying to wrestle the knife out of Carl's hands. I pocket my gun, get behind him, take him round the neck, cut off his air supply and lower him to the ground.

As he turns purple, I lean into his face and say, 'Take your friend and get out of here. Now!'

Charlene holds the knife at his neck as he gets to his feet with his hands raised in surrender. Baldy is still out cold and Carl has difficulty lifting him. I open the back door of the van and between us we dump him on the greasy floor and slide him in among the hanging sides of beef and boxes of hamburger meat. Carl looks sheepishly at Charlene and seems about to say something, but thinks better of it and gets into the van.

As he starts the engine, Charlene walks to the window and says, 'You don't say nothing about this, Carl Mercer. You hear?'

Carl looks at her for a moment and then nods.

'You and that fat gut hayseed in there.'

'I hear you, Charlene.'

The van moves a few feet and then stops. Carl leans out of the window, looks balefully at Charlene and says, 'Can I have my knife back?'

'You get your skinny ass out of here!'

The van moves off and Charlene turns to me. 'Where did you learn to punch like that?' she asks.

I show her the gun and say, 'I had a bit of help.'

'Oh, right. I'm glad you didn't shoot him.'

'I reckon he is too.'

She laughs but I can see she's been shaken by what's happened. 'Are you OK?' I ask.

'Just fine. Are you?'

I nod and say, 'It was good of you to help me.'

'Don't mention it, honey. I've been waiting for a chance to whop them assholes for years.'

I notice that she's not wearing her apron and ask, 'Are you finished now?'

'Yeah, that's me done for the day. I'll go on over and get the bus.'

'Let me give you a lift.'

'There's no need.'

'It's really no trouble,' I say, as I open the car door for her.

• • •

As we drive, she asks me where I'm from and where I'm headed and I tell her that I've been visiting my brother in Dallas and am on my way to meet friends in Acapulco, to celebrate a wedding anniversary. We leave the highway, wind along country roads for a few miles and pull into a trailer park in a wooded area bordered by farmland. Charlene points to a medium sized Winnebago trailer with a table and chairs in front under a dark red awning. I park beside it.

She turns to me and says, 'You want to come in for a while?'

I'm not sure if her look is promising more than simple Southern hospitality, but I feel I want to find out.

'Why not?' I say.

She unlocks the door, shows me into the worn upholstered interior and switches on two fans, one at each end of the living area. I enjoy the cool breeze while she goes to the fridge, takes out two bottles of beer and offers me one. When I accept, she cracks them open against the work top, hands one to me and sits on the sofa. When I sit down beside her she leans back, crosses her legs and takes a long pull at the bottle.

'That was kinda wild back there,' she says.

'It was.'

'I ain't never seen a woman take care of a situation the way you did.'

'It's lucky they were so stupid.'

'You were so fast.'

I try to smile modestly.

She puts her arm on the back of the sofa, uncrosses her legs and takes another drink. After a pause she says, 'You look so slim and pretty, like you couldn't hurt a fly.'

She leans her head back and I sense her relaxing. I put my arm on the back of the sofa and move my hand towards hers. Our fingers touch and she is still for a moment. When I stroke the back of her hand, she moves it away, takes a deep breath and leans forward on the sofa. The silence is uncomfortable, but when I start to get up she puts a hand on my arm.

'Don't go,' she says.

I sit back and she looks at me and smiles.

'I like you being here but … that ain't me, you know?'

'I'm sorry.'

She looks as if she's on the edge of tears and I know

she wants to tell me something. The sassy waitress with the smart lines has become a lost girl. I look around the trailer and see a photograph of a man in military uniform on top of the TV that I wish I'd noticed before. He has a kind open face and a warm smile. She sees me looking at the picture.

'Is that your husband?' I ask.

'He was killed.'

'I'm sorry.'

'Vietnam.'

'When did it happen?'

'Six months ago.'

'How did he …?'

'He was injured. The field hospital he was in up country got bombed by our guys.'

'American bombs?'

'Right.'

'That's terrible.'

'It happens a lot.'

'I didn't know.'

'It isn't reported.'

'Have many died like that?

'No one really knows, but they think maybe a third of US casualties in 'Nam have been from friendly fire.'

'That's awful.'

'They think it's near twenty thousand.'

We sit in silence for a time and I think about the stupidity of wars and the people who make them, and wish they could feel the misery of this heartbroken girl.

'Did you live here together?' I ask. Charlene sits back and dries her eyes.

'We was living with his folks on their farm. I never really got on with his mother and after Joey was killed, she turned real sour towards me, like it was my fault or something, so I moved here.'

A truck drives past outside and a dog barks. I look at the tired condition of the furniture and the limp curtains filtering the setting sun, and I feel the loneliness of her grief.

'You have someone back home?' she asks.

I think how long it's been since I saw Lizzie and say, 'Not really.'

Sitting next to Charlene, feeling her sadness and hearing the odd sounds outside of dogs and people coming and going and living their lives, the thought of finally resting somewhere and living a simple life of plain love and ordinary concerns tugs at me for a moment.

I notice the time on the clock next to the husband's picture and realise that I should get back on the road. I stand up and take the car keys out of my pocket.

Charlene says, 'You have to go now?'

'I really should.'

'You can stay over, if you want.'

She stands, moves towards me and then hesitates. I can see that she doesn't want to be alone and I am tempted to stay with her, but then I think of Lee alerting the Texas Police if I don't cross that border on schedule.

'My friends are expecting me so I ought to get going,'

I say.

She nods and as I turn towards the door, she leans forward, gives me a brief kiss on the cheek and giggles. I kiss her back and we laugh together as she opens the door for me.

I step down onto the grass, turn and say, 'Will those meat boys give you any trouble?

'Nah. They'd never admit to being beaten on by a woman.'

I get into the car, start the engine and return Charlene's wave as I drive towards the road.

12

I'm at the hospital before twelve and Georgie's with me. Neither of us has slept much. I've tried to make her go to school but she wouldn't, so I've said she can come. We go in the main entrance and a black woman sitting behind a glass partition tells us how to get to the children's ward. We climb two flights of stairs and go along a corridor with green walls and a shiny floor. Nurses and people in white coats go in and out of doors, and look at us as if we shouldn't be there.

The ward is at the far end. I can hear children coughing and crying as we get near the door. There are rows of beds on each side with children in every one. Some are sitting up talking to visitors that have come and others are lying down alone. Some have their arms or legs in plaster, strung up above the bed on pulleys. I move out of the way of a little lad in a wheelchair who's lost one of his legs, and go to a nurse who's standing at the end of one of the beds talking to a smart- looking old couple.

'Excuse me,' I say.

She turns and gives me a sour look. 'Yes?' she says.

'Can you tell me where Jack Walker is please?'

'Is he a patient?'

'Yes.'

'Are you relatives?'

'We're his sisters,' I say.

She sighs, turns to the smart couple and says, 'Would you excuse me a moment?'

The man nods and smiles. The nurse walks towards a desk at the end of the ward and signals us to follow her. As we get to the desk, she looks at me crossly and says, 'Those are trustees, you know.' She takes a book off the desk. 'What was the name?'

'Jack Walker.'

She turns a page and runs her finger down it.

'He's in isolation. Go through that door and wait for someone.'

She snaps the book shut and marches back to her trustees, whatever they are. We go through the door she showed us into a narrow, dimly lit hallway with two doors leading off it. We sit on a bench against one wall and wait. After a bit, a tall man in a white coat, with dark hair that falls over his forehead, comes out of one of the doors.

He sees us and says, 'Are you waiting to see someone?'

'Jack Walker,' I say.

He looks at us a moment as if he's not sure about something. Then he opens the door he's just come out of.

'Come in.'

We go in through the door. There's one bed in there, and Jack's lying in it with a plastic mask on his face and a needle in his arm that's on the end of a tube that's hooked over a stand at the side of the bed. His eyes are shut and he looks as if he's asleep. I can see that he's breathing, so I know he's alive. I turn to the doctor, who's leaning against the wall with his hands in the pocket of his coat.

'How bad is he?' I ask.

He takes a hand out of his pocket, brushes his hair back and says, 'He's got a severe case of Pertussis. What you would call whooping cough.'

'Will he be all right?'

'We don't know yet.'

'How soon will you be able to tell?'

'Difficult to say. His vital signs are weak. He's on antibiotics, which should kill the bacteria in time, but he may not survive the treatment. Children from slum conditions often don't.'

'Why's that?'

'Malnutrition, damp atmosphere and dirt all contribute to a weakened immune system and reduced capacity for recovery.'

Georgie snivels. There are tears falling down her cheeks. The doctor takes a wad of tissue paper from a trolley beside the bed and gives it to her.

'We'll do what we can, of course,' he says.

The nurse who we saw last night comes in and goes to Jack. She pushes the needle further into his arm and he stirs a bit. She goes round to the other side of the bed, takes his mask off and puts a small glass tube into his mouth. She holds his wrist, looks at a watch she's got pinned to her apron and writes something down on a piece of paper that's clipped to a board. Then she wraps something round his arm above his elbow and squeezes away at a rubber ball thing she's holding in her hand, which makes the thing round Jack's arm blow up. Then there's a hissing sound and it goes down again and she's looking at a dial and writing something else down on the board. She unwraps the thing round his arm and takes it off. She takes the little glass tube out of his mouth and looks at it then she writes something else on the paper on the board and hands it to the doctor.

He looks at what she's written and then he hands the board back to the nurse. He goes to the side of the bed and folds down the sheet that's covering Jack. He takes the same thing the doctor last night had out of his pocket, and puts the two ends in his ears and the metal end on Jack's chest. He moves it to different places, then he puts it back in his pocket and goes to the door.

'Will he be all right?' I say.

'Too early to say,' he says, as he walks out of the door.

The nurse tucks the sheet back up again and says, 'You must go now.'

'I want to stay,' says Georgie.

'Visiting time is over now.'

'Can't you give us a few minutes?' I say.

She looks at us and then at the watch on her chest and says.

'All right. But you don't touch anything, and when I come back you go.'

She hangs the board on the end of the bed and goes out of the door.

We sit on each side of the bed and I look at Jack's pale face. I put my hand on his forehead and I can feel how hot he is.

Georgie holds his hand. She leans in close to him and whispers, 'You're going to be all right, Jacky, I know you are.'

Jack's head moves under my hand and I can see his lips opening under the mask, as if he's saying something. I want to lift the mask to hear him, but I don't dare in case it's bad for him. His lips stop moving and his head is still again. We sit with him for a few minutes and then the nurse comes back in.

'You must go now, or I'll be in trouble,' she says.

'OK,' I say.

'You can come tomorrow.'

She holds the door open for us. As we pass her, she puts a hand on Georgie's arm and says, 'Try not to worry, dear.'

Georgie looks up at her and says, 'Take care of him, please.' The nurse smiles at her.

'Of course, darling.'

We walk back through the ward. The visitors have gone and a couple of nurses are trying to calm down a little girl who's crying really loudly and thrashing about. We go down the stairs and out of the main door onto Harrow Road. We walk up to the traffic lights, cross over and go down Great Western Road towards the bridge.

I say to Georgie, 'Fancy a walk along the canal?'

'No. I want to go to school now.'

'You sure?'

'Yes.'

I walk with her to the school, getting her a bacon sandwich from the caff on the corner of Lancaster Road on the way. She says she doesn't want it, but I make her eat it. It's still the lunch break when we get to school and I leave her in the playground. Walking away, I see her standing by herself near the fence with her head bowed.

• • •

I go over the railway bridge and turn the corner into our street. Claire and Sammy are sitting on the steps above Claire's. She sees me and comes along the pavement to meet me.

'Dave was here looking for you,' she says.

'Yeah?' I say.

'He's in the British Oak.'

'OK.'

'What's going on, Reen?'

'How should I know?'

'Twice in two days?'

'Maybe he's not a queer after all.'

'I'm coming with you.'

'Don't.'

'Are you sure?'

'Yeah.'

'Come round ours after.'

'Yeah.'

Claire looks at me and says, 'You all right?'

'Jack's in the hospital. Whooping cough.'

'The poor little mite. How is he?'

'He ain't good.'

'Are they looking after him?'

'I think so. I'll go back up there later.'

A football bounces onto the pavement between us. Claire kicks it back to the boys in the road.

'I'd better go and see Dave,' I say.

'Be careful.'

I nod and she goes and sits beside Sammy. I turn and walk away, wondering if I should tell her about Dave and what we've got planned. I'd like to, but she's my good friend and I don't want to put her in any more danger than she's in already.

I get to the British Oak and look in the window. The lunchtime drinkers are mostly old geezers slumped behind their pints and a few younger blokes reading papers or listening to the racing on the radio behind the bar. I hear a car horn toot behind me. I turn and see Dave sitting at the wheel of a black Jaguar. He reaches over and opens the passenger door.

I get in and he says, 'Get your head down.'

I lie down on the seat and the car moves off. We drive for a bit, make a couple of turns and stop. I can hear a dog barking. Dave switches off the engine.

'OK,' he says.

I sit up. We're parked in the middle of a scrap yard. An Alsatian is straining against a chain attached to the wall of a shed that's squatting among piles of twisted bits of metal. The door of the shed opens and a man with a crew cut and a big beer belly steps out and looks at the car. After a nod from Dave, he yanks the dog's chain, bellows something at him, and goes back into the shed. The dog lies down, puts its head on its paws and looks grumpily at us.

Dave reaches into his overcoat pocket, takes out a sheaf of notes, and puts it on the seat between us.

'That's two hundred,' he says. 'The Baileys are opening an all-night drinker on Walmer Road tonight. Nick'll be there in his best bib and tucker with his firm.'

'How am I going to get to him through that lot?'

'He likes a young dolly.'

'Is that a fact?'

'Me and the lads are going to drop in after closing time and stir it up a bit.'

I pick up the money, put it in my pocket, and open the car door. 'Where in Walmer Road?' I say.

'Corner of Runcorn Place.'

The dog gets to its feet and gives a weak bark as I head for the gate.

Dave gets out of the car and walks towards the shed.

I need to see Jack.

I grip the money in my pocket and walk back to the hospital. I go in through the main entrance and the woman behind the glass partition asks me what I want. I tell her I'm waiting for someone and stand near the double doors. A few minutes later she drops her pen on the floor, bends down to find it and I slip through the doors and up the stairs to the children's ward.

It's quieter now. Most of the kids seem to be sleeping or lying staring up at the ceiling. A little boy cries out and a nurse gets up from a desk at the far end and goes to him.

I go through the door behind the desk while she bends over him and open the door to the room Jack was in before.

I go to his bedside and look at his pale little face behind the plastic mask. His breathing sounds weaker than it was and his forehead still feels hot. The door opens and the nurse who sent us away earlier comes in.

She shuts the door behind her and puts her hands on her hips. 'You, girl! You must not be here!' she hisses.

'He's worse, isn't he?'

'You've got to get out. Doctor's coming now and if he sees you we're both in big trouble.'

'I've got to see the doctor.'

'You can't do that. He's a very busy doctor. You must go.'

The door opens and the doctor from yesterday with the dark hair comes in. He sees me and says to the nurse, 'It's not visiting time is it?'

The nurse says, 'She sneak in somehow. I tell her to go but she won't.'

The doctor looks at me.

'Nurse, kindly remove this girl so that I can attend to this patient,' he says.

'I can pay,' I say.

'What?' he says.

'For his treatment.'

'He's being treated already.'

'It's better if I pay though, isn't it?'

'Since you ask, it makes no difference. He's receiving intravenous antibiotics and corticosteroids and he's isolated in a sterile environment, at least he was, until you burst in and began contaminating the atmosphere with the filth of the backstreets. All this is presently being paid for by Her Majesty's Government and I'd advise you to be grateful for that and leave immediately, so that I can instruct the nurse to clear his airways.'

The nurse opens the door and I go into the corridor. She follows me out and says, 'Don't you worry, dear. He's a very good doctor. You come back tomorrow. Visiting hour.'

'Will he be all right?'

'Come back tomorrow.'

• • •

I come out of the hospital onto Harrow Road. Cars and lorries and carts are pushing and shoving in a hurry to get somewhere. I start to cry. I want to run back and pick Jack up and bring him with me, jump on one of these lorries and take him off to the country or the seaside and make him better. I sit down on the pavement and lean back against the wall of the hospital. I dry my eyes and tell myself that he's best where he is with the snooty doctor and the big cuddly nurse.

A tall woman in a fur coat coming out of the hospital stops and looks at me. It's the trustee lady who was talking to the nurse when I came this morning.

She comes over to me and says, 'Is something the matter, dear?' I look away from her.

'Are you ill?' she says.

I wipe my eyes and stand up. 'No,' I say.

'You look distressed.'

She opens her hand bag, searches for something and says, 'Is there anything I can do?'

'I'm all right.'

I turn to walk away from her but she puts her hand on my arm. 'Here, have this,' she says.

She puts sixpence in my hand. I look at her worried face, full of pity and half a smile. I throw the tanner on the floor and walk away.

'Well, really!' she says.

At the traffic lights I look back and see her getting into the back of a long black car.

The traffic stops and I cross the road. I feel dirty and shabby suddenly. I grip the money in my pocket. I want to go up West to the posh shops and doll myself up, but I've been wearing these same old threads for years and with what's going off tonight, it might not be so shrewd to look like I've suddenly got money to throw around. I'll go to Claire's later and get the loan of a tight blouse and a pencil skirt and some shoes. For now, I'll settle for a hot soak up Silchester Baths before I pick up Georgie from school. I need to make sure she doesn't go to the hospital and get herself taken into care.

I get to the baths and hand fourpence to the old cow on the desk. She gives me a towel and half a bar of carbolic and writes number seven on a ticket. I find my cubicle, go in and close the bolt on the door. I take out the bath plug, turn on the cold tap and wash some hair and grime out of the bottom of the bath. Then I turn on the hot tap, sit on the wooden chair beside the bath and watch the steam rising. When it's full, I take my clothes off and step into the warm silky water. As the heat seeps into my bones I start to feel sleepy, and I hold my breath and let my head slide under the water. I stay under as long as I can, then I breathe out and come up and rest my head back and feel the cool edge of the bath against my neck.

I feel so bad about our Jack. I should have taken him to the doctor before, but I never knew it was the whooping cough. I know that kids die from it. I'll go up again tomorrow. I can only hope he's all right.

I look down through the lovely warm water to where he hurt me. The bruises on my thighs are turning blue now. I brush my fingertips over them ever so lightly and then I stroke myself between my legs. I remember the feel of the soft skin on Lizzie's neck when she put her arms round me when I'd killed Johnny and I want her to hold me again and kiss me; the feeling's growing and getting stronger and it's spreading out all over me and I'm crying out suddenly and there's a banging on the door and a voice.

'You all right in there?'

It's her from the desk. I grip the sides of the bath, take a deep breath and say, 'Yeah, thanks … I slipped over on the soap.'

I can hear her walking away. I top up the hot water and lie back again for a bit. I wash my hair with the soap, and then I wash the rest of me. I step out onto the cork mat beside the bath, dry myself and dress. I dab what's left of the carbolic with the towel, put it in my pocket and go back to the desk. When I offer the wet towel to the old bag, she frowns at me and points at a bin beside her. I lob the towel in and walk out into the sunny street.

I pick up Georgie and take her home. She wants to go to the hospital, but I explain what happened when I went back earlier and she agrees to wait until the morning. When we get home, I make her a boiled egg and bread and marge. She eats half the egg and none of the bread. When I try to feed her, she jumps down, goes to the bedroom and sits reading a book she's brought from school.

Mum's sitting on her mattress with a drink, mumbling and looking round the room. I boil her an egg, show it to her and put it on the table. I try to sit her at the table, but she won't move, so I leave her to it and eat the egg myself. I push the plate away and sit looking at the rotten state of the place, the mould on the grey walls and the clapped-out furniture, and I think it's a miracle we're not all ill with the whooping cough.

I hear a dog bark and voices downstairs. I go out onto the landing and look over the bannister. The rent collector is standing by the front door in his sharp suit, with his stick and his dog. Three black men carrying suitcases and carrier bags walk past him and go through the door into the ground floor front room. The rent collector goes in after them.

I go back into ours and sit down at the table. The dog's barking downstairs and someone's shouting. I decide I'm going to get us out of here as soon as I can. I go into the bedroom and tell Georgie to stay indoors while I go round to Claire's.

13

I reach Laredo and follow signs to the Mexican border. After leaving the interstate and driving downtown in the gathering dusk, I stop at a hardware store and buy a roll of duct tape. I take the gun from under the front seat, crawl under the car and tape the gun to the topside of one of the chassis members. I check the map, drive across a four lane bridge over the Rio Grande into one of several separated traffic lanes at the far end, and tell the gum chewing Mexican customs official who examines my passport that I am meeting my husband in Acapulco. When he looks in the boot of the car and questions my lack of luggage I tell him that American Airlines lost my suitcase. He waves me through and I drive into Mexico.

A mile or so into Nuevo Laredo, I see a sign for Highway 85 to Monterrey. I am soon clear of the town and rolling south again. I glance at the fuel gauge, see that the needle is flickering on empty and stop at the next gas station. The pump attendant is a busy little middle-aged guy with a cheeky smile who talks non-stop, in staccato Spanish, while he fills the tank, cleans the windscreen and takes my money, seeming not to require any response from me as he does so. I can still hear him chattering away as I get into the car and drive off. By midnight I reach the outskirts of Monterrey and pull into a motel. There is a lone pick-up truck in the car park. A lumpen receptionist sits behind a counter, smoking a cigar and watching baseball through a snowstorm on a small TV. I get his attention, point to the tariff on the wall and make the international mime gesture for sleep. He takes a key from a hook on the wall and mutters something ending in pesos. I hand him a note and he digs in a drawer for change. He takes me along a dark corridor to a room with a small double bed, a Formica sideboard and a tattered armchair. He hands me the key, points to a bathroom a couple of doors away and goes back to his baseball. I lie on the bed and take in the drab brown wallpaper and the sour smell of rancid bedding. I think of Charlene in her trailer and wonder if she's sleeping. I wish I could be with her, giving her any comfort that I could, and feeling a warm body beside me.

I am woken by a knock at the door. I see that it is light outside and I am lying on the bed fully dressed. I am suddenly afraid that Lee has come after me for some reason and I curse myself for not bringing the gun from the car. I pick up a metal table lamp from the sideboard, hold it behind my back, move to the door and open it quickly. A small birdlike woman holding a mop and a plastic bucket is looking up at me. She says something that sounds like an apology and backs away. I put down the table lamp, point to my wrist and ask her what the time is. She shows me her watch and I can see that it is ten thirty. I smile at her, beckon her into the room, take a towel and the car key from the sideboard and cross to the bathroom.

The cold shower clears my head. As I dry myself, I notice that the tiles on the walls are almost the same pale blue colour as the ones in my bathroom at home, and I wonder how things are there. Georgie and her boy-friend Graham were staying at my house when I left. When they arrived, I was shocked to see how thin and listless Georgie was. Graham told me she's been working obsessively on her thesis in Cambridge and refusing to stop for meals. I tried to talk to her about why she wasn't eating, but she refused to engage with me. I nearly cancelled the trip, but Martin gave me a hard time and threatened to put it about that I'd lost it, so I filled the fridge with food and told Graham to look after her and not let her work too hard. I suddenly need to know that she's all right.

I dry myself, dress quickly and walk through to the reception desk. The man who checked me in is now slumped in his chair reading a newspaper. I point at the payphone on the wall and tell him I want to call London. He has just enough English to understand that I want the dialling code and a lot of change. He finds the phone book and shows me the code. I feed coins into the machine and dial. After some clicking and crackling, I hear a distant ringing tone, and eventually Graham answers.

I push more coins in and say, 'Graham, it's Rina.'

'Oh … Hello.'

'How are things?'

'Well, er …'

Graham is a Divinity student. He's a sweet boy with a fine intellect, but he's not the world's greatest communicator.

'Can I talk to Georgie?'

'Well, um …'

'You're very faint, Graham. Can you speak up?'

'Oh, right, sorry.'

'Let me talk to Georgie.'

'She's not here.'

'Where is she?'

'She's been taken into hospital.'

'Hospital? Why?'

'She collapsed last night and I called an ambulance and they're keeping her in.'

My head swims. I grip the receiver and push my forehead into the wall.

'What's wrong with her?'

'Malnutrition, they said.'

'Oh God.'

'I tried to make her eat but she just wouldn't, she'd take a mouthful and not be able to swallow it and say she felt sick. I tried soup and everything, but she couldn't swallow. Then last night, I went into the bathroom and she was standing in front of the mirror, with no clothes on, looking at herself and I asked her if she was all right and she turned to me and then she just fell down on the floor. I couldn't wake her so I phoned for an ambulance.'

'Did she come round?'

'Yes.'

'Thank God you were there.'

'I wasn't sure …'

'You did the right thing. How are they treating her?'

'There's a tube thing that goes into her mouth and they've restrained her arms so that she can't …'

I visualise her being force-fed and I want to scream. At least they are keeping her alive.

Graham says, 'When are you coming back?'

I fight the urge to smash the phone and decapitate the receptionist, who's looking at me as if he's never seen a woman before.

I breathe deeply and say, 'I'm in a remote part of the world, and flights aren't frequent, so it might take a couple of days, but I'll be there as soon as I possibly can.'

'Right.'

'Can you stay with her, Graham?'

'Oh, absolutely. I'm just going in to see her now.'

'Where is she?'

'The Royal Free.'

'Take care of her.'

• • •

To hell with Lee and his tracking devices, I'm going to get to an airport, steal a passport and get on a flight right now. I knock on the counter and ask the receptionist for a map. He finds one and I spread it out on the counter and check the route to Mexico City. It looks like a day's fast drive. I fold the map and walk towards the car under the dazzling sun. I turn the key in the lock and get a good burn from the handle as I open the door.

As I sit on the hot seat, an arm goes round my neck and hard metal presses into my temple. In the mirror, I can see Guido, with a black eye patch, smirking at me. I twist round and try to grab the gun, but he jumps over onto the front seat, takes hold of my face and jams the gun against my temple.

'OK, fucking bitch, you give me your gun now,' he says.

'It's underneath the car.'

'You get it, and you don't fuck with me. OK?'

'OK.'

Guido pockets his gun and gets out of the car. He opens the door for me and, as I move, he puts his hand on his pocket and fixes me with his good eye.

'You don't fuck,' he says.

'I thought you knew that by now,' I say.

He looks at me with utter loathing and says, 'Yeah, you funny fucking bitch. You get gun.'

I crawl under the car, rip off the tape and take hold of the gun. I reach out, grab Guido's ankle and smash his leg against the side of the car. He falls down and I roll out, land my full weight on him, get a hold on his neck and hit him in the face. As he goes limp beneath me, a military jeep on the far side of the parking lot starts up, surges towards us and skids to a stop inches away. Through clouds of dust, I see four men with guns get out and surround us. I stand up, throw the gun down and raise my hands.

One of the men grabs Guido by the hair, pulls him to his feet and bundles him into the back of the jeep. The passenger door on the far side opens and a short figure wearing a leather flying helmet and a white T-shirt steps down, walks round the front of the jeep, and stands in front of me. The fabric of the T-shirt strains against a rippling landscape of bulging muscle and a pair of large, udderish breasts. She's about as broad as she's tall and the face that glowers at me from under the flying helmet is ugly enough to leave an orangutan suicidal. The face is bulbous and swollen, with pitted skin like ancient varnished oak, black eyes beneath brows as dark as crows' wings, a broad flattened nose and lips like two car tyres lying on top of one another. When the lips stretch into a smile and then open to emit a dry laugh, exposing a graveyard of rotting teeth, I expect a plume of bile to spew forth.

Her laugh rattles on for a moment, then she looks me up and down, turns to the men and says, 'Hey, it's my twin sister!'

The men laugh and she holds out a horny hand. We shake and she says, 'OK London, gimme your keys. We need to talk.'

I hand the car keys to her and she throws them to one of the men, nodding towards the jeep. As I get into the rear seat, I see the receptionist closing the front door of the motel very slowly and pulling down a window blind. Muscle woman gets in beside me and the jeep pulls out of the parking lot with my car following.

As we accelerate onto the highway, she turns to me and says, 'I'm Carmela.'

I look straight ahead and ignore her.

'It's cool, honey. We're on the same side,' she says.

She's probably mid-thirties and although she's clearly Hispanic, or maybe Indian, her American accent tells me she's not local. We drive into Monterrey. The heat is intense, and a smell like burnt kippers soaked in urine is coming off Miss Universe. The mid-morning traffic hoots and weaves around us as we reach the centre and cross a large square. We turn into a side street between high sided white buildings and pull over. I am escorted along the narrow pavement, through a wooden door and up three flights of stairs into a small sitting room with a brown leather sofa and two armchairs around a low table. A ceiling fan turns slowly, barely disturbing the trapped air.

Carmela indicates an armchair and says, 'You want a beer? Coffee?' I shake my head and she dismisses the men and sits in the armchair opposite me. She takes off the flying helmet, releasing a cloud of jet black hair that has the buoyancy and shiny texture of a nylon fright wig from some novelty shop. She uses both hands to try and flatten it down.

'Bet you wish you never came, huh?' she says.

I say nothing. She opens a cigarette box on the table, takes one and pushes the box towards me. As she picks up the lighter, I consider attacking her while she's distracted, but although there aren't many people who frighten me, I might reconsider my chances against this one.

She exhales smoke, leans back in her chair and says, 'He stitched you up pretty good, huh?'

I wait a moment before I say, 'What do you want?'

'I want to tear out Lee Master's asshole and make him eat it.' She gives me a reptilian smile and adds, 'You want to give him his balls for dessert?'

I say nothing.

She leans towards me and looks into my eyes. 'OK, London. Here's the deal. Guido's mine and he's told me the plan for you to set up Manuel for Lee. I want both those bastards, and you want out and back home. So, you go with Lee's plan and get the deal together with Manuel. You give me where and when it's going down, I join the party, I get Lee and Manuel and you get home.'

She's completely repulsive and more animal than human, but there's something about her that makes me believe her. Even if I can get away from her, my chances of solo escape are slim at best.

I say, 'Why do you want Lee?'

'He has agents woven into my operation and I need to know who they are. He also knows too much about a whole lot of stuff that I'm into.'

'Manuel?'

'He fucked me with the authorities. It's routine shit, but I have to kill him anyways.'

'To encourage ...'

'Right. Also, I pick up his business, which is cool.'

'So why not just kill him?'

'Too noisy with the amount of protection he carries. This way, it's quiet and I get them both.'

She stubs out her cigarette and flexes her neck from side to side until it gives a loud click.

'I need to work out.'

She stands, rolls her shoulders back and forth and says,

'You ready to do this thing or you want to spend a couple months in my cellar?'

'How do I get home without Lee?'

'Easy. I give you a new passport when it's done and you step on a plane.'

'How do I know you won't kill me?'

'I sell to London. You could be good for me there. Besides, you're too beautiful.'

I try to rid myself of a nauseating thought picture as I remind myself that Lee will turn me in without doubt when the deal is done, and that Manuel may decide to kill me too. La Grotesque here is looking like my best option.

I say, 'I go on to Manuel's with Guido and we communicate through him?'

'Yes.'

'How do you know he isn't going to tell Manuel?' I ask.

'He's mine.'

'Are you sure?'

'Manuel killed his sister.'

'What if Manuel refuses the deal?'

'He won't. He's a greedy son of a bitch and he lost a few fields a while back.'

'I want to see the passport before I go.'

'We'll get that started.'

She opens the door and speaks to someone in the corridor. She turns back and says, 'They'll come take your picture and get the details they need to get it together. You want to work out while you wait?'

I decline and watch her overdeveloped thigh muscles

rubbing against each other as she waddles out of the room. Minutes later a wizened old man in a cream linen suit arrives carrying a camera and a tripod. He plants the tripod in front of the window and mounts the camera on top of it. He smiles at me and points at a spot on the floor in front of the camera. I move into position and he clicks the shutter a couple of times. Then he hands me a pen and a sheet of paper.

'Name. Address. Date of your birth please,' he says.

I decide to be Sarah Collins from Wolverhampton and knock a couple of years off my age for good measure. I hand the pen and paper to him. He smiles at me again, picks up the camera and tripod and leaves.

I sit back in the armchair and wait. After a while the door opens and Guido walks in. He takes the seat that Carmela vacated, gives me his habitual look of loathing and says, 'You don't do what she say, she kill you.'

'I know.'

'She tougher than all the men.'

'Really?'

'I know her in East LA. She one mean bitch.'

'I get it.'

We sit in silence. I think about poor Georgie lying in a hospital bed, and wonder how the hell I'm going to shake off Carmela, as well as Lee, Manuel and the Texas Police, and get back to her. The door opens and the old boy in the linen suit comes in and hands me a passport. It looks and feels exactly like the real thing. He offers me a pen. I hesitate a moment and then sign the passport as

Sarah Collins. The old boy stands smiling as if waiting for my opinion. I nod to show my appreciation and he looks pleased and leaves.

Guido takes the passport from me and says, 'We need to go.'

The door opens and Carmela enters, wearing a pink bathing suit.

I look away from the nauseating sight of tumescent muscle crawling with swollen veins. Sweat drips from her chin and her elbows, making pools on the wooden floor. She wipes her face with a towel and I retreat slightly as she approaches. She turns to Guido, takes the passport from him and looks first at it, then at me.

'We cool?'

'Yes,' I say.

'See you at the shindig.'

She leaves and Guido shows me out of the door and down the stairs to the street. We get into the car and I attempt to follow Guido's increasingly hysterical directions as we penetrate the cut and thrust of Monterrey's morning traffic. He eventually leads us out of the city and onto the highway that will take us past Mexico City to Manuel's fortified mansion in the hills north of Acapulco. After a while I ask Guido if he wants to drive. He shakes his head and raises the gun he's holding to remind me that he's in control.

The highway is straight and fast and the mountains on either side make a jagged horizon beneath the deep blue sky. Country music wafts comfortably from a Texas radio station. By early evening, we're beyond Mexico City and taking the exit from Highway 95 for the final approach to Manuel's place, climbing up the mountain road.

As the house comes into view above us I look across at Guido and say, 'Did you lose that eye?'

'No.'

'Will it be OK?'

'Maybe.'

'You'll know better next time.'

'Fuck you.'

'No, fuck you, you stupid little dwarf!'

He swings the gun at me. I stamp on the brake and he lurches forward and hits his head on the windscreen. I grab the gun from his hand, smash it into his face, open the passenger door and kick the ignorant pig out onto the road.

I drive the last couple of miles, stop in front of the wrought iron gates and wait. A side gate opens and a guard with an AK 47 walks slowly towards the car. I wind down the window.

'I want to see Manuel.'

14

Little Richard's screaming out Lucille as I go down the steps to Claire's, and I can see her jiving with Sammy through the window. I knock and she twirls round, sees me and comes to the door to let me in. We go in her bedroom and she turns the record player down. I say hello to Sammy and he offers me a fag.

'You know I don't,' I say.

'Yeah, of course,' he says and lights one up himself.

Claire takes one from his packet and says, 'What about me then?'

Sammy laughs and lights her up as well. He turns to me and says, 'Did you see my new motor?'

'That old wreck that's parked outside?' I say.

'That's a fucking good car, that is. Morris Eight. One of the best cars on the road.'

Claire says, 'Hop off down the pub, Sam, and I'll see you later.'

'I thought we was going out for a drive?' says Sammy.

'I want to talk to Rina about something.'

'About what?'

'Never you mind, you nosey sod.'

'Who are you calling ...'

Claire takes a ten bob note out of a drawer and waves it in front of his face.

'Now you be a good boy and toddle off down the pub,

and we'll see you later.'

Sammy takes the ten bob note off her and says, 'You robbed a bank or something?'

'Yeah. Now piss off before I change my mind.'

Sammy puts on his coat and combs his Brylcreemed hair. He turns the back of his head to us.

'How's my DA then?'

'If I was a duck, I'd be proud of an arse like that,' says Claire.

'Gertcha,' says Sammy and smacks her on the bum. He opens the door, waves the ten bob note at us and says, 'Tara, girls.'

The door slams and Claire puts a Johnny Ray record on the Dansette, a nice slow song I haven't heard before.

I say, 'How come he's got a car? I thought he was on the National Assistance.'

'He had a good little tickle in the week.'

'What sort?'

'Him and a mate done a chemist up Willesden.'

'I never knew Sammy went robbing.'

'He does now.'

I hear the car splutter into life and move off. 'I need to borrow some clothes,' I say.

'What for?'

'I'm going out.'

'Dave again?'

'No, it's a mate of his who's ...'

'Don't give me that malarky, Reen. I want to know what's going on.'

'You don't.'

'I know he's rumbled you did Johnny.'

'How …?'

'It's bleeding obvious, isn't it? He snaps his fingers and you jump.

Twice in two days.'

I sit on the bed. I feel very tired. Claire sits down next to me and I tell her the score. When I've finished, she looks away as if she's thinking.

Then she says, 'You ain't got no choice.'

'Not much.'

'Can you do it?'

'I reckon.'

'As long as that's the end of it.'

'I hope.'

The door opens and Claire's mum looks in. Her face is swollen on one side and I can see she's tried to hide a bruise with makeup.

'Hello, Rina love. You all right?' she says.

'Yes, thanks, Mrs Welch.'

'How's your Jack?'

'He's not too good at the moment.'

'Poor little mite.' She turns to Claire and says, 'Go up the pub and see if your dad's there and tell him his dinner's spoiling.'

'Oh Mum …'

'Now.'

Mrs Welch shuts the door.

Claire looks at me and says, 'He came back drunk at

seven o'clock this morning. When she asked him where he'd been, he punched her in the mouth, picked up his lunch, and went to work.'

'Blimey.'

'I'd better try and find him.'

She opens the wardrobe and says, 'Take anything you want except my red dress.'

'Thanks.'

'And watch out.'

I open Claire's wardrobe. She's got some really nice clothes. All nicked over the last couple of years. We're the same size, so I know anything will fit me. I take a tight black skirt, a white V-neck sweater, a pair of high heels and a handbag. I roll them up in a sway back jacket and go back to ours.

Mum's at the kitchen table with a bottle, muttering to herself. She doesn't see me as I walk through to the bedroom. Georgie's in bed, reading her book.

'You all right?' I say.

She nods without looking up from the book.

I go behind the head of the bed and lift up the floorboard in the corner. I take out the gun, put it in my jacket pocket, put the floorboard back and say, 'I've got to go and help Claire with something. I don't know what time I'll be back. I'll ask Lizzie to look in later. You get off to sleep now.'

I take the book out of her hands, but she grabs it back off me and puts it under the blanket next to her, then she turns away from me and closes her eyes. I say good night to her and go into the kitchen. Mum's lying on the mattress now. I put the gun in the oven, change into Claire's clothes, brush my hair and go up to Lizzie's. The high heels are really hard to walk in and I nearly fall off them on the stairs. I listen at Lizzie's door; I can't hear anything so I knock quietly. In a minute the door opens and she's there in the pink dressing gown and the black undies.

'Well, look at you, gorgeous!' she says.

'I need a favour.'

'You're going out.'

'I've got to.'

'I should say you have, looking like that.'

'Can you look in on Georgie for me?'

'Of course I can. Who is he?'

'It's not like that.'

'Oh yeah? Come in a minute.'

'I've got to go.'

'Won't take a second.'

She pulls me over to her dressing table and sits me down in front of the mirror.

'Close your eyes,' she says.

I feel her brushing make up onto my eyelids.

She says, 'Open your eyes. Now, pull your lips back like this.'

She widens her mouth. I do the same and she puts lipstick on me and then powders my face. I look in the mirror while she brushes my hair into waves with a round type of brush I've never seen before. She finishes my hair and steps back to look at me in the mirror.

'There's my glamour girl,' she says.

I stand up and turn to face her. She's looking at me and I see her eyes get softer behind her smile. I move closer to her. She takes my hand and pulls me to her and there's that soft skin on her neck again and her arms are round me and I'm pressing against her lovely warm body.

Someone's banging on the door. Lizzie pulls away from me. She puts her finger to her lips and goes and opens the door.

'A gentleman to see you.'

It's the rent collector's voice. The door opens wider and the Alsatian's head appears, looking round with its piercing eyes and sniffing the air as if it's suspicious of something. Lizzie stands to one side as a very fat man in a pair of dungarees and a donkey jacket comes in. The rent collector pulls the dog back and shuts the door.

The man looks at Lizzie and then at me and says, 'It's a team, is it?'

Lizzie says, 'This is my sister. She's just leaving.'

'I'll pay more.'

Lizzie lets her dressing gown fall open, puts her arm round the man's neck, reaches down below his fat gut and says, 'I wouldn't want to share a lovely big hunk like you with anyone.'

She walks him towards the bed, lays him down on it, climbs on top of him and starts kissing him and whispering in his ear. I back away towards the door and she raises a hand behind her back and waves at me. I close the door quietly and go down the stairs to our kitchen.

I get the gun out of the oven and push it into the back of the waistband of my skirt. I look at my reflection in the window and check that the loose fold of the jacket hides it. I make sure Georgie's asleep and go down to the street. Some boys on the other side whistle at me as I wobble a bit on the heels.

As I get to the end of the street, Claire comes round the corner with her old man holding on to her arm. He slips off the pavement into the gutter and staggers into the road cursing and swearing. I step up into a doorway so he doesn't see me. Claire goes to pull him back onto the pavement and he shoves her aside and weaves his way up the middle of the street. A van comes round the corner and he shakes his fists and shouts at the driver who just manages to swerve round him. He aims some more abuse at the disappearing van and then lurches off towards his basement. Claire follows him down the steps and I go on to the end of the street, hoping she's not going to get hurt tonight.

I keep my head down as I walk towards Walmer Road. It's Friday night, the pubs are chucking out and there's a good few skirmishes and punch-ups on the way. Outside the pub on the corner of Portobello, two women are going at each other and a group of men are laughing and egging them on. One of the women swings a punch and the other one takes her shoe off and whacks her on the head with it. The men cheer as her victim falls onto the pavement.

Walmer Road's quiet and I can see a couple of Teds standing near to the corner where the club's supposed to be. One of them's big and powerful looking, the other one's short and looks older. I can hear music as I get nearer. A car pulls up by them and I step into a doorway. Three men in dark suits get out of the car. They talk to the Teds and then go through an iron gate and down some steps.

I walk up to the gate. The bigger one of the Teds steps in front of me.

'Where the fuck do you think you're going?' he says.

'I've got a message for someone,' I say.

'Who?'

'Mr Bailey.'

'Which one?'

I'm wondering what to tell him when his mate says, 'Don't be a cunt, Reg, they need a bit more skirt in there.'

The big one looks at him as if he doesn't like being challenged. The older one holds his look then opens the gate and says, 'Go on love, you're all right.'

I go down the steps and push open a door. I weave my way through a press of bodies around the door into a long room with a low ceiling. There's a bar down the one side, made out of packing cases with a couple of wooden planks on top. There are tables along the wall opposite, with a card game going at one of them, and a juke box at the far end. Older men in expensive suits and younger ones wearing the drape are talking at the bar. Groups of men and women sit at the tables. The women are mostly young and there's a lot of beehive hair, rock'n roll skirts and stiletto heels. The whole place reeks of villainy and ill-gotten gains and I can see my dad at home here, if only the silly old sod hadn't got himself killed.

Old man Bailey's holding court at the table at the far end. He's a round little pig of a man with a bald head and small squinty eyes. They say he once ate a live mouse between two slices of bread in a pub one night and then spat the innards into his pint and drank it off. There's a beautiful dark-haired girl next to him who can't be much older than me. She could be his daughter, but I don't see his wife anywhere, so I think maybe she isn't.

Nick Bailey's at the end of the table next to his younger brother and an older geezer with white hair who's with a brassy middle aged woman. Nick's good-looking with blonde hair, sharp blue eyes and an easy way with him. The old geezer says something and they all laugh. Nick puts his arm round the old boy and raises his glass to him.

I go to the bar and buy a whisky, and then I move towards the back of the club where I can see a door that's half open. When I get to the table, Nick's turned away, talking to his brother. As I get beside him I drop my handbag by his feet and kneel down to pick it up.

'Oh, sorry,' I say.

He turns and sees me. I stay on one knee and smile up at him.

He has a good look down my V-neck and says, 'The way you're dropping things, I'll take you home tonight.'

I laugh and get up.

He clocks my tits again from below, stands up and says, 'What are you drinking?'

I show him my whisky and say, 'I've just got one, ta.'

'Well, have another one.'

He takes my elbow and guides me to the bar. The suits make way when they see who's coming and he shakes a few hands while we get drinks.

He leans on the bar and says, 'Who are you with tonight?'

'One of them over there.'

I nod in the direction of the group of lads by the door.

'Boyfriend?'

'Just a mate.'

He leans closer and says, 'You live round here?'

As I'm saying the name of our street, there's a commotion by the door and the two Teds who were outside earlier are being pushed and jostled into the club by people I can't see. The bigger one falls forward onto the deck and there's a man behind him holding an iron bar. Everything goes quiet and nobody moves, then a Bailey boy smashes a bottle over the head of the man with the iron bar and the whole place erupts. Chairs are flying. Women are screaming. Knives are slicing. Blood's flying and bodies are thumping on the floor. I dive over the bar out of the way, but then the bar's toppling towards me and I'm going to be crushed against the wall. I vault back over and catch an elbow in the face. I fall on top of someone and a heavy weight lands on my legs, then I'm picked up and crushed against someone's chest and pulled through a mangle of heaving bodies until I can't breathe. I reach round for the gun, but it's gone and then there's cold air on my face and then a bump. I'm sliding down a brick wall and it goes black.

'Come on, girl, get up!'

Someone's lifting me up and shaking my shoulders. Dave's holding the gun in front of my face.

'He's coming after me. Fucking do it!' he hisses.

The runt's got one hand round my neck. I snatch the gun off him and bring my knee up into his bollocks. As he doubles over and staggers away, Nick Bailey comes out of the door and aims a kick at his head that has him bouncing off the back wall of the yard and landing on the cobbles. I hide the gun behind my back as he picks Dave up, swings him round and chucks him over the wall.

Nick walks towards me looking wild and breathing heavily. He leans against the wall beside me.

'It's all right,' he says. 'Don't be scared, that's the last of them. It's all over. Fucking liberty!'

He stands in front of me, pulls me to him and kisses me. I can feel him trembling. The bell of a police car jangles in the distance. I press my body into him and slip my tongue into his mouth. His hands close round my tits and I feel his cock harden. I open his flies, take hold of his cock and rub it back and forth with one hand while I raise the gun behind his back until it comes level with the side of his head. I pull the trigger. There's an almighty bang and the bullet goes straight through his head and smacks into the wall with a splatter of blood and muck. I push him off me onto the ground. Blood's spewing out of his head onto the cobbles.

I wipe the gun on my skirt and drop it. I run across the yard, kick off my shoes and try to climb the wall. The skirt's so tight I have to hitch it up to my waist to get over. When I'm astride the top of the wall, a copper comes out of the door flashing a torch about. I swing my leg over before he sees me and drop down onto the bomb site that's at the back of Walmer Road.

Dave's out cold, lying on a pile of rubble. I haul him up, put his bony little body over my shoulder and carry him away across the bomb site. There's a broken down shed near the road. I lay him down behind it, kneel beside him and look back at the club. A copper's looking over the wall and shining his torch around. Dave comes round and starts moaning. I put my hand over his mouth. He looks at me pleadingly with his squinty little eyes and goes quiet.

I take my hand away and he whispers, 'Did you get him?' I nod.

He says, 'Where's the gun?'

'I dropped it back there.'

'Good.'

'Where's my three hundred?'

'Meet me outside the yard, tomorrow at six.'

He stands up slowly and leans against the wall of the shed. He holds his head with one hand and his balls with the other. There are tears in his eyes and I think how pathetic he is.

'Can you walk?' I say.

'Yeah.'

I look back at the club. There are bright lights in the

yard but no coppers in sight. I straighten my skirt and head for Ladbroke Grove.

• • •

The night air feels cold and clean on my face. I've got that pure, empty feeling that came on me after I killed Johnny, like I can do anything and I'm not scared of anybody. I look up at the moon all that way away and I feel as if I could fly up there if I wanted.

When I get back to our street, that lumpy Jamaican music that you can't quite dance to is thumping through the window underneath ours. I go up the stairs and into the kitchen.

Claire stands up from the table and says, 'Come and look at this!' She takes me into the bedroom.

'He's nearly fucking killed her this time!' she says.

Claire's mum is lying on the bed next to Georgie. One of her eyes is blackened and closed and there's a cut on her forehead. Her nose is swollen and pushed sideways and her lips are covered in dried blood. Claire takes a cloth from a bowl by the bed and wipes some of the blood away.

'She's black and blue all over. He went berserk when he got in and now he's passed out drunk on the floor, so I've brought her here.'

'You've done right.'

'I'm sorry.'

'Don't be daft. Has he had a go at you?'

'He never touches me. He saves it all for her.'

'Is he still at yours?'

'Yeah. I've taken his keys and locked him in.'

'Good. You're stopping here.'

'Thanks, Reen.'

I look at Georgie sleeping next to Claire's mum and I wonder what else she will have to be in bed with in her life.

I say to Claire, 'Did our Mum wake up?'

'No. She was raving something terrible when we first got here and I thought she was awake, but she was asleep.'

'Good.'

'Lizzie was here. She said to go up and see her when you got in.'

'OK. I'd better go up. Will you be all right?'

'Yeah. You go on..'

Claire sits in the armchair with one arm and I go through to the kitchen. Mum's quiet and sleeping on her mattress.

I go out onto the landing and sit on the stairs. The music is still pulsing up from the Jamaicans' front room. I'm thinking about what Claire's dad's done, and all those men in that club tonight with their tough guy look and their gangster suits, and I think how small and stupid they really are. All they do is make people afraid of them so they get their respect, but in actual fact it's just fear. I'll respect that doctor at St Mary's if he cures our Jack, but I'll never respect some bloke who can do nothing but be cruel to people.

I go up to Lizzie's and listen at the door. I can't hear anything, so I go in. I can see her red hair on the white pillow in the moonlight coming through the window. I look at the moon again through the window, then I stand by the bed and take off my clothes. My feet are bruised from running over the rough ground of the bomb site. I lift the sheet and slip underneath it. Lizzie turns towards me and wraps me in her arms. I find that soft skin of her neck and press my lips into it. I feel her breathing getting deeper. I press myself into her lovely warm body. She takes my head in her hands and kisses me.

15

The gates swing shut behind me. I drive towards the familiar façade and stop the car under a palm tree opposite the front door. I lean back, close my eyes, inhale the sweet evening scent of subtropical flora and listen to the high-speed clicking of cicadas. The pool glistens through the trees and I long to peel off my stale denim and dive in. The front door opens and Manuel, wearing a white silk shirt and black trousers, walks towards the car. I get out and go to meet him.

He offers me his hand. 'This is a pleasant surprise, Señorita Walker.' I smile and shake his hand.

He says, 'I did not expect to see you again so soon.'

'I don't have too many friends in Mexico.'

'And none at all in Texas, I think.'

'That's true.'

'I am glad if you think of me as one, Señorita Walker.'

I hear footsteps on the gravel behind me and turn to see Guido limping towards the front door. Manuel barks an order at him and he disappears inside.

Manuel takes my arm and says, 'Please, come. We sit by the pool.'

At the table, he summons a guard. I ask for whisky and a glass of water. Manuel orders tequila.

'You are hungry?' he asks.

'No, thank you.'

I'm starving, but I need to be clear and unencumbered for what's to come. I always lose weight when I work. I try to push away thoughts of Georgie being fed from a tube.

Manuel gives a laconic smile and says, 'Congratulations on your escape.'

'Thank you.'

'There have not been many from that prison, I think.'

The cicadas suddenly fall silent, as if impressed by the information.

'I am sorry for what happened to the car of the minister before.'

'Do you know who did it?'

'Of course.'

'Who was it?'

'Another organisation that Gonzales was receiving money from, that had been attacked by the army.'

'Like you?'

'Yes. The difference is that they want it to be known that they have killed him so that the next one they bribe will play ball and protect them. I do not. That is why I send you to take out Gonzales quietly.'

'So how do you get the next one to play ball?'

'I give him money wrapped in the face of Gonzales.'

As I consider the undeniable pragmatism of the strategy, a familiar figure approaches carrying a tray.

Juanita smiles at me as she puts the drinks on the table and says, 'Good evening, Señorita.'

'Hello, Juanita,' I reply.

Manuel says, 'Señorita Walker has returned and I think

will be staying with us.'

He looks inquiringly at me. 'Thank you,' I say.

'Please make her comfortable.'

'Si, señor.'

Juanita bobs a curtsey and returns to the house. I take a sip of whisky and listen to the warm breeze riffling the leaves of the palm trees.

After a while Manuel says, 'So. You do not drive all this way to have drink by the pool, I think.'

I turn and look at the guards lounging against the wall of the house. Manuel signals to them to leave us and they walk away.

I let a few moments pass before I say, 'My late associates left behind some unfinished business.'

'I understood they came here to kill a man.'

'And buy a million dollars' worth of cocaine.'

Manuel sips his drink, looks at me and says, 'And you wish to complete this business?'

'Yes.'

'You have the money?'

'I know where it is.'

'Here in Mexico?'

'El Paso.'

'Ah.'

'I need you to get the coke over the border and meet me there.'

'I see.'

Manuel looks thoughtful. As he raises his glass to his lips, a burst of machine gun bullets rip holes in the paving stones in front of us. Manuel pitches forward into the pool. I throw myself onto the ground. The water in the pool turns red. Bursts of gunfire and shouts come from inside and around the house. Hands grab each of my arms and legs, carry me face down across the grass into the house, and throw me into a chair. The muzzle of a machine gun wavers inches from my face. Guido leers behind it, shaking with rage.

'No Manuel no more, gringo bitch. I the king! I the boss! No Manuel, no Carmela, I Guido! I the top now!'

I can see four or five guards standing behind him with AKs and machine guns, and three dead guards on the floor. Guido stands back from me and raps an order to a couple of the guards. They grab me and take me through the door into the entrance hall. There are bursts of gunfire from above and outside the house as one of them unlocks a door at the back of the hall and we go down a flight of stairs to a dimly lit passageway with metal doors leading off it. A door is unlocked and I am pushed into a dark room. The door shuts behind me and I struggle to see anything at all in front of me.

As my eyes become accustomed, I see a large, low-ceilinged room bathed in a dim orange light with another room leading off it. Four or five shadowy figures are sitting or lying on beds that line the walls, along with various chests and cupboards. They look up at me with varying degrees of interest and I see that they are all young women. One of them is holding a baby at her breast. Another comes in from the adjoining room holding a bowl of something hot. She glances at me, sits beside the one with the baby and offers the bowl to her. I linger by the door, take in the listless atmosphere and breathe the faintly perfumed air.

A slender girl rises from a bed in the far corner and comes towards me. She has long black hair, olive skin and dark eyes that have a ghostly faraway look. She wears a short white silk shift and I guess that she is about twenty.

She takes my hand, leads me to a bed and motions me to sit down. She settles next to me and says, 'You are American?'

'English.'

'I am Pilar. What is your name?'

'Rina.'

One of the other women, a slim teenager with auburn hair, moves closer to look at me.

Pilar says, 'Why have they put you here?'

'I was captured.'

She nods and looks around at the others. 'As are all of us.'

'For a long time?' I ask.

'Some of us long time, others not.'

'For Manuel?'

'Of course.'

I feel a wave of revulsion, and then joy as I remember that he is lying at the bottom of his swimming pool with bullet holes in his silk shirt. I want to know these girls' stories, but this is no time for conversation.

I say, 'You know he is dead?'

She is suddenly alert. 'What you say?'

'Manuel has been shot.'

'When?'

'About ten minutes ago.'

She repeats the news and all the girls surround us. Pilar puts her arm round the one holding the baby and I can see that it is tiny and has its eyes tightly closed. Its mother looks about fifteen years old and none of the other girls seem much older.

Pilar looks at me and says, 'What has happened?'

I relate the sequence of events to Pilar, who appears to be the mother hen, and she translates for the others. They react to Guido's name with revulsion and then talk animatedly for a while, before gradually subsiding into a morose silence and drifting back to their beds.

I look at Pilar and ask, 'What were they saying?'

'They are glad Manuel is dead, but they think that Guido is worse.'

'And you?'

'We will see.'

I look around for a means of escape. There must be an air supply to underground rooms like these. I go through the door behind the beds and find a bathroom with a stove and a refrigerator and a table in one corner. There are shelves stocked with tinned food and a metal grill in the ceiling above the table. I go over to take a closer look and see a ventilation shaft inside the grill, which looks just wide enough to crawl along. The sound of distant gunfire reminds me that if Guido has killed most of Manuel's armed guards, security will be disorganised, but not for long. I stand on the table and inspect the grill.

Pilar comes over and says, 'It will not open. We have tried.'

I take off my belt and loop it over one of the metal cross pieces. I grip the belt, pull down hard and the metal bends a little. Pilar joins me on the table and takes hold of the belt higher up. We pull together and the frame of the grill squeaks in protest. Some of the other girls come to see what's happening and one of them climbs up and adds her weight to the belt. We swing in mid-air, like some overweight trapeze act, until the remaining girls push the table away, put their arms round our waists and pull. There is a clang as the grill breaks free of the ceiling and we collapse in a heap on the floor. The grill lands on top of us in a shower of plaster and brick dust.

I roll out of the melée, get to my feet and brush the dust from my hair. The baby starts crying in the other room. The faces around me are now alight with excitement and anticipation. I put my belt back on, retrieve the table, stand on it and put my head into the mouth of the shaft. I can see that it climbs gently for a couple of yards and then levels off. It is just big enough to get along by lying flat and using elbows and forearms for traction. Some light is creeping along it, which indicates other hatches along the way and a possible exit.

I say to Pilar, 'Wait here while I take a look.'

Pilar nods, gets onto the table and makes her hands into a stirrup. I place my foot in it and climb into the shaft. I pull myself up the initial gradient and onto the flat run.

A welcome current of air envelops me and I see that the length of the shaft is punctuated by three grills that look similar to the one I have entered by. Light shines into the shaft from the two furthest away. I slither towards the first one, cross over it and see nothing but darkness below.

I crawl to the second grill and look over the edge. Racks of rifles and machine guns line the walls of the room below. Cases of grenades are stacked on tables next to rows of hand guns. A long white cabinet that looks like a deep freezer lies against the wall beside the door.

I make my way to the next grill and look down. A black plastic box with a dial on the front, which could be a radio but for the electrodes dangling from its sides, stands on a table next to a stretcher with leather straps buckled across it. There are chains and manacles bolted to the walls of the cell along with various hooks and spikes. A chainsaw lies in a corner next to an electric drill.

I move on and wonder what other facilities this corridor might have to offer in addition to a harem, an arsenal and a torture chamber. I reach the end of the straight section, manoeuvre myself around a tight right-hand bend and come up against a metal grill with a fan turning slowly behind it. Beyond it is daylight and the trunk of a palm tree.

I shake the grill. It is absolutely solid and of much heavier construction than the one the girls and I ripped apart. I look at the welded edges and conclude that there is no way through it. I make my way backwards, finally reaching the grill above the armoury, which I can see is bolted to the rim of the hatch from inside the shaft. I try to loosen the bolt nearest to me, but it is rusted in and will not shift. The one to my left is loose and unscrews easily, as does the one furthest away. The one to my right is more obstinate but finally gives way. I move back and as I bend the grill up and towards me it snaps off at the edge. I drop it through the opening into the cell, ease myself down after it and land on the floor.

As I am surveying the array of guns, I hear movement in the shaft above, and Pilar's head appears. She jumps down from the hatch and is followed by three other girls. The last one to land reaches up to the hatch and a small bundle is lowered into her outstretched arms. The bundle gives a faint squeak as its mother drops through the hatch, takes it in her arms and gives me a sheepish smile. A tiny hand emerges from the bundle and reaches up towards her face.

I say to Pilar, 'I told you to wait.'

'We have been waiting for years.' Pilar brings the mother and baby to me and says, 'This is Paloma and Tomas.'

I look at the baby's pink little face and think of Jack when he was first born. He snuffles in his sleep and I want to hold him, then I remind myself that this is not the time to be cuddling babies. Pilar names the other three girls as Lucía, Adriana and María and we exchange nods and smiles.

While the girls look around the cell and take in the grenades and the weaponry, I check out the lock on the door and find it solid and heavy duty and unlikely to give way to a blast from an AK 47, which would be dangerous anyway because of the ricochet. I check the armoury and find plenty of ammunition for the AKs. I search the boxes of grenades and handguns and then open the freezer. Gold bars and bundles of thousand dollar bills are stacked next to a padlocked metal box. I put the box on the floor and smash the padlock with a rifle butt. I feel excitement mounting as I open it and find waxed paper packages with the familiar words Polar Ajax stamped on them. I have found a store of good old fashioned gelignite, which will blow the door open nicely if only I can find a detonator. I get Pilar and the girls to open the remaining boxes, but find nothing but more grenades and guns.

I am about to give up when I notice a small canvas bag at the back of one of the gun racks. I open it and find two aluminium detonators with fuses attached and a battery operated one that is shaped like a twelve bore cartridge. If we can find some matches we are in business.

'Pilar, can you see any matches?' I ask.

'There are matches in our cell,' she replies. She rattles off some Spanish to Lucía, who goes next door to fetch them.

I open one of the packs of gelignite and begin to pack the explosive into the keyhole using a small stick to push it all the way into the key cavity. I unravel the fuse of the detonator and gently push the metal tip, containing the ultra-sensitive base charge, into the gelignite.

Lucía arrives with the matches and I turn to Pilar.

'This will blow the lock out of the door and we'll be able to get out.'

'That is good,' she says.

'So far as it goes.'

'I understand, yes. We could be killed.'

'Yes.' I look at Paloma and Tomas, then I say to Pilar, 'How old is the baby?'

'Almost one month.'

'Is it Manuel's?'

'Who knows?'

I try not to imagine what the girls must have gone through. 'Are you sure you want to do this?' I say.

'Wait a moment.'

Pilar speaks to the girls, who have been standing in a silent group, watching me check the place out, and unleashes a torrent of comment and argument. María, a sandy-haired waif who can't be more than thirteen, picks up a hand gun and gesticulates with it to reinforce her point. Pilar finally shouts at them and they fall silent. A more reasoned debate seems to take place in which Paloma takes an active part.

Pilar finally turns to me and says, 'They are resolved to go with you if you will allow it.'

'Wouldn't they be safer back in the cell?'

'There is no safety in that cell, only abuse and humiliation for them.'

Seeing the force of her argument, I say, 'Can they handle guns?'

'I am sure, if you show them. They know guns. They

are the children of farmers.'

I weigh the odds of getting out of here with five young girls and a newborn baby, and every instinct tells me to blow the door and leave them behind to take their chances.

I look at the young but old faces around me and know that I can't.

16

When the undertaker showed me the coffin I thought it looked too small, but he said he'd measured our Jack and it was the right size for him.

Two days later, I'm standing with Georgie and Lizzie beside the grave in Kensal Green Cemetery, with Claire and her mum on the opposite side. The sky's full of dark clouds and there's a cold wind blowing the leaves up around the gravestones. The sexton and his assistant lower the coffin into the grave with two straps that go underneath it. The vicar from St John's is reading from a book. We're all crying so much I can hardly hear what he's saying. I think it's something about a woman called Martha and she's talking about Jesus arising again from the grave. I put my arm round Georgie and I can feel her shoulders shaking as she weeps into a handkerchief.

The coffin lands on the floor of the grave and the vicar stops reading and closes the book. I think of little Jack lying inside the coffin and I cry out in anger at the unfairness of it all. Georgie grips my arm and looks up at me. I bow my head and watch the men drop the straps into the grave on top of the coffin. We stand quiet for a bit and then the sexton hands the vicar a trowel and he scoops up some earth and drops it onto the coffin. He gives the trowel to me and I do the same and pass it on to Georgie and the others. The vicar shakes hands with each of us and says how sorry he is for our Jack's passing, then he says goodbye and walks towards the gate with his black robes billowing out behind him. The men start to shovel earth into the grave.

As we're walking away, I go to Claire's mum. She's wearing that much make up to cover the cuts and bruises on her swollen face, I can hardly recognise her.

'Thank you for getting the vicar to come, Mrs Welch,' I say.

'That's all right, Rina love.'

'It was …'

I can't finish what I'm saying. She puts her arm round me. 'Call me Maureen, love.'

We walk through the gate and along Harrow Road to where Sammy's waiting in the car. Claire gets in the front and the three of us squeeze into the back. We drive in silence down Ladbroke Grove, turn into Kensal Rise and on to our street.

• • •

I pour out the sherry for everyone and give Georgie some orange juice. Mum's up at the table now and Maureen's trying to talk to her, but Mum's just staring into her lap and not saying anything. Maureen doesn't drink and so I offer her a cup of tea. Claire and Lizzie are talking and looking out of the window and Georgie's gone into the bedroom to read her book. I go to the cooker and light the gas under the kettle. I see Jack's face in the shine of the kettle and start crying again. I put my finger into the gas flame and I feel the burn and the pain shoots up my arm and then I'm all right.

Sammy comes over, stands next to me and says, 'I'm sorry, Reen.'

'Thanks for coming, Sam.'

'No bother.'

'Nice to have the car.'

'Yeah.'

He looks at me and lowers his voice.

'This ain't really the time but …'

'Go on.'

'I've got a message for you.'

'What about?'

'A bit of an accident that happened down Walmer Road the other night.'

'I don't know what you're on about.'

'Yes, you do.'

I turn and look at him.

He says, 'Dave Preston's been grassed for it. He's at the nick and he's saying he was down the Malibu with you.'

He's talking about a club in Westbourne Grove. I look at Sammy and I know he's being straight.

'I never knew you were on their firm,' I say.

'I am now.'

'How come?'

'I done a bit of work with a mate. They found out, we had to give them a taste and that was it.'

'How do they know what he's saying in the nick?'

'They've got a copper on the take in there.'

'Who's grassed him?'

'One of the Bailey mob, I reckon. They're saying Nick done Johnny Preston and Dave shot him for it.'

'Sounds about right.'

'I never knew he had the bottle.'

There's a loud knocking at the door. Everyone goes quiet. Claire's pointing down into the street. I go and look through the window and there's a police car parked. There's more knocking and I open the door and there's a tall man with a thin face in a grey raincoat and a trilby hat with two uniformed bobbies standing behind him.

'Rina Walker?'

'Yeah,' I say.

'Detective Inspector Davis. You're coming with me.'

'Can I get my coat?'

He nods, comes into the room and has a look round. Sammy's nipped into the bedroom and shut the door. Claire and Lizzie are looking scared.

Maureen stands up from the table and says, 'What's this about? Where are you taking her?'

'Notting Hill Police Station. She's wanted for questioning.'

'She's just buried her brother.'

'I can't help that,' says Davis.

'How long am I going to be?' I say.

'That depends on you.'

I take my coat off the back of Maureen's chair. 'It's all right,' I whisper to her.

The copper walks over, takes my arm and says, 'Come on, you.'

I throw a look at Claire as I go through the door and she mouths something that I can't make out. I walk past the copper and down the stairs. The policemen follow me. One of them goes past me on the front steps and opens the door of the police car. Davis gets in the front and I go in the back with a copper on each side of me. One of them tries to look down my tits but I pull my coat round me and he looks out of the window instead. We get to the police station and I'm taken to the front desk. A red-faced copper standing behind it swings this big book round towards me.

'Can you write, miss?' he says.

The other plods chuckle. I look round for Davis, but he's not there. The comedian hands me a biro and says, 'Put a cross on there, love.'

I sign my name in the book, then I'm taken along a corridor, down some stairs to the basement and past the cells. I've been here before with Mum. We came to see Dad once when I was little. There's snoring coming from one of the cells. Dave's sitting on a bunk in another one. He comes to the bars as I walk past. They put me in a room at the end of the corridor. It's bare except for a table and four chairs.

One of them says, 'Wait in here. He'll be along.'

He shuts the door. I sit on one of the chairs and run my hand along the metal edge of the table.

The door opens and Davis comes in carrying some papers. He's wearing a grey suit and a striped tie. He looks about forty. He's got a hooked nose and a thin moustache underneath it. His face is lined and his hair's receding and going grey. He pulls a chair out, sits opposite me and puts a photograph of Dave on the table.

'Can't you do better than that for a boyfriend, nice looking girl like you?' he says.

I smile at him and say, 'You should see him dance.'

'On the end of a rope, if you've got any sense.' He leans forward over the table. 'Accessory to murder. I'll put you down for ten fucking years. By the time those old girls in Holloway have finished with you, your cunt'll be stretched wide enough to park a lorry in it.'

He sits back and shuffles through his papers until he finds a blank one. He takes a pen out of his top pocket, unscrews the cap and writes something on the top of the paper. He sits back in his chair.

'Unless,' he says, 'you give me a statement that you saw him shoot Nick Bailey.'

'I didn't.'

'I don't give a fuck if you didn't. I've got a witness who's placed you with Dave Preston out the back of an all-night drinker in Walmer Road, where he shot Bailey.'

'We was never there.'

'Well, I know you were, and I know I'll get him for it. All you've got to worry about is whether you go down with him or not.'

'Get stuffed!'

He reaches across the table and slaps me. I hit the floor and scream then I grab the table and shove it into him.

He falls backwards onto the floor and I jump on him and punch him in the face. The door opens and two policemen run in. They grab me off him, throw me onto a chair and handcuff me behind my back. They go to help Davis up, but he shrugs them off and gets to his feet. One of the coppers is smirking as he picks up the papers and the table and chairs. Davis looks at them.

'Out,' he says.

They go out and shut the door. Davis sits down opposite me and rubs his cheek.

'Harry Walker's girl,' he says. I nod.

He chuckles and says, 'A chip off the old block.'

I think about my Dad and what a good laugh he could be when he wasn't angry about something. Then I think of poor little Jack and I hate this grey streak of piss in front of me. I want to kill the bastard. I twist my wrists around against the sharp metal handcuffs until I get the pain.

Davis folds his arms on the table and leans forward. 'Do you really want to go your dad's way?'

I want to gouge those grey eyes out but I say, 'Of course I don't.'

'Handsome girl like you, you could do something with your life.'

'I know and I'm going to.'

Just as soon as I've stuffed that metal chair up your arse.

'Just make a statement that you saw Preston shoot Bailey behind a club in Bramley Road last Friday night and then stand up in court and tell the jury.'

'But you see, Mr Davis, that would be lying because I never saw him shoot anybody.'

'Now, Rina …'

'We were dancing in the Malibu club on Friday night and then he came back to ours and stayed.'

He sits back and gives me a thin smile. He knows I'm in it now because I've supported the alibi that Dave's given him and if he can break that he's got the both of us. He reaches for the paper and picks up his pen.

'You're prepared to make a statement to that effect?' I nod and he unscrews the cap of his pen.

'Name?'

'Katherine Walker.'

He asks me where I was on the night I killed Nick Bailey and I give him the story about being with Dave at the Malibu. I know I'm risking being done for accessory by backing Dave up, but if I don't, he could end up grassing me. Davis writes down my statement, calls one of the coppers back in and tells him to take my handcuffs off. I sign the statement. Davis signs it as well, puts it in his pile of papers and stands.

He looks down at me and says, 'You're about as ignorant as your old man was.'

He goes to the door and turns to the uniformed copper.

'Get her out of here,' he says and walks off down the corridor.

I follow the copper past the cells and give Dave a wink as I reach him. I get taken to the front door and, as I go out onto the street, I turn back. Davis is looking at me from a window near the corner of the building.

• • •

Sammy and Lizzie are gone when I get back. Claire and Maureen are sitting one each side of Mum at the table drinking tea.

Maureen looks up and says, 'Thank God for that. Are you all right?'

'I'm fine,' I say.

I pour myself a cup of tea from the pot and sit at the table. 'Where's Georgie?' I say.

'Lying on the bed reading,' says Claire.

'Lizzie?'

'Working.'

Mum takes a drink of her gin and stares at the table. Maureen's looking at me.

'What happened?' she says.

'Nothing, really.'

'It didn't look like nothing.'

'Don't, Mum,' says Claire.

Maureen's still got her eye on me. After a bit she says, 'It's to do with that night you brought the kids round late to mine and then took the pram away, isn't it?'

No one speaks. I look at Claire and she's biting her lip and staring at the fireplace.

Maureen looks at her and then at me.

'You'd better tell me what's gone on,' she says.

There's the sound of people going down the stairs and

the door opens and Lizzie comes in.

Maureen says, 'Not now, Lizzie.'

'I want her here,' I say.

Lizzie stands by the door for a moment then she comes to the table and sits down next to me. I feel her hand on my leg.

Maureen says, 'Let's have it then.'

I'm just about to say something when Mum jerks upright, grabs hold of Maureen's hair and wrenches her head back. She shouts in her ear, 'You leave my girl alone, Maureen Welch, or I'll rip your fucking head off!'

I run round the table and get hold of Mum. Claire pulls Maureen away and sits her down. Mum's flailing her arms about and screaming at me to let go of her and I'm grappling with her and then Lizzie joins in and we get her onto the mattress and hold her down. She thrashes about a bit and then she quietens.

'Jesus Christ, Alice!' says Maureen.

'She's all right now,' I say.

Mum starts sobbing and crying. She reaches her hand round my neck, pulls me to her and says, 'That bastard hurt my little girl, he hurt my little girl.'

'All right, Mum,' I say.

'Hurt my, hurt my, hurt my …'

Her voice tails off and she closes her eyes. I feel her body go limp and her breathing settles down. I wipe her eyes with my sleeve then I get up and sit at the table. Lizzie and Claire sit down too. Maureen's rubbing her head where her hair's been pulled. I pour everyone a glass of sherry. I take a good drink myself and then I tell her what's happened.

• • •

A bit later, Maureen's looking like she's had the shock of her life. One thing's led to another and I've told her about Johnny and Nick Bailey as well and how Dave made me do it. I get up and pour a cup of tea. I put it in front of her and sit down at the table. Claire and Lizzie are looking at her.

She sips her tea and then she says, 'I can't believe you'd …'

She stops speaking and we all sit there in silence, waiting for what she's going to say. She takes a couple more sips of her tea then she looks straight at me.

'I admire you for what you did to that beast, Rina, and the other one you had to do because you were forced to. You did what you had to for your Jack and Georgie and no one will hear anything about it from me, may God strike me dead.'

'Thanks, Maureen,' I say.

'That kind are filth,' says Claire.

Maureen puts her arm round her daughter and I pour out the last of the sherry.

I hear someone running up the stairs. There's a knock at the door and I go and open it. Sammy's leaning on the bannister, breathing hard.

'Are Claire and her mum still there?' he says.

'Yeah,' I say.

I let him come in and he goes straight to Maureen.

'I've just been in the pub and your Ron's been in a rare old ruck with a couple of black blokes. He's fighting mad and he's smashed up your gaff and I think he's going to come looking for you.'

Maureen goes to the window and looks out. Claire says, 'He doesn't know we're here, does he?'

'I reckon he might,' says Sammy.

'Have you told him, you stupid …?'

'Of course I haven't. Now come on, both of you, the car's downstairs.'

Sammy opens the door and Maureen and Claire put on their coats. 'Where are you going to go?' I say,

They look at one another then Claire says, 'We'll be all right, don't …'

The downstairs door crashes open and someone's running up the stairs. Sammy closes our door and puts his weight against it. Before I can get there to add mine, the door flies open and Sammy's thrown on the floor.

Claire's dad stands swaying in the doorway. He's a big man and his forehead's dripping blood. He sees us standing behind the table and he starts grinning and then laughing. He walks towards Maureen, and stretches out his arms as if he's going to give her a cuddle. I back away from her and, as he swings back his arm to hit her, I grab the frying pan off the draining board and smash it against the side of his head. He falls onto the table, it breaks in half, and he lands hard on the floor.

The bedroom door opens and Georgie's looking at

Claire's dad bleeding onto the floorboards. There's a deep cut on the side of his head where I've caught him with the edge of the frying pan. He shifts onto his back and starts to come round.

Lizzie's right by him. She says, 'Upstairs. All of you. Come on.'

Georgie's gone back in the bedroom. I go to get her and she whines and tells me to leave her be, but I pull her by the arm and tell her she can bring her book. When we go back through the kitchen, Claire's dad's up on all fours shaking his head and wondering where he is. We get out without him seeing us and follow the others upstairs.

Lizzie locks and bolts her door and me and Sammy help her to move her wardrobe in front of it. Georgie sits on the floor in the corner and opens her book. Lizzie takes a bottle of Scotch out from under her bed and gets cups from her kitchen. While I'm watching her pour us all a drink, I remember I've left Mum with Claire's dad. I'm wondering whether to go down again when I hear a crash from downstairs and a dog barking and two men shouting. I go to the window. It's dark now, but I can see Claire's dad rolling down the steps onto the pavement. I beckon to the others and we see him lie still for a minute, then he pulls himself up on the railings and limps off along the street.

Sammy opens the window and leans out, then he shuts it and says to Claire, 'He's gone into yours.'

Lizzie hands us cups of whisky.

'Do you want a drink of milk, love?' she asks Georgie. Georgie shakes her head without looking up.

Maureen sits down in a chair and sighs like she's really tired. Claire pulls up a chair next to her and puts her arm round her.

Maureen leans her head against Claire and says, 'He wasn't always like that, you know.'

'I know, Mum,' says Claire. 'It's the drink that's got him.'

Claire turns her mum's head towards her and says, 'You can't go on with him anymore, you know.'

'Where can we go?'

'You're staying at ours,' I say.

'That's the first place he'll come to,' says Claire.

The dog barks outside on the landing and there's a knock at the door.

Lizzie says, 'That's Aleksy. I'll see what he wants.'

We shift the wardrobe and she unlocks the door and goes onto the landing. I can hear them talking and then Lizzie comes back in with the rent collector with his sharp suit and his Alsatian.

She says to me, 'It's you he wants.'

The rent collector looks at the four of us and then at Georgie. He points at me with his stick and says, 'You go downstairs please. I talk.'

The dog gives a growl and I say to Lizzie, 'I'll be back in a minute.'

Aleksy opens the door for me and I go down the stairs with the dog panting behind me. When we get into our kitchen he looks at the broken table and Mum sleeping and the blood on the floor and says, 'You make shit hole, no?'

'Accident,' I say.

He looks at Mum and says, 'You, her and kids out in two weeks.'

'What?' I say.

'Landlord want flat. Repossess. You out.' He turns to leave.

'Hang on,' I say.

I go to the bedroom and take the money I got from Dave out of the back of the armchair with one arm. I peel off a couple of fivers and put the rest in my pocket. I go back in the kitchen, hold the notes out to him and say, 'How about a couple of months' rent?'

He shakes his head and says, 'Out. Two weeks.'

Mum was right. Johnny was keeping us here rent-free by threatening Bielsky, who Aleksy collects rents and clears out for. Now he's gone, they can move five Jamaicans in and get more rent. I look at his pointy shoes and his silk tie and his silver top cane and his sneering look. The dog starts licking at the blood on the floor. He pulls it to him.

'Two weeks, or we come.'

'Wait,' I say.

He stops in the doorway.

'Tell Bielsky I want to see him.'

He turns and looks me up and down then he says, 'Mister Bielsky don't see scum.'

'Fuck you!'

'You only good for suck men's cock. You want suck men's cock, make money, you come to me.'

There's a scuffling sound over by the gas stove. The Alsatian darts across, dives underneath the stove and scrambles out with a rat wriggling and squealing in its mouth. The dog chews it up and swallows it in one. Aleksy goes across, picks up its lead and pats its back.

'You get your dinner. You good boy.'

He takes the dog out onto the landing. As he turns onto the stairs he says, 'Two weeks, or we come.'

17

I pick up an AK 47, look at Pilar and say, 'Once loaded with a full magazine, it's basically point and shoot.'

Pilar repeats this to the girls in Spanish. I pick up a full magazine and slide it into place in the magazine well.

'You can fire single shot or automatic by moving this selector switch here. Middle position for automatic, lower position for semi-automatic. The upper position is safety which means you can't fire the gun.'

I show them the switching action and put the gun to my shoulder. 'Then you take aim by lining up the sights and pull the trigger, or you can shoot from the hip if your target is close to you.'

There's a burst of machine gun fire and then single shots from somewhere above. I give a gun and a full magazine to Pilar and each girl, except for Paloma. When she sees that she has been excluded, she knots the ends of Tomas's shawl to make a sling, puts it over her head and swings him round so that he lies at her back, then she takes an AK from the rack and loads it with surprising efficiency. The girls form a line, check their selector switches, shoulder the guns and look along the sights. María and Adriana are clearly excited by the prospect of action. Paloma and Lucía have more of an air of quiet resolve about them. I feel tearful for a moment as they stand before me cradling lethal weapons in their slender young arms and I curse the men who have twisted their innocence so brutally.

Paloma puts a question to Pilar, who says, 'How many bullets in a magazine?'

'These look like standard ones, so it should be thirty rounds.'

I hear more gunfire from above and decide that we have to make our move. If I'm going to die today, it may as well be among a group of abused women rising up against their tormentors. I check the gelignite in the lock and the fuse, and tell Pilar to get the girls to crouch down behind the freezer and put their fingers in their ears, and to flatten herself against the wall beside the door.

Once I see that everyone is in place and that Paloma has Tomas's ears covered, I kneel down in front of the lock and check that the detonator is pressed firmly into the gelignite, then I bite into the fuse cord and tear it off six inches from the detonator. The matches are damp, but after a few attempts, I fire one up, light the fuse and press myself against the wall of the cell.

The explosion is deafening. Bits of metal smack and ping against the walls and floor but the door swings open. I leave the cell with Pilar and the girls following behind me. The passageway is empty and pitch dark. We feel our way along it. Light bleeds around the edges of the door to the main hall, which is at the top of the stairs at the end of the passageway. We reach the door and I light a match and inspect the lock.

One shot busts it open.

The hallway is quiet and deserted. I motion to the girls

to stay where they are and make my way to the windows which overlook one side of the building where Manuel was shot. There is nothing there to show that a massacre has occurred. The poolside furniture is neatly in place and the water in the pool is a clear blue colour.

As I cross the hall to rejoin Pilar and the girls, I catch sight of the heel of a boot through a partly open door, adjacent to the one we entered by. I turn to the girls, put a finger to my lips and beckon them over. I indicate the boot and that we are going to take a look. The girls form a semicircle around me and we creep towards the door with guns raised. I ease it open very slowly to reveal that the boot is attached to a foot sticking out of a pyramid of bodies that almost touches the crystal chandelier hanging from the ceiling.

As we take in the sight of so much dead flesh, a door opens above us and a peal of laughter echoes around the hall. I hear footsteps on the gallery above. I lead the girls into the room of bodies and we conceal ourselves behind the fatigue-coloured pile. A group of laughing men whoop down the stairs and through the door to the basement that we have just come from. We can hear them jostling along the corridor and then falling silent as they reach the open door and go down to the cells.

I move towards the door and into the hall. Pilar and the girls follow me. I close the door to the basement, turn to them and say, 'Those men will see that we're gone and come looking for us.'

Pilar translates and I continue.

'We need to be ready for them when they come through that door. You stand in line, pick one man and aim your gun at his head.' María says something. I look at Pilar.

'Like a firing squad,' she says.

'Yes,' I say.

I turn to Pilar.

'You tell the men that if they make a sound they are dead, then you tell them to lay their guns on the floor and we take them in there.' I indicate the room we have just left. I point at Lucía and Adriana and and say, 'You two, pick up their weapons and follow us in.'

I hear footsteps on the stairs and motion the girls to stand in line a few feet from the door. I indicate to Paloma to take Tomas into the room of bodies and she does so. I move to the side of the door, raise my gun to my shoulder and the girls do the same. The door opens and three guards walk through it and freeze.

One of them reaches for a holster. I kick him in the stomach and he falls forward onto the floor. Pilar issues her instructions. The men lay down their weapons and the girls herd them into the room of bodies. Lucía spits in a guard's face. I take their handcuffs, cuff them together and make them sit on the floor.

I take Pilar aside and say, 'Find out where Guido is and what the set-up is now.'

Pilar approaches the older of the men and asks him various questions. He overcomes his reluctance to answer her when Lucía shoves the barrel of her gun in his ear.

After a short conversation, Pilar returns to me.

'Guido is in the dining room. He sent them down to fetch us and take us to him. There are three other guards with him.'

One of the guards says something. I turn and see Adriana swing her rifle butt at his head. He sinks to the floor unconscious. I look at Pilar.

She says, 'He called her a slut.'

I say, 'We need to get upstairs.'

I take a bandana off a corpse in the pile and gag one of the guards. Pilar and Adriana do the same to the other two and we take belts from the bodies and bind their wrists and ankles. The girls follow me into the hall. I put a finger to my lips and we creep upstairs to the gallery. As we move along it, I hear voices coming from behind what I remember is the dining room door. I stop outside the door, group the girls around me and indicate that we are going in. We raise our guns and I boot the door open.

Guido and three men are sitting at a table groaning with food and champagne bottles. Guido looks up from his plate and chunks of fish fall from his mouth. We walk towards them and they stand and raise their hands in surrender. I push Guido against a wall and shove my gun barrel under his chin.

I press myself against him, look him in his good eye and say, 'I want my passport and the keys to a car right now, or I blow your fucking head off!'

He nods as much as he can with his head clamped between the wall and the gun barrel, and I release him and push him towards the door.

'Stay here and look after our friends,' I say to Pilar, as I leave.

Guido leads me along the gallery to a door at the end. We enter an oak-panelled office with a large mahogany desk at one end with a throne-like swivel chair behind it and leather armchairs in front. The wall behind the desk is lined with wooden filing cabinets. I sit in an armchair while Guido opens various desk drawers, rifles through them, comes up empty and then opens a filing cabinet. Half way through the second drawer, he finds a bunch of four or five passports and throws them onto the desk as if he has completed his assignment. I stand and raise my gun.

'Find it,' I say.

He looks through the passports and hands me one. It is mine. I tell him to put the others back. I pocket mine and say, 'Car keys.'

Guido leads me out of the room, along the gallery and down the stairs to the hall. We go through a door into a long corridor that leads to door at the back of the building. We pass a door to a large kitchen. I glimpse two or three figures huddled behind some boxes under a worktop. We emerge into a courtyard where various cars are parked. I point to a Ford station wagon that will accommodate myself and the girls and Guido takes me back inside and gives me one of several keys from a drawer in a small chest inside the door.

I open the door, point at the car and say, 'Start it up.'

He crosses to the station wagon and gets in. It starts

with a satisfying growl and relieves itself of a black cloud of exhaust gas. As I am taking the key from him, I hear a shot from upstairs. I push Guido into the passageway and urge him back to the hallway, up the stairs and into the dining room.

One guard is lying on the floor with a bullet hole in his forehead. Another is sprawled unconscious in a corner, bleeding from the nose. The third one stands naked against the wall. His outstretched hands are skewered into the oak panelling with table forks. His head hangs forward, resting on the bone handle of the knife that sticks out of his neck. His penis dangles from his mouth, dripping blood onto the gold crucifix nestling among his chest hair.

Pilar, Adriana and María sit together on a red velvet banquette against the wall next to Paloma, who is breastfeeding Tomas. They watch impassively as Lucía cuts into the crucified guard's scrotum with a carving knife. She sees me and stops.

Pilar says, 'He made her pregnant when she was twelve.' I nod. 'Then he killed her baby.'

I look at Lucía and see the loathing and the lust in her face and I want to tell her something, but I don't know what it is.

Pilar says, 'These other two used to …'

'We don't have time,' I interrupt.

I point to Guido.

'I'm going to lock him up. Do what you have to do and meet me by the Ford station wagon in the yard at the back.'

The amputee will bleed to death from the groin in

about ten minutes and I don't like to contemplate how they'll finish off the other one. I stab Guido in the back with the gun barrel and we go downstairs to the cells. I shoot the lock off a wall cabinet in the corridor and take out a bunch of keys. I find the key to the torture chamber, unlock it and throw him into it. He whines and wrings his hands as I slam the door on him and lock it. Much as I'd like to turn his lights out, something tells me that killing one DEA agent is enough for one trip. I go to the cell we escaped from and open the freezer. I take six bundles of notes, one for each girl and one for me, and put them in an empty grenade box. I look ruefully at the gold for a moment and then select a snub nosed Colt Cobra, load it and slip it into my back pocket. I pick up the grenade box, head back along the passageway, throw the keys into the cupboard and climb the stairs.

Guido's cries for help recede as I reach the courtyard at the back of the building. Pilar and the girls are waiting by the car holding their guns. I realise I have no idea what to do with them once we get away from the house. I decide to think about that later. I tell Pilar to make them put the guns in the back of an old pick-up truck that stands in a corner of the yard and get into the car. They protest at losing their weapons, but Pilar insists and they reluctantly dump them in the truck. I put my AK in there as well and open the grenade box. I hand a sheaf of notes to Pilar and each of the girls. They stare in disbelief at however many thousand dollars they are holding for a moment and then beam at me and chatter excitedly.

Pilar flicks a few notes, sees that all the bills are thousands and says, 'This is amazing!'

'You've earned it,' I say.

I unlock the car. Pilar sits beside me in front and the others squeeze into the back seat. I hear Tomas gurgle and sigh and look round to see him contentedly sucking at Paloma's breast. I start the engine and drive out of the courtyard, round the side of the house and on to the gravel drive. We pass the pool and approach the main gate. Pilar gets out and opens the gates and we pass through onto the road.

Pilar turns to me and says, 'Where are we going?'

'I need to get to Mexico City airport. What about you?'

Pilar confers with the girls and says, 'We will go to Mexico City as well.'

'Is that where you're all from?' I ask.

'No.'

'Don't you want to go back to your families?'

'They are all dead.'

I look at Pilar's slender young frame on the seat next to me and wonder what will become of her in Mexico City.

There is a whoop of joy and a chorus of excitement from the back seat.

Pilar says, 'Adriana has counted the money. Each has fifty thousand dollars!'

18

Georgie's pulling at my arm and saying it's time for school. I open my eyes and I'm looking at a pair of feet. I lift my head and see that I'm lying across the bottom of Lizzie's bed. She's asleep next to Maureen, and Claire's curled up in the armchair by the fireplace. I look round for Sammy, then I remember he went home before I came back up last night.

I get up, take Georgie downstairs and she goes to the privy while I make her a piece of bread and margarine. The milk's gone sour, so I give her a glass of water. She gets her books from the bedroom and we set off to school. As we're going along Golborne Road, I ask her if she's all right, but she won't speak. I ask her again but she says nothing.

I stop and pull her round to face me, then I shake her. 'You've got to talk to me, Georgie!' I say.

She looks at me and after a bit she says, 'I want to be somewhere else.'

Tears are welling up in her eyes. I put my arms round her and pull her to me. I say, 'I know, Georgie, I know.'

She's really sobbing and crying now, so I pick her up and carry her back towards home. When we get to our street, she's still crying but she says she wants to walk. I set her down and give her a handkerchief. She dries her eyes and says, 'I want to go to school.'

'Are you sure?'

'I'm going,' she says, as she walks away from me.

I catch her up and say, 'I'll take you.'

'No.'

She runs round the corner into Golborne. I follow behind her to make sure she's all right. She crosses the roads carefully and when I see her catch up with a group of other kids from the school, I turn and walk back to our street.

I come round the corner and see Sammy's car parked outside ours. Sammy's leaning on the railings, smoking. He sees me, flicks his fag into the gutter and walks towards me.

'Dave's out,' he says.

'That was quick.'

'He wants to see you.'

'Where is he?'

'He's waiting for you at the yard.'

'Claire and Maureen upstairs?'

'They're at yours. Lizzie's got a visitor.'

'Stay with them, all right?'

'Do you want a lift?'

'Stay with them.'

Sammy nods. I wait until he's gone inside and then I walk towards Westbourne Park Road.

• • •

At the scrap yard, I can see the back end of Dave's Jaguar sticking out from behind a pile of wrecked motors. The dog's lying beside the hut with its head on its paws. I rattle the gates and it goes into a barking frenzy and rears up on its back legs, pulling against its chain. The shed door opens and the bloke with the crew cut and beer belly comes out, yanks the dog's chain and growls something at it. The dog lies down again and beer belly unlocks the gate and nods towards the Jag.

I go over to the car and hear the Everly Brothers smoothing it up as I get there. Dave opens the passenger door and I slip into a warm pocket of polished wood and leather. Dave switches off the radio.

'You owe me three hundred quid,' I say.

He takes an envelope out of his pocket and gives it to me. I flick through the notes inside and say, 'Davis knew I was lying.'

'Of course.'

'He said he had people to say we were there.'

'Like hell he did.'

'Is that it then?'

'I got the governor of the Malibu and a couple of others to say we were there all night, so I reckon we're all right.'

'You did all that from the nick?'

He gives me a snidey little smile, reaches across me, opens the door and says, 'It's finished. I don't know you. You don't know me. Now fuck off.'

I slam the door shut, grab him by the collar and smack his head on the dashboard. I push him up against the door and say, 'Don't you fucking tell me what to do or I'll get straight up that nick and put you in so much shit, you'll drown in it.'

I feel under his jacket and round his belt for a gun or a knife but he's not carrying. I check the glove box and then I let him go.

He holds the side of his head and says, 'You're a fucking piece of work, you are.'

'Shut up and listen.'

He looks at himself in the driving mirror, takes a black handkerchief from his top pocket and dabs at his face.

I sit back and let him preen a bit then I say, 'I want to see Bielsky.'

'What for?'

'Where do I find him?'

'Not round here.'

'Where then?'

'There's a Polish restaurant down Princes Gate. He's always in there.'

'Take me over there.'

'Who the fuck do you think you are?'

'I'm the one who done a murder that you wanted the credit for but didn't have the bottle to do yourself, because you're a cowardly little pansy who's trying to act the hard man. I'm also the only person without form that can give you an alibi for that murder, so if you've got any sense, you'll do what I tell you.'

He looks through the windscreen, breathes out slowly and sinks down in his seat. I look past him and see the dog raise his head as if he's sniffing the air and then rest it on his paws again and close his eyes.

Dave turns to me and says, 'All right.'

'When we see Bielsky, you tell him you want to buy a flat.'

'Eh?'

'For you and me.'

'What?'

'I need a new place and I don't want him or anyone else to know I've got money, so I'm having you as a front.'

It takes him a minute to grasp the idea but finally he says, 'You're not as stupid as you look.'

'Wouldn't do any harm for you to have a nice young girlfriend, eh?' He manages a tight smile as he starts the engine.

I say, 'I want you to put a bit of work my way.'

'Going to rob a bank now, are you?'

He hoots the horn and swings the car round towards the road. The beer belly comes out of the shed and opens up for us.

As the car pulls away I say, 'When can you give me something?'

'I'll have to speak to my Dad.'

'No.'

'Nothing goes off without Dad's say so.'

'It stays between us.'

'You don't know what he's like.'

'Everyone knows what your dad's like.'

'Rina …'

'Just fucking do it, or *I'll* speak to your dad.'

He turns to me, but I don't look at him. We drive along

Holland Park Avenue towards town, past the fine houses and the posh people walking along under the trees.

I say, 'What do you reckon to Sammy?'

'He ain't done much, but he seems all right.'

'It'll be me and him.'

'You'll need three.'

We stop at the lights at Notting Hill. I can see the date in the window of a bank. It's the fifth of March. I'm sixteen today.

At Lancaster Gate, we turn into the road that runs through Hyde Park and I watch the nannies in their uniforms pushing prams along the paths giving the little ones their fresh air and I think of our Jack as he lay in that hospital bed with the mask and the tubes going into him. I uncross my legs and push the heel of one of Claire's shoes into my ankle until the pain's slicing up my leg. I close my eyes and let out a long breath.

The car lurches suddenly and I open my eyes. Dave says, 'Fucking idiot!'

A taxi's stopped for a fare in front of us. Dave pulls out and passes him and the driver puts his arm out of the window and gives us two fingers. We turn into Princes Gate and stop outside a restaurant with some foreign name that I can't read.

Dave pulls on the handbrake and says, 'This is it.'

A doorman in a black overcoat opens the door of the restaurant and an old man and a younger woman in a fur coat come out. The old man nuzzles up to the young woman and says something in her ear. Her beautiful dark hair bounces on her shoulders as she laughs and nudges him with her elbow. The fur coat falls open and I see her pearl necklace and the tight black dress that grips her figure. The old man puts a tip in the doorman's hand and he pockets it, touches his hat then steps out into the road and hails a cab. I look down at my dirty old jacket and skirt and feel my matted hair. A cab pulls up, the doorman opens the door and says something to the driver. The couple get in and the cab pulls away. Dave opens his door.

'Wait,' I say.

'What's the matter?'

I feel the notes in my pocket and say, 'Take me down to Brompton Road.'

'You what?'

'Brompton Road. Now.'

'You said you wanted to see …'

'I do, but I need something first.'

'I'm not your fucking chauffeur.'

'Shut up and go!'

• • •

It costs me two quid to get past the doormen at Harrods, and the snooty assistant in the ladies fashion department just about holds her nose as she serves me. I buy a black dress like the one the woman outside the restaurant was wearing, and a dark grey coat, a pair of sheer nylons, a suspender belt and black high heels. I go in the Ladies, have a good wash and get the dirt out from under my nails, then I put the new outfit on and go down the escalator to the hairdressers on the lower ground floor and have a shampoo and set. I buy some lipstick and eye make up on the ground floor and get the girl to put it on for me.

When I walk out past the doormen, one of them says, 'Good afternoon, madam.'

Men look at me as I walk along Brompton Road. I see a litter bin by a bus stop and I'm just about to dump the Harrods bag with my old clothes in it, but then I decide to keep hold of it. If I walk down our street looking like this, people are going to be asking questions that I don't want to answer.

Dave's parked the car round the corner in Hans Road. When I get there, he's asleep behind the wheel. I get in beside him and shut the door.

He jerks upright and says, 'Who the fuck ...?' Then he recognises me and his eyes open wide.

I put on a posh voice and say, 'Now you can take me to that nice Polish restaurant, darling.'

He laughs and says, 'You're a fucking turn out, you are.'

We drive back to the restaurant. The doorman shows us in to a long room with a high ceiling. There's a row of round tables with white table cloths down the middle and two rows of smaller tables along the walls. Most of the tables are occupied by men in dark suits with the odd woman here and there. It's really warm and it smells of hot dinner and perfume. I can see Bielsky sitting at a table at the far end of the restaurant talking to two men. A bloke in a suit and a dicky bow comes and takes our coats.

Dave says, 'Mr Bielsky.'

The man nods, hands our coats to a girl standing behind him and leads us towards Bielsky's table. When we get near, Bielsky looks up and says, 'David!'

He offers his hand. Dave shakes it. 'Hello, Feliks,' he says.

Bielsky looks at me and says, 'You bring beautiful lady!'

Dave looks embarrassed so I smile, reach out a hand and say, 'I'm Rina. Nice to meet you, Mr Bielsky.'

He stands, takes my hand and says, 'The pleasure is all mine my dear, I assure you. You will join us, no?'

The two other men stand up. One of them exchanges words with Bielsky in Polish, and they shake hands with him and leave. Bielsky pulls out a chair for me and I sit next to him with Dave on the other side of me. He is a big man with a round face, a long nose and bushy eyebrows. He wears a pair of black rimmed glasses with thick lenses that make his eyes look as if they are sticking out of his head so he can see you better. There's a bottle of vodka on the table and a couple of plates of sliced sausages and little pastry things. Bielsky waves to a waiter and says something to him in Polish. The waiter brings two glasses to the table. Bielsky picks up the vodka bottle and pours us drinks, then he raises his glass to us and downs it in one.

I take my first sip of vodka and it burns my tongue. Dave's staring at the table cloth, trying his best to look like a gangster.

Bielsky says to him, 'Your father is good?' Dave nods without looking up. 'Please give respects and say that I am sorry for your brother,' Bielsky continues.

Dave nods again and keeps staring at the table cloth. I kick him in the leg and he looks at Bielsky.

'I need a new gaff.'

'From me?' says Bielsky.

'What have you got?'

'You want buy or rent?'

'Buy.'

'House or flat?'

'Flat.'

'Most of flats are rented now with many waiting.'

'You must have something.'

Bielsky's looking at me. He's probably wondering if Dave's got me on the game and what kind of sweetener he'll get if he is.

He says, 'I have two floors, Portland Road.'

'How much?'

'For you, David, I make eight hundred.'

I stand up from the table and say, 'Excuse me.'

I walk behind Bielsky's chair and nod to Dave, then I make for the Ladies.

When I get back, Dave says, 'We're going to Portland Road.'

• • •

The flat has its own front door half way up the stairs of a four storey house at the far end of Portland Road, near to Walmer Road and the club where I shot Nick Bailey. It's got a kitchen and two rooms on one floor and three rooms up above. I try not to look surprised when Bielsky opens the door to a bathroom with a hot water boiler on the wall above the bath. The rooms are all wallpapered and it's dry and pretty clean. There's a couple of beds and a few sticks of furniture, but it doesn't look as if anyone's lived there for a bit.

I pull Dave to me as Bielsky goes down the stairs and peel a hundred off the three that he gave me. I put it in his hand and say, 'Offer him seven hundred and give him this for starters, but only if he can wrap it up inside a fortnight.'

'Where are you going to get the rest?'

'We'll talk about that.'

We go down to the kitchen and I tell Dave I'm going to wait in the car. He gives me the keys and I shake hands with Bielsky and leave before he can start questioning me.

I have a look through the bay window on the ground floor, but I can't see much except some pictures of the countryside on the walls and a couple of armchairs. I sit in the car and wait. I turn on the radio. Some posh bloke's all steamed up about some canal or other that belongs to Sue or someone. I turn the dial, but I can't find anything but talking or orchestras so I turn it off. Bielsky's car is parked on the other side of the road and the two men from the restaurant are in it, both looking at me from under their hat brims. Dave and Bielsky come out of the house. They shake hands and Bielsky goes across to his car, gets in the back and they drive off.

Dave gets in behind the wheel and I say, 'Well?'

'All done.'

'Seven hundred?'

'Yeah.'

'In two weeks?'

'That's what he said.'

'Good. Let's go.'

'Wait a minute.'

'What?'

He turns round in his seat and says, 'You want me to buy the gaff?'

'Yeah.'

'With your money?'

'Yeah.'

'I don't get it.'

'I'll tell you once more. I need a new place and I don't want no fucking landlord who can chuck me out, but I don't want anyone to know that I've got money enough to buy it. So, the place is yours but we both know it's mine. All right?'

He looks at me as if I'm two bob short of a quid, then he sighs and says, 'All right.'

'So what happens next?'

'His brief and mine will meet as soon as I tell him when, and they do it.'

'And that's it?'

'If I have the money.'

'You'll have it.'

'When?'

'As soon as you tell me where I can steal it.'

19

I pull the station wagon out of a sharp bend in the road that winds down from the mansion to the highway and narrowly miss a truck coming the other way. I glance round and see that the girls have not noticed. They are still fingering their thousand dollar bills and chirruping away while Tomas sleeps in Paloma's arms. Pilar is leaning back in the seat next to me, smiling with her eyes closed. Her long, silken legs stretch into the footwell, parted invitingly at the knees. I try to keep my concentration on the road and enjoy the breeze blowing through the window and the fresh scents of propagating greenery. Through the trees, I catch glimpses of the azure sea nestling into the gentle curve of the coastline.

I look in the mirror and see a truck, identical to the one that we nearly hit before, coming up fast behind us. Its green radiator grill fills the mirror suddenly and the car slews sideways as the truck hits our rear end. I wrench the wheel over to correct the skid, floor the accelerator, throw the car into the next bend and pull away from the truck. On the downhill straight that follows, I see the truck come out of the bend and start gaining on us, horn blaring and lights flashing. As I slow for the next bend, it pulls out, comes alongside us, slams into us and forces us into the side banking. I stand on the brakes as my window shatters and the door bulges into my side. We come to a stop wedged at an angle between the truck and the bank. Pilar is on top of me and the girls in the back are tangled up and screaming.

Metal scrapes on metal as the truck moves forward and away from us. The car lurches down the bank and comes to rest with two wheels on the road. The truck stops a few yards away, the rear doors swing open and the tailgate crashes down. Six men with guns jump down and surround the car, sliding the bolts of their AKs. I put my hands up. In the mirror, I see the girls doing the same. Paloma slides down into the well between the seats and manages to stifle Tomas's cries just as the passenger door of the truck opens and Carmela climbs down from the cab. She says something to one of the armed men, walks slowly to the car, reaches in through my window and takes the key out of the ignition.

She takes in the girls and says, 'Quite a meat wagon you got here.' She tries to open the door, but it's jammed shut. When a couple of her men step forward, she waves them back, drop-kicks the door handle, puts a foot against the rear door and wrenches it open. I get out.

She takes the Colt from my back pocket, finds my passport and money and says, 'Get in the truck.'

I climb into the cab. Carmela gets into the driver's seat. 'I was coming to find you,' I say.

'Sure you were.'

She looks straight ahead for a moment then says, 'What did you do with Guido?'

'He's locked up at the house.'

'I never knew he was that stupid.'

'He took Manuel out, so now you can take over his business.'

'And all the other DEA snitches that were in bed with him?'

'Most of them won't be getting out of bed again.'

'I saw that, but there's a whole lot more.'

'Let those girls go and I'll get Lee for you.'

'You think you can bargain?'

'Do you want the DEA snitches?'

'Sure I do.'

'How else are you going to get Lee alive?'

She thinks for a moment then she turns and gives me a cold look. 'OK, we go with the plan.'

I nod and catch her smell again as she leans towards me and says, 'If you even think about trying to fuck me, I'll kill you.'

While I'm wondering how she intends to circumvent the fact that the main player in the plan to get Lee is dead, there's a scream from behind the truck. Carmela turns to look out of the window. I see in the wing mirror that one of her men has Pilar up against the car.

Carmela jumps down from the cab and I follow. She wrenches the man off Pilar, lifts him above her head like a barbell, throws him onto the tailgate of the truck and grabs his balls. He rears up, screaming in pain. She chops the bridge of his nose, throws him onto the ground and gives him a vicious kick in the stomach. She snaps an order to the remaining men and they pick him up, lift him into the back of the truck and get in after him. Carmela closes the tailgate, turns and leans on the truck and looks at me.

'If I let these gals go, what am I going to give these guys for entertainment?' she says.

Tomas starts to cry. Carmela hears him, walks to the car and looks at each of the girls who are still and silent in the back seat. She opens the rear door sees Paloma and Tomas on the floor. As she looks down at them, I see a sudden tension grip her neck and shoulders.

Just as I'm moving closer and deciding how I'm going to kill her if she makes a move, she smiles and says, 'Well now, will you look at this little guy?'

She picks Tomas up, rocks him gently and makes soothing noises until he stops crying. Paloma gets out of the car. Carmela jiggles Tomas on her bosom for a moment then she kisses his forehead, hands him to Paloma, throws the car keys to Pilar and says, 'Get out of here.'

Pilar looks at me and I say, 'Go.'

Pilar hesitates and then gets into the driving seat and tries to shut the broken door. One of the girls in the back seat reaches out of the window and holds it closed. Pilar starts the engine and looks at me again.

'Go,' I say.

After a couple of attempts, she starts the engine and the station wagon lurches onto the road and rolls on down the hill.

Carmela opens the door of the cab. As I'm about to climb in, a white Cadillac whooshes up the hill forcing us back behind the truck. Carmela slams the door shut and says, 'Oh fuck!'

'What?' I say.

'Manuel's brother.'

'Are you sure?'

'He's supposed to be in Colombia.' She thinks for a moment and then says, 'It may be cool, in fact. Come on.'

We get into the truck, Carmela turns it round and we grind up the hill to the mansion. As we approach the gates, Carmela stops the truck.

'Wait here while I go talk with him.'

She says something to the men behind us and gets out of the cab. One of her men climbs over, sits in the driver's seat and points his gun at me. Two men get out of the back of the truck and walk with her to the gates. Carmela speaks to one of the two guards. He opens up for them and they go in through the front door of the house.

I look behind me. The remaining men are slumped morosely over their weapons. The oldest one looks to be no more than twenty. He sees me looking and raises his AK. The one with the shattered nose and the battered manhood lies on the floor between them with his knees drawn up, moaning and making gurgling noises. I lean back, close my eyes and think about those lovely girls and that little boy, bowling along the highway with money in their hands and a shot at freedom. At least something good came out of this whole mess.

A shout wakes me and I see Carmela standing in front of the house waving us forward. The gates open and we drive in and stop next to the white Cadillac. I get out of the truck, join Carmela and we enter the hallway. The door to the room of bodies is open.

She glances at the pyramid and says, 'We have a little house cleaning to do.'

She calls to her men and they gather round her. She indicates the pile of bodies and issues some instructions. They move reluctantly towards the corpses.

'There's more upstairs,' I say.

'I saw already. Never mess with teenage girls.'

She leads me upstairs and says, 'Come meet brother Rodrigo. He's cool with the plan.'

'How come?' I ask.

She stops at the top of the stairs and says, 'He wants to work with me because he's changing his operation from marijuana to cocaine and he needs a partner with solid contacts in LA, which is cool with me because I can use what he has going with coke from Colombia. We both want Lee, so we can clean out all the snitches from Rodrigo's end, as well as mine.'

I follow her to the study at the end of the gallery and she opens the door. I walk in and see a skinny figure with a mop of long black hair crouched over the mahogany desk. After a loud nasal inhalation, the hair is flicked back to reveal a gaunt face with high cheekbones and deep-set eyes, that burn momentarily and then soften as their owner smiles, pushes the mound of white powder on the blotting pad across the desk towards me and offers me a rolled-up dollar bill. I return his smile and shake my head. I can see a resemblance to Manuel but his mean, cadaverous look is a long way from his late brother's cultivated elegance. He passes the confection to Carmela, leans back in the chair and puts his feet on the desk. 'You going to set up the American?' he says.

'Yes,' I reply.

Carmela takes a long snort, shakes her head, jumps up and says, 'Fuck, that's good!'

'I told you,' says Rodrigo.

'How much you get?'

'Plenty. Sit down, fuck's sake, we talk about the American with ...?'

'Rina.'

'I, Rodrigo.'

Carmela takes a deep breath, sits and says, 'OK. Sure, but we've gotta move this ...'

Rodrigo raises a hand and says, 'Until we find the assholes ...'

'Yeah,' says Carmela, reaching for the coke again.

Rodrigo swipes the blotting pad away from him and puts it in a desk drawer. He stands and leads us to the leather armchairs grouped round the fireplace at the other end of the room, his long scrawny body contrasting sharply with Carmela's elective deformity.

He sits and says, 'I am glad you locked up the chief asshole. I always knew he was dangerous, but my stupid brother insisted on keeping him because his old man saved my brother's life once.'

'I assumed we'd need Guido to communicate with Lee,' I say.

'Sure,' says Rodrigo.

He gets up and crosses to the fireplace.

Carmela says, 'She's into doing a little business with us from London also, once we're clean.'

Rodrigo says, 'That's good. With Manuel gone, Carmela and I are getting things together and we need someone in London. You have connections there?'

'Yes.'

'Cool. We'll talk.'

The last thing I want is to get involved in the drug trade, but if they think I can do them some good they might be less likely to kill me once they have Lee.

Rodrigo tugs at a bell pull hanging beside the mantlepiece, turns to me and says, 'Go relax for a while, and we'll see you later for a drink on the terrace after we figure out a few details.'

I smile and nod, delighted at the prospect of getting out of my Haight Ashbury costume. The door opens and Juanita enters, looking neat and trim in her white uniform.

'Take Rina to her room,' says Rodrigo.

I follow Juanita out onto the gallery. Below I can see Carmela's men carrying bodies across the hall and out through the main door. As we approach the door to the dining room, two more of his team emerge carrying the mutilated body of the crucified guard. We follow them down the stairs, across the hall and out of the door onto the drive where the corpses are being loaded into the back of the truck, like so much merchandise. I see that the gates are shut and guarded once more. We walk past the pool.

Juanita says, 'Your room is as you left it.'

'That's good,' I reply.

Juanita unlocks the door to the bungalow and we enter the familiar interior. I feel strangely relieved to be back. I head for the drinks table and pour three fingers of whisky.

'Would you like a drink, Juanita?' I ask.

'I should not really.'

'Tequila?'

'Just a small one. I have to help in the kitchen.'

I give her a drink and we sit on the sofa. I say, 'How come you weren't killed?'

'Guido is my husband.'

'I see.'

'He did not kill the servants, they are nothing to him, only Manuel and the guards who were not with him.'

'Did Carmela know what he was planning?'

'No.'

'So she just happened to be on her way here?'

'I telephoned her, also Rodrigo, and told them what Guido had done.'

'Why?'

'I thought that they would kill him when they found out, and kill me as well unless I told them first.'

'You did the right thing.'

'My husband is crazy.'

'Aren't you afraid he'll find out?'

'They will not tell him. I am too useful to them.'

I see what she means. I'm about to probe further into

the nature of her relationship with Carmela when she says, 'They will kill him after they get the American.'

'Is that OK?'

'I hate him.'

She finishes her drink.

'I have to go now.' She smiles and walks to the door. 'If you need anything, just ring the bell and I come.'

I watch Juanita walk alongside the pool, sure-footed and purposeful with her neat hair and her neat figure in among all this killing, and wonder what kind of future she has in mind for herself. I take my clothes off, take a hand mirror from the dressing table and stand with my back to the full length mirror beside the wardrobe. In the hand mirror I can see the small round scab between my shoulder blades, left by the insertion of the transmitter. I think of Georgie in the hospital and how much I want to be out of here and on a plane. I reach up my back with one hand and down with the other, but although I can join my fingers, I have no strength in them in that position and there's no way I can get it out.

I go into the bathroom and run a bath. While it fills, I pour another whisky and look at the clothes in the wardrobe. I take out a white cotton dress, lay it on the bed and select a pair of silver slingback shoes. I go into the bathroom and sink into warm, welcoming water.

I feel a tingling in my ankle, and then I am swimming underwater through a foul swamp. The slimy water is sucking at my arms and legs. Reeds are clinging round my neck and my waist, pulling me down towards the blackness far below where tumescent bodies writhe and slither over and under one another. I try to resist and swim up towards the light, but I am pulled down and down past craggy buildings with ancient cadaverous faces staring through lit windows. I plunge into the roiling stew of sopping flesh. A fin curls round my neck and wrenches me up and up. A gargoyle face lunges at me screaming …

"Rina! Rina!"

Pilar is pulling me out of the water. I sit up, cough violently and vomit water. I scramble out of the bath and sit on the edge, gulping air.

Pilar is holding my head and saying, 'It is OK … it is OK … you are all right now.'

She gives me a towel. I bury my face in it. My head is swimming. I feel a burning pain in my left leg. I can see a swelling like a red boil on the outside of the ankle. As I reach down to touch it, Pilar kneels in front of me, clamps her mouth over it and sucks. She spits something gloopy onto the floor, sucks and spits again and then presses her thumb on the wound. My head starts to clear. Pilar ties a hand towel round my ankle. She reaches into the bath, ladles a handful of water onto the floor and stamps on it.

'A spider,' she says. 'You were bitten. Some of them go in water.' She sits next to me and puts her arm round me. 'It is OK now.'

I put my head on her shoulder and say, 'I passed out.'

'It happens sometimes.'

'From a bite?'

'For some people, yes. The poison is gone now.'

'Thank you.'

I am beginning to feel my strength returning. The pain is fading and my head is clear. I try to stand. Pilar puts her arm round me and leads me into the bedroom. She sits beside me on the sofa.

I say, 'Are you alone?'

'Yes.'

'Why did you come back?'

'It did not seem right to leave you.'

I feel her fingertips stroking the inside of my forearm. 'You saved our lives.'

Her fingers walk up my arm and caress my breasts. She teases a nipple with her tongue, while her hair wafts over the tops of my thighs. I close my eyes and let go of myself as she kisses my stomach and says, 'I must put you to bed, I think.'

She takes my hand and guides me across the room. I slide between the silk sheets and wonder at her perfect body as she undresses.

20

I'm sitting in a stolen Ford Consul with Sammy and Claire, watching the Post Office in Jamaica Road. It's three o'clock in the morning and there's a light rain giving a shine to the tarmac. Claire's fallen asleep in the back of the car and Sammy's nervously drumming his fingers on the steering wheel. I'm not feeling too calm myself, but I decide it's time to go and I lean over and give Claire a shake. She wakes up and looks out of the window.

'All right?' I say.

'Yeah, sorry,' she says.

Sammy turns round to her and says, 'Give us the tools then.' Claire passes a canvas bag over the front seats to him.

'Can you stay awake?'

'Of course I can.'

Me and Sammy get out of the car. Claire gets into the front behind the wheel. She lets the handbrake off and we push the car over the road, onto the pavement and hard up against the front of the Post Office. Sammy takes a jemmy out of the tool bag and climbs onto the roof of the car. He reaches up to the alarm box on the wall and levers it open. The bell gives a muffled ding as he clips a length of wire inside the box. He gets down onto the pavement and we push the car back onto the road. I get another jemmy out of the tool bag and work the forked end in between the edge of the front door and the frame, just below the lock. Sammy nudges his jemmy in above the lower lock. We lever the door open as quietly as we can and we're in.

The safe's an old Phoenix, on the floor behind the counter at the back. I turn on the torch, lift the flap in the counter and we crouch down beside the safe. I take out the drill and a diagram of the drilling points that I've bought off an old peterman mate of my Dad's. He can't do safes any more, not since he had his knees smashed for grassing.

I plug the drill into a powerpoint under the counter and buckle the soundproofing cover onto it. I hold the torch in my mouth, put the diamond tip of the drill bit against the front plate of the safe, just above the combination dial, and squeeze the trigger. I drill through the shell of the safe and get to the steel plate that protects the lock gates. I lean hard on the drill and after a while it goes through the plate and I pull out the bit. I shine the torch into the hole and I can see the lock gates inside. I turn the combination dial back and forth until I see the lock fence fall and release the bolt. I turn the lever on the front plate and swing the door open.

Sammy reaches into the safe and takes out three bundles of notes and some plastic bags of coins and puts them in the bag. I find a sheaf of Postal Orders that he's missed and put them in my pocket. I put the drill in the bag and wipe the front of the safe over for prints. There's a creaking noise from upstairs. Sammy picks up a jemmy and stands beside a door by the end of the counter. As I take the other jemmy out of the bag, I hear someone coming down the stairs. I slip my balaclava over my head and Sammy does the same. The footsteps stop at the other side of the door. A key turns in the lock and the door crashes open, knocking Sammy against the wall. A small man with a shotgun comes towards me.

I flash the torch in his eyes, whack the barrel away with the jemmy and make a dive for his legs. He hits the floor and Sammy grabs the gun and kneels on his back. We turn him face upwards. He's an old boy with long grey hair, in his pyjamas and dressing gown, and he's shaking like a leaf. Sammy points the shotgun at his head. The old geezer starts squirming and whimpering underneath me.

'Take it and get out,' he says.

Sammy cocks both barrels and says, 'Shall I kill you first?'

'That's enough now,' I say.

I pick the old boy up and sit him in a chair. He's no more than a bag of bones.

He pulls his dressing gown round him and says, 'That's pensioners' money, that is.'

'Keep quiet and you won't get hurt,' I say.

'You're a woman,' he says.

'There's no flies on you, eh Grandad?' says Sammy.

I put the jemmies in the bag and shine the torch round the safe. It looks clean and I turn to the old boy and say, 'Where's the phone?'

He just stares at me. I look around and spot it at the end of the counter. I go over and rip the phone wire out of the wall. I stand in front of the old man, shine the torch at the door and say, 'Get back upstairs and stay there.'

Sammy raises the shotgun and the old boy gets up and goes to the door.

He turns, looks at us and says, 'Slags.'

Sammy laughs and lowers the gun. The old boy whips round, grabs the gun and whacks him in the balls with it. He raises the gun towards me and I charge at him, grab him by his scrawny neck and smash his head down on the counter. His skull cracks open and he drops onto the floor.

Sammy crawls over to him, looks at him and says, 'He's dead.'

I look down at the twisted wreck of him. His legs are folded underneath him and he looks no bigger than a child. There's blood and some grey stuff oozing out of his head into his grey hair. 'Pick him up,' I say.

Sammy gets up slowly and leans against the wall, holding his balls and shaking his head. I duck under the counter, open the front door and look up and down the street. No one's about, so I signal to Claire to back the car up to the door. I go behind the counter, put the old man over my shoulder and tell Sammy to pick up the bag and the shotgun. He follows me out to the car and shuts the door of the Post Office behind him. I open the boot and put the body in. Sammy puts the bag and the shotgun in after it, closes the boot and opens the driver's door. Claire moves over and Sammy gets behind the wheel. I slip in the back seat and we're off up Jamaica Road and onto Tower Bridge.

I tell Sammy to stop half way across. I take the body out

of the boot, drop it into the river and throw the shotgun and the balaclavas in after it. I sit back in the leather seat, breathe deeply and look out over the river. The moonlight's shining like silver on the water and I think about the old boy lying on the mud underneath. I reckon he would have shot me if I hadn't stopped him, but I wish he'd stayed in his bed.

We drive to Bethnal Green where we nicked the Consul and left Sammy's car. He tells Claire what happened with the old man as we drive. She seems half-shocked and half-excited. When he tells her about getting the shotgun in the balls she laughs, then she reaches over and strokes him between his legs.

When we get to Bethnal Green, none of us can remember the name of the road and we have to drive round a bit until Claire recognises a bombed-out house on a corner with yellow wallpaper hanging off an upstairs wall. We find Sammy's car, dump the Consul and drive west. Sammy drops me outside Kensal Green Cemetery and I tell them I'll see them back at Portland Road. I get the bag out of the boot and watch them drive off.

I throw the bag over the wall and climb over after it. I pick up the bag and walk to the far end of the cemetery where there's a big family grave under a tree. I kneel down at the back of it, push two fingers into a hole where a piece of masonry is chipped off and get a grip on the edge of a stone slab. I pull the slab towards me, reach inside the grave and pull out an old army ammunition box. I take the money and the Postal Orders out of the bag. I count the notes and make it one thousand seven hundred pounds. I peel off the seven hundred and put it in the money belt round my waist. I put the rest into the box on top of the other cash, and remind myself that I must have a proper count up one of these days. I shut the box and put it back in the grave. I stuff the bag with the tools in there as well, push the slab back in place and rake over the leaves where I've been kneeling.

Dawn's breaking as I walk back among the gravestones. I stop at our Jack's grave and I feel calm and peaceful. I listen to the breeze rustling the leaves and I look up at the stars way above through the branches of the trees and, for a moment, I can feel Jack with me. I remember how tiny he was in my arms when he was a little baby, and how proud I felt when he started walking. I feel so bad that I didn't get help for him sooner. I sink down beside the grave and I'm crying and telling him that it's my fault that he's dead and I'm so sorry.

Then something tells me to look up and I can see his face in the tree above and he's smiling at me and telling me something that I can't make out and it's almost like he's glowing and he looks peaceful and happy. Then he fades away and he's gone. I feel calm again and somehow I know he's all right. I wipe my tears away and walk on.

There's a milk cart rolling up Portland Road on its way to Holland Park. I recognise the driver with the red face I used to nick from. I think about giving him a few quid to make up his losses, but then I reckon he's probably doing all right on some fiddle of his own. The houses are in a bit better nick than our old street but it's still a slum, thanks to Bielsky and his mates keeping it like that so that they can overcrowd the houses with blacks and Irish who can't get lodgings in the better parts.

I can see lights on in the flat. I go in the front door, past Georgie's new bike in the hall, and up the stairs. I can hear the radiogram rocking and rolling in the front room. I go in and Sammy and Claire are asleep on the sofa with their arms wrapped round each other. I lift the needle off the record and turn off the radiogram. I pick the bottles and glasses up off the coffee table, take them into the kitchen and put the kettle on.

I stand at the window and watch the sun coming up over the houses opposite. The kitchen clock says it's nearly half five, too late to go to Lizzie's and get back in time for Georgie. I turn off the kettle, make myself a cup of tea, go through to the front room and shake Sammy awake. He grunts and rolls off the sofa onto the floor.

Claire sits up and says, 'What's happening?'

'Pay day,' I say.

I put my tea down and give Sammy a nudge with my foot. He moans a bit, then he pulls himself up onto the sofa and sits next to Claire.

I take the two hundred out of my pocket, hand it to Sammy and say, 'There's a ton each.'

He leafs through the notes and says, 'How much did we get?'

'About seventeen hundred.'

'Not bad,' he says.

He hands Claire her share. She takes it and says, 'What about the rest then?'

'After I've squared Dave, there'll be about another two hundred each for you two, but go carefully with it. I don't want you splashing it about and raising suspicion. The rest is my share and expenses.'

Claire looks a bit put out.

I say, 'You could always go and work in John Lewis.'

She laughs and says, 'Not after we've robbed it.'

Sammy stands up, takes her hand and says, 'Night night, Reen.'

They go through the door and up the stairs to Claire's room. I sit down on the sofa, drink my tea and sink back into the soft cushions. A bird tweets outside the window and I feel myself drifting off.

The old man with the grey hair comes through the door in his pyjamas holding a dead bird. He grins as he spreads out the bird's wings and comes towards me. I try to get up but I can't move. He stands beside me and holds the bird above my feet and grins at me, then he moves it slowly up over my body until it's above my head. I try to scream but I can't make any sound. He lowers the bird down and presses it onto my face. I feel its beak pushing into my eye and its claws digging into my cheeks and my mouth's full of feathers. I try to breathe and I suck feathers down my throat and into my lungs and I know I'm dying and the old man's laughing and saying, 'Scum ... scum ... scum ...'

I feel pain in my shoulder and a voice is shouting.

'Come! You've got to come, she's smashing herself up!

Georgie's standing over me and shaking me. I hear a crash of breaking glass. I run through the kitchen into the back room. The window's smashed and mum's on the floor lying on broken glass in front of it. There's a gash on her forehead and a big bit of glass sticking out of her neck. I pull out the glass, tear a piece off her skirt and wrap it round her neck to try and stop the bleeding. I feel for her breathing, but there's nothing there and I know she's gone. She must have tried to get out through the window in her madness, trying to get back to our old kitchen. I cradle her head in my hands and close her sad eyes. I kiss her forehead and I feel all the unfairness of it.

Georgie's standing by the door crying. 'I was in the kitchen and I heard her,' she says.

'It's all right. Go in the front room now,' I say.

There are footsteps on the stairs. Maureen comes in. 'Oh my God, Rina. She's not …?'

I nod my head. Maureen comes and kneels beside me. She feels for a pulse in Mum's neck then she shakes her head. She helps me into a chair and sits holding my hands. I look at Mum lying on the floor and at the little room with the mattress and the metal box beside it. She wouldn't have a proper bed upstairs like the rest of us when we came here, only her old mattress on the floor and her box. She'd become like a child, sucking at her gin bottle and throwing her tantrums. Now and again she'd come to her senses, like the night when I done Johnny, but she'd been well gone ever since we moved here. Maureen and me had tried to get her to the doctor, but she fought us off and screamed the place down every time we tried.

We lay her on the mattress and Maureen puts a blanket over her. I go through to Georgie. She's sitting on the sofa with a book on her knee. I sit next to her and put my arm round her. She leans into me and I stroke her hair.

I say, 'Mum's gone.'

'She wasn't very well.'

I hold her tighter and I can feel her crying. I want to cry too, but I can't get my breath. I feel like there's a metal band round my chest that's getting tighter. I start to sway and I feel as if I'm going to pass out. I rest Georgie against the sofa cushions and make myself stand up. I go in the kitchen. Maureen's pouring boiling water into the teapot and the sound of the water pouring's getting louder and the room's going round. I sway against the table and slide down onto the floor.

I come round and see Maureen's kind face in front of me. She holds the back of my neck and gently pushes my head down between my knees. My head clears and I sit up slowly. I'm at the kitchen table. Maureen's rubbing my neck and shoulders.

'Why did she have to do that?' I say.

'She was in a bad way, love.'

'I should have tried more to help her.'

'You did all you could for her.'

'She never wanted to come here.'

Maureen puts her arms round me and says, 'Don't blame yourself now.'

I lean against her and feel the wool of her cardigan against my cheek getting wet with my tears.

She strokes the back of my neck and says, 'There now, you're all right.'

'Where's Georgie?'

'She's just in there. I'll get her.'

Georgie comes in from the front room carrying her book. She sits down and puts the book on the table in front of her. She looks at me. Her eyes are dry and she has that cold look that she gets. I know I should speak, but I don't know what to say to her. She opens the book and starts reading.

Maureen pours three cups of tea and puts them on the table. She sits next to Georgie, puts her arm round her and says, 'I'm afraid it was her time, love.'

Georgie looks at Maureen and repeats, 'She wasn't very well.'

Then she looks down at her book again.

I take a drink of tea and say, 'No school today.'

'I want to go.'

'Not today, love,' says Maureen.

'I'm going,' says Georgie. She gets up, closes her book and goes to the door.

Maureen follows her, takes her arm and says, 'You can't, love, not today.'

Georgie twists away from her. 'I'm going!' she says.

I stand up and say, 'At least have something to eat before you go.'

Georgie snatches an apple off the sideboard and goes

out of the door. Maureen starts after her.

'Leave her,' I say.

Maureen turns and says, 'Will she be alright?'

'It's where she wants to be.'

I go to the window and wait until I see Georgie wheeling her bike out of the front door and onto the road.

'She's on her bike,' I say. 'It doesn't seem ...'

'I know.'

We sit at the table and drink our tea.

Maureen says, 'I'm really sorry she went the way she did, love.'

'At least it was quick,' I say.

'After you moved us all in here, to this lovely place. It seems a shame.'

'I don't think she knew where she was.'

We sit quiet for a bit, then Maureen says, 'You stay here with her and I'll go down the undertakers in Westbourne Grove.'

'Is that what you have to do?'

'I think a doctor has to see her for the death certificate, but they'll know how it goes.'

'I'll come with you.'

'No, love, you've been up all night. You stay here and rest.'

I hear a knock at the door. I go and look through the spy hole and see that it's Dave. I bring him into the kitchen.

Maureen goes to the cooker and says, 'Hello, Dave. Do you want a cup of tea?'

'Ta, Maureen,' he says, taking off his Crombie. He's

got himself a new dark blue suit with a velvet collar and a pair of suede brothel creepers with thick rubber soles that give him an extra inch or two that he can do with. He looks in the mirror above the sink and combs his hair. He flicks his quiff with the end of the comb so it hangs over his forehead and sits down at the table. He looks like a miniature gangster.

Maureen puts his tea in front of him and says, 'I'll get off then, Rina.'

'OK,' I say.

'Bye, Dave.'

'Bye, Mrs Welch.'

Maureen shuts the door behind her. Dave crosses his legs. 'Go all right?' he asks.

'Apart from the old boy coming downstairs in his pyjamas waving a shotgun.'

'What?'

'Game old bugger.'

'What happened?'

'He won't be going upstairs again.'

'Who the fuck was he?'

'You tell me. You sussed the place.'

'I don't fucking know.'

'Postmaster?'

'He lives in Bow, goes home every night.'

'So who was he?'

'Fucked if I know. Where is he now?'

'In the river.'

'Did you leave anything?'

'Of course not.'

'You done the safe?'

'Yeah.'

'How much?

'Seventeen hundred and a few postal orders.'

'Not bad.'

I take out the five hundred and put it on the table. 'There's a monkey. That puts us square on this place.'

'Yeah.'

He puts the notes in his inside pocket, takes out his poncy silver cigarette case and his lighter and lights up a fag. He takes a long drag and sits back.

I say, 'I need a gun.'

'Yeah.'

'That could have gone bad last night.'

'I know.'

'And I want a big score and out.'

'With them two?'

'They're alright.'

'She's been round the clubs a lot looking like she's won the pools.'

'I'll tell her to keep it down.'

'Sammy sort that alarm?'

'Yeah.'

He stands up and puts his coat on. He has a quick look in the mirror and says, 'Meet me at the Elgin tonight.'

We go into the hall and I see him out.

When I go into the kitchen, I feel dizzy again. I grip the side of the table, sit down, put my head between my knees and after a few moments I feel better and sit up. My head clears, and I know that I want to be with Lizzie.

I'm not sure she'll be alone now, but I decide to go and see. I leave a note on the table for Maureen, saying I'll be back later, pick up my jacket from the hall and let myself out.

21

Pilar is calling my name and shaking me gently.

I wake and she says, 'Juanita is coming.'

I get out of bed, look around for something to put on, and pick up the white cotton dress from the floor. Pilar's legs disappear beneath the bed as Juanita knocks at the door.

'Come in,' I say, as I slip the dress over my head and step into the silver slingbacks.

Juanita enters and says, 'Carmela and Rodrigo are waiting for you on the terrace.'

'Thank you. Tell them I'll be there in a few minutes.'

Juanita nods and leaves. Pilar slithers out from under the bed and we laugh as she puts on her underwear. She is so beautiful. I want to tumble her back into bed right now and to hell with Carmela and Rodrigo.

'How did you get in here?' I ask.

'There is a way.'

'That's a high wall.'

'I can climb a palm tree.'

'Perhaps you should teach me.'

'I will.'

'The girls?'

'They went to Mexico City.'

At the dressing table, I apply a quick layer of makeup to my face and smooth some foundation cream over the bite mark on my ankle.

'I have to have dinner with Carmela and Rodrigo.'

'I thought I would find you in a prison cell.'

'I managed to get myself upgraded.'

'That is good.'

I find a pair of white silk pants in a drawer of the dressing table and put them on.

'I must go. Will you be here?'

'Yes.'

We hold each other and kiss. I go to the door and say, 'Shall I lock you in?'

'Anytime.'

I laugh, close the door, turn the key and slip it into the pocket of my dress. As I shade my eyes from the evening sun, I notice a black van parked on the drive near the gates. My partners in crime are sitting at a table by the pool. Rodrigo is now wearing a seersucker jacket, jeans and cowboy boots. His hair is tied back in a ponytail. Carmela glowers and bulges next to him in her sweat-stained singlet and shorts.

Rodrigo indicates a glass on the table. 'Whisky?'

'Thank you,' I reply.

I sit down and he says, 'Lee Masters.'

'Yes,' I say.

'Carmela tells me he's going to give you a million bucks to pay Manuel at the border for coke, so he can bust him in possession.'

'On the US side,' I say.

'Right. Did he give you a location?'

'No.'

'A time?'

'He said Guido would call him, take instructions and set things up.'

'We'll get him out now and make him do it.'

Rodrigo gets to his feet. 'Wait a second,' I say.

He turns. 'What?'

'Lee is expecting to do a deal with Manuel, and last time I looked he was dead.'

'He is.'

'I don't understand.'

'Come.'

Rodrigo leads the way through the French windows and across the hall to a room next to the front door. Inside the room, two men wearing white overalls and gloves are bent over a body, partly covered in a sheet, lying on a long table. One man has a syringe in his hand and the other holds a small brush and an artist's palette. They straighten up as we enter and one of them addresses Rodrigo in Spanish. I approach the body and see that it is Manuel. Rodrigo indicates that they should continue, and we watch as the man with the syringe slides the needle into Manuel's cheek and slowly pumps fluid into it. The needle is withdrawn and his colleague mixes a colour on his palette and brushes it onto the cheek. He adds a couple of strokes to the forehead and chin and then stands back. The other man lifts Manuel's eyelids and pushes a small metal clip under each of them so that Manuel appears to be staring vacantly at the ceiling. The men look to Rodrigo for his approval. He takes a close look at Manuel's face, nods and asks them a question. They remove the sheet covering Manuel's body and stand at each side of his head. At a nod from the taller one, they each put one hand under his neck and the other beneath his shoulder. There is a metallic clicking sound as they lift Manuel up to a sitting position and let go. He remains upright.

One of them lifts his right arm until it is level with his shoulder and it remains raised when he lets go of it.

Rodrigo shows no sign of being disturbed by the sight of his dead brother gesticulating at him in full make up. The men take Manuel off the table and with more sounds of clicking and ratcheting they bend his legs at the knee and sit him in an upright chair. The effect is macabre. I am reminded of a shop window mannequin with a bad case of haemorrhoids.

Words are exchanged with Rodrigo, and the men pack jars of fluid, surgical instruments and various sinister-looking cogs, bolts and strips of metal into cases. Rodrigo ushers them into the hall and I see him hand one of them an envelope and shake their hands as they leave by the front door.

He joins us and says, 'Good enough?'

'From a distance,' I say.

'That's all it needs,' says Carmela.

Rodrigo turns, walks across the hall and says, 'Let's talk to Guido.' We go through the door and down the steps to the basement.

Rodrigo opens the wall cabinet and takes out the bunch of keys.

He is breathing heavily as he looks at me and says, 'Where is he?'

I remember that I put him in the torture cell and say, 'Third door.'

He walks to the door and tries several keys. Finding one that turns the lock, he opens the door. I can see Guido cowering in a corner of the cell. Rodrigo rushes at him and throws a flurry of vicious punches at his head. Guido ducks and covers. Rodrigo hacks at him with his pointed boots and Guido rolls onto the floor. Rodrigo picks up the chainsaw lying against the wall and pulls maniacally at the starting cord, producing impotent whimpering sounds from the machine.

Carmela strides across the cell, grabs the chainsaw and slaps his face. She shouts a command, shoves him against the wall and holds the blade of the chainsaw against his neck. Rodrigo's fury subsides and Carmela releases him, picks Guido up off the floor and sits him in a chair. Guido whimpers and looks anxiously at the electrodes lying on the table in front of him.

Carmela says something to Rodrigo and he nods, pulls Guido to his feet and pushes him towards the door. Guido falls to the floor. Rodrigo and Carmela pick him up and drag him along the corridor and up the stairs. I follow them to the hallway. They carry Guido up to the office and dump him in a chair next to the desk. Rodrigo immediately leans over him and starts to fire questions at him until Carmela moves him gently but firmly away from his victim and indicates the chair behind the desk. Rodrigo sits glowering at Guido while Carmela goes to a tray of drinks and pours a glass of brandy, puts it to Guido's lips and coaxes him to take some.

Carmela pulls up a chair next to him and begins gently to interrogate him. I lean against the wall by the door and watch, impressed by her technique. After a while, seeming satisfied with the information she has received, Carmela goes to the mantelpiece, tugs at the bell pull and says something to Rodrigo.

He looks over at me, indicates Guido, and says, 'He killed my brother.'

'I understand,' I reply.

Juanita knocks at the door, enters and says, 'Dinner is ready in the dining room.'

'I need to call London,' I say.

Carmela looks at Rodrigo and says, 'I don't think so.'

'My sister is sick and I need to check on her.'

Rodrigo goes to the desk, unclips an earpiece from the back of the telephone, shows it to me and says, 'You permit?'

I nod, pick up the receiver and dial. After a few clicks and buzzes, the line connects. I listen to it ring and ring. It's morning in London, Graham must be at the hospital. I replace the receiver.

Rodrigo puts back the earpiece and says, 'Your sister is seriously ill?'

'I'm not sure yet.'

Carmela gets up and says, 'Let's eat dinner.'

• • •

Carmela and Rodrigo help Guido up and take him into the dining room. As we enter, I look for any lingering signs of the morning's violence, but can see none. Carmela takes off her belt, ties Guido to a chair, and we sit at the round table. I see that the skeleton of Santa Muerte is still in pole position in the centre, although she no longer glows. I wonder if she'll continue to protect me.

Juanita enters with a large round metal dish and places it on the table. I can see shrimps and mussels and chunky-looking bits of meat poking out of a bed of yellow rice. Rodrigo picks up a serving spoon and offers it to Carmela.

She ploughs the spoon into the pan and distributes generous helpings to each of us. Juanita pours wine and I pick up a fork, hoping it did not feature in this morning's crucifixion. Although it looks unfamiliar to me, the food tastes delicious and I quickly empty my plate and wish I could smuggle some back to Pilar.

As Juanita pours more wine, Rodrigo sits back and says, 'Guido's going to call Lee Masters, tell him that Manuel has agreed to do the deal with you, and get the location of the drop. He thinks it will be north of the border, near El Paso, in Texas. He'll also be told where you need to go to meet with Lee and get the money, probably also in El Paso.'

'How far to El Paso?' I ask.

'To drive, two days.'

'Do you have the coke?'

'Of course. For one million dollars, you get two hundred fifty kilos of pure. Special bargain price. The first of many deals we will make, no?'

'Sure,' I say.

Rodrigo speaks to Guido, then he says, 'He'll call now. We go to the office.'

We leave the table, Carmela releases Guido and we go next door. Guido goes to the telephone on the desk, picks up the receiver and dials. Rodrigo stands beside him, unclips the earpiece from the back of the telephone and opens a notebook on the table next to the phone. He puts the earpiece to his ear and makes notes as he listens. Guido, after a few inaudible opening remarks, gives the occasional affirmative grunt and then replaces the receiver.

Rodrigo clips the earpiece back in place and writes in the notebook.

He turns to me and says, 'He'll meet you in El Paso at eight p.m. day after tomorrow at a gas station on the corner of Alameda Avenue and Prado Road. He'll drive a blue Ford Pinto. You're to arrange to meet Manuel at nine p.m. that evening at an old farmhouse thirty miles south of El Paso, east off Highway 10, to make the deal.'

He tears a page out of the notebook and hands it to me.

'It is all there, including directions to the farmhouse. I have a copy.'

'Will you be there?' I ask.

'Guido'll bring Manuel and the coke, which is yours,

along with your passport, once we have Lee. Also, we can help you get the coke to London if you want.'

'And the money?'

'We keep.'

Carmela moves towards me, looks steadily at me and says, 'Be at the farmhouse with the money and you get the coke.'

They clearly have some notion of burning me or killing me, but it is nothing more than I expected. They are both entirely ruthless and only concerned with honing their business operations without further penetration by the DEA. I know that I will have to rely on Lee and my own resources on the day. In the meantime, I want to get back to Pilar.

Carmela says, 'You need to leave early tomorrow.'

'What about a car?' I ask.

Rodrigo says, 'We show you in the morning.'

'What does a Ford Pinto look like?

'Small ugly sedan,' says Carmela.

There is a general move to the door. Rodrigo heads towards the far end of the gallery. Carmela, Guido and I walk down the stairs to the hallway. Guido melts away behind us and Carmela says, 'Walk you home?'

'OK.'

We step out into the hot night air. The cicadas are clicking at orchestral volume and various night birds squawk and hoot in avian protest at their domination of the airwaves. A light breeze rustles the palm fronds and wafts delicate scents to and fro around us.

Carmela says, 'Rodrigo tried to kill you before and he will again.'

'He shot up the minister's car?'

'Sure. He hated his brother. Rodrigo was the one who paid Gonzales to have his marijuana fields destroyed.'

'You'd never know he hated his brother from the way he set about Guido.'

'Showtime.'

'Why would he want to kill me?'

'He thinks you know too much about him and he's a major league paranoid.'

'I'll bear it in mind,' I say.

We cover the short distance to the door to my room and she turns to face me, looking into my eyes.

'You knock me out.'

She moves closer to me.

I take out my key, look down at her and say, 'I have a long drive tomorrow.'

She presses her body into me and I feel her doughy breasts and then hard muscle and the heat of her breath on my chest. She rises onto her toes, puts her lips next to my ear and whispers, 'Just a little comfort for a little girl?'

When I feel her tongue snaking around my ear lobe, I suppress a wave of nausea, ease her away from me gently and say, 'Business first?'

She kisses my cleavage and, just as I'm about to inflict great pain on her, she pulls back and says, 'Later.'

She turns and walks away and I wait for her foul flavour to leave me before unlocking the door. When she reaches the concrete path beside the pool, I go inside.

Pilar is lying on the sofa, still in her underwear. I join her and we melt into each other's arms.

I nuzzle her ear and say, 'How about a trip to the United States?'

'Tell me more.'

'Later,' I say, as we slide onto the floor.

22

I wake up in Lizzie's bed, stretch my arms and legs out over her slippery silk sheets and reach for her, but she's not there. I turn over and see her sitting in the glow from the fire, looking so beautiful. When these sort of feelings started in me, I knew I only wanted to be with girls, but I was too scared to let on to anyone. I love Lizzie for the way she's understood me and helped me to become myself.

She comes over, sits on the bed beside me and kisses my cheek. 'What time is it?' I ask.

'About half four.'

I get up on one elbow and say, 'Have I been asleep since …?'

'You've had a nasty shock, finding her like that.'

'I've got to get back. There's undertakers coming, and I should be there.'

I get out of bed and put on my clothes. Lizzie reaches under the bed and pulls out my shoes. She sits me on the bed, rubs my feet and then puts them on for me.

'Are you sure you're all right?' she says.

I can feel the faintness for a moment but then it passes. 'I'm fine.'

'Do you want me to come with you?'

'It's OK. Maureen's there.'

'She's a brick, that one.'

'Yeah.'

I stand up and put my jacket on.

'I should go.'

She takes me in her arms, kisses me and whispers, 'Come back soon, you lovely thing.'

• • •

It's almost dark when I reach Portland Road. I get to the house, go in the front door and shut it behind me. As I go up to the flat, I hear a car pull up outside. The bell rings and I go back down and open the front door.

DCI Davis is standing on the step with two uniformed coppers and a bloke in a brown raincoat carrying a briefcase.

Davis looks me up and down and says, 'Well, well. If it isn't Miss Walker.'

Maureen comes down the stairs behind me and says, 'They're here about your mother, Rina.'

I stand back and they go past me and up the stairs. I shut the door and follow behind them. Maureen shows them into the flat and they go into the back room where Mum's lying. I pull Maureen into the kitchen.

'What are the coppers doing here?' I ask.

'The undertakers phoned them. They said they have to if there's been an injury.'

We go into the back room. The bloke with the briefcase bends down and pulls back the blanket covering Mum. Davis has a look at her and then at the broken window and the blood on the floor.

He turns to me and says, 'That's your mother?'

'Yes,' I say.

'Who found her?'

'I did.'

'Where was she?'

'Lying under the window.'

'Why did you move her?'

Maureen steps forward and says, 'We both moved her.'

'Why?'

'She'd passed away. It seemed wrong to leave her lying on the floor.'

Davis takes out a notebook and says, 'Your name is?'

'Maureen Welch.'

'Address?'

'I live here.'

Davis looks at the two of us and then he closes his notebook. The bloke with the briefcase gets up.

Davis says, 'This is Mr Watson from the Coroner's office.'

Watson nods at us and goes over and looks at the window and the blood on the floor.

'What do you reckon?' Davis says.

'Probably heart failure, but we'll need an autopsy.'

Davis looks at the window and the blood again, then he kneels down and looks at Mum's neck.

Maureen says, 'She'd lost her mind. We reckon she was trying to climb out the window and she cut herself and fell down.'

Davis stands up and says to Watson, 'Accidental?' Watson hesitates and then looks at the window.

Davis goes over to him and says, 'Saves a lot of paperwork.'

Watson looks over at Mum and then nods. He takes a piece of paper out of his briefcase, turns to me and says, 'Full name of the deceased?'

'Alice Ivy Walker.'

He writes on his form and puts it in his briefcase. Davis turns to the uniformed coppers.

'Get the undertakers up,' he says. The two coppers leave.

Watson picks up his briefcase, looks at his watch and says, 'I'll be getting along then.'

'Thank you, Mr Watson,' says Davis.

Watson nods at him and leaves. When he's gone there's a knock at the door.

Davis says to Maureen, 'You show the undertakers where she is while I have a word with young Miss Walker.'

Maureen opens the door to two men in black suits. One of them's holding a stretcher and the other has a blanket. Davis follows me into the front room. He shuts the door, then he throws me down on the sofa.

'Did you kill her?' he demands.

'Of course I fucking didn't!'

'How come scum like you can afford a nice place like this, eh?' He's got my by the collar and he's shaking me. 'Nice little earner from Dave Preston for a false alibi, was it?'

He tightens his grip on me. His eyes are bulging and he's going red. I stare back at him and say nothing. He lets go of me and goes and looks out of the window.

He says, 'Who else is here?'

I cough and loosen my collar. 'My sister and Maureen and her daughter.'

'What's your sister's name?'

'Georgina.'

'And the daughter?'

'Claire.'

He writes something in his notebook and says, 'Anyone else?'

'Not now.'

That seems to remind him about why he's here. He looks down at the street and then at his watch. He turns and looks at me as if he's trying to make up his mind about something. I'm wondering if he knows anything more than he's letting on.

After a bit he says, 'Alright.'

He goes to the door and opens it. The undertakers are bringing Mum through the kitchen on the stretcher. After they go past us and down the stairs, Davis turns to me.

'I'm sorry about your mother,' he says. He goes out the door. Maureen shuts it behind him and we go into the kitchen. She says,

'Did he put those marks on your neck?'

I pull my collar up and say, 'It's alright.'

'Are you in any trouble, love?'

'No.'

'You've been so good to us, Rina, I don't know what we would have done without you and I'm so grateful, but if you're in trouble because of it …'

'I'm not in trouble.'

Maureen goes to the sink and fills the kettle. She knows I was out all night with Claire and Sammy and I reckon she knows why. She'll have sussed that I robbed the money to get this place for us as well, but I know it's safer for her if we don't speak about it.

I say, 'Is Georgie upstairs?'

'She had her tea and went straight up.'

'Claire and Sam?'

'They left before the police came.'

'I've got to go out. Can you mind her for me?'

'Of course, love.'

As I get to the door she says, 'Hang on a minute, Reen.'

She puts the kettle down and comes over to me. She dabs at her eyes with the edge of her apron, then she takes my hand.

'You're a good girl,' she says.

I smile at her and we hug each other.

• • •

On the way to the Elgin, to meet Dave, I pass a pub with a couple of placards leant against the wall outside. One says Keep Britain White and there's a couple with the lightening flash in the circle. The fascist mob will have had a meeting somewhere and the lads'll be in there getting pissed up before they go out looking for Jamaicans to beat up.

The Elgin's full of people and noise and the same old

singer's crooning away about Carolina being finer or some such rubbish, while the old bint on the piano thumps away behind him. I squeeze through the crowd to try and find Dave. He's sitting at a table at the back with a couple of young Teds and an older bloke who looks like a villain. I stand near and catch his eye and then I push my way back to the door and out into the street.

Dave comes out and walks past me and round the corner to where his Jag's parked. I follow him and get in the front seat beside him. He looks around and then he reaches under the seat and pulls out a gun.

'How's that?' he says.

I take it and weigh it in my hand. It feels good. Not too big and not too heavy.

'That's a 51 Beretta that is. Italian. Good little gun.'

He takes it from me and shows me the way to load the magazine and unlock the safety catch, and how to cock it by sliding back the top part. The magazine holds eight rounds.

I say, 'I'll need more bullets.'

'That's a hundred and twenty you owe me already.'

'You'll get it. When's the next one?'

'Soon as you like.'

'Where?'

'Hatton Garden.'

'Jewellers?'

'You're moving up in the world.'

• • •

I walk up the Grove and go along the canal towards the old gasworks. It's dark on the towpath and I'm glad I've got a gun tucked in my knickers. I can only just see the edge of the canal by the light from a few windows in the buildings on the other side. I climb over a brick wall and walk between two derelict factories, then I'm over another wall and in the old gasworks. The moon comes out from behind a cloud as I walk between the two big gasometers toward the railway line.

I find an old door that's fallen off one of the sheds and stand it up against the wall in front of the railway tracks. I take out the gun, push the safety over, pull back the slider and fire a shot at the centre of the door. The gun kicks more than I expected and I miss the door completely. I plant my feet firmly and grip the gun with both hands. I breathe slowly, aim carefully, and put four shots dead centre.

I put the gun away and leg it back to the canal. When I get there, I see someone looking out of an upper window. I put my head down and hurry towards the bridge. Just as I reach it, someone opens a window on the other side and chucks an old sack full of something in the canal.

It's gone midnight and I'm walking past a pub on the way to Portland Road when I see him. Claire's dad, staggering drunk and leaning on the wall of the pub. His head's down and there's drool hanging out of his mouth. He looks up and sees me. I go to cross the road and he roars at me. 'Come here, you fucking bitch!'

A car comes past and stops me crossing. He lunges at

me and we fall into the road. He's like a ton weight landing on top of me. He tries for my neck, but I grab his hair, wrench his head back and roll out from under him.

He rears up on his knees and shouts, 'You fucking hurt me, you fucking …!'

I kick him hard in the face. He falls backwards, cracks his head on the pavement and lies moaning and twitching in the gutter. I think about finishing him, but I can see an old couple coming towards us, so I turn and walk on. I get to the corner and look back. He's still in the gutter and he's not moving. The old couple cross the road to avoid him. I'm glad he was after me and not his wife and daughter.

Sammy and Claire are still up when I get back. I go and check Georgie's asleep and join them in the front room. They sit up when I come in.

'I'm really sorry about your mum, Reen,' Claire says.

'It's a real shame,' says Sammy.

'She was in a bad way,' I say.

'You should have woken us up,' he says.

'So you could say hello to the law?'

'Oh … yeah,' he says.

'Any trouble?' says Claire.

'I don't think so,' I say.

There's a bottle of whisky and one of gin on the table that looks like it's one of Mum's. The TV's showing the test card. The little girl reminds me of what Georgie would look like if she'd ever smile.

I turn the TV off, pour myself a whisky and say, 'I've

just seen Dave.' Claire leans forward. 'I've told him I want a big score, then out,' I say.

'Has he got one?'

'Jeweller's in Hatton Garden.'

Sammy's woken up as well. He says, 'Sounds good.'

I take the gun out and put it on the table. I say, 'You'd better get yourself one of these.'

He picks up the gun.

Claire takes it off him and aims it at the TV. 'Make it two,' she says.

23

A shaft of early morning sunlight creeps across the bed towards Pilar's tender young body. I think of her imprisoned underground for years like a piece of livestock, and wonder how long it's been since she was woken by the sun. I kiss her shoulder and she stirs and opens her eyes. She reaches for me and I fold her into my arms.

As she ripples against me, I summon every reserve of self-control and say, 'You have to leave now.'

'Mmmm?'

'Can you get over the wall and wait for me down the road?'

She is suddenly wide awake and standing beside the bed. She hurries into her clothes and says, 'It is late. I should not have slept.'

The clock on the bedside table says six a.m. I follow her to the bathroom. She stands on the basin and opens the small window above it.

'Will you be all right?' I ask.

'Look for me on the road.'

She looks out of the window and then turns her back to it, raises her leg behind her and pushes it through the window. She leans forward, places her hands on the basin, puts her other leg through the window and springs out backwards.

I go back to the bedroom, ring for Juanita and review the contents of the wardrobe. I select a pair of straight Fiorucci jeans, a simple white cotton shirt and a light calf-skin jacket. Although the heat is already approaching blistering, I choose a pair of low-heeled, ankle-length boots with a solid square toe.

Juanita arrives with a tray of fresh coffee and two cups. She sees that the bathroom is empty and gives me a look of mild amusement.

I try to look enigmatic and say, 'You don't miss much.'

'She is a lovely girl.'

'Yes.'

Juanita pours a cup of coffee and hands it to me. She picks up the second cup, walks to the door and says, 'They are waiting for you in the living room.'

'Thank you, Juanita.'

She looks at me for a moment and says, 'Be careful.'

She closes the door and I sit on the sofa and drink coffee. Beyond the pool, I can see a truck driving in through the gates. The driver lets down the tailgate and six or seven men climb down and walk towards the house. The truck drives away and the gates close behind it.

I walk through the already burning sunshine to the house and go in through the French windows. Carmela and Rodrigo are sitting beside a small table with coffee and several plates of sticky pastries. Rodrigo offers me coffee and a pastry. I accept and sit down.

He says, 'For the drop, we're going to use two pick-up trucks that are the same.'

'Identical,' says Carmela.

Rodrigo glances at her and continues, 'You'll go in one truck and the coke in the other, but by different routes. We put the coke in metal containers and weld them inside the front and back fenders of one truck, also in a compartment underneath the gas tank, so the dogs can't smell it. When you meet with Manuel, you check that the coke's there and then swap trucks and license plates so that Lee sees that the deal is made. You understand?'

Rodrigo pours himself a cup of coffee.

'You have the trucks?' I ask.

'They're out back.'

'Who will drive Manuel's truck?

'Guido.'

'With Manuel beside him?'

'At the meeting place, yes.'

'Where will you be?'

'Don't worry about it,' says Carmela.

'OK,' I say.

Carmela says, 'Once we have Lee Masters, you can take off with the coke.'

'And find myself a welding kit,' I say, biting into a pastry.

'We'll give you a guy in El Paso who'll take care of it.' Rodrigo stands. 'Come see the trucks.'

We go downstairs and out into the yard behind the house. Rodrigo leads us to an outbuilding and opens one of a pair of heavy wooden doors. Inside are two identical white pick-up trucks. A man with a metal visor and an oxyacetylene torch is welding at a bench. I avert my eyes from the glare. Two others are fitting a fender to one of the trucks. One lies underneath the truck, the other kneels in front, holding the fender in place. The welder switches off the torch, lifts his visor and stands back. We move to the bench and inspect his work. Metal tubes, about the size of thermos flasks, have been attached to the inside of the fender with metal straps welded to the chrome.

I notice a toolbox on the floor under the bench. While the men are bent over the fender I reach down, take a box cutter knife from the upper tray of the toolbox and slip it into a pocket. The two men who were fitting the front fender to the pick-up come over, collect the newly finished fender and carry it to the back end of the truck. Rodrigo says something to them and one of them pulls a hydraulic jack over to the truck, pushes it under the rear end and raises it a few feet.

Rodrigo kneels under the rear wheel and beckons me to him. I kneel beside him. He points to what looks like the petrol tank.

'That's where the rest of the coke is.' He indicates a seam half way up the side of the tank. 'The join is there. We'll cover it,' he says and stands up.

It is clear that this is all designed to make sure I show up at the farm house, so I try to look suitably impressed, although I have absolutely no intention of trying to leave the United States with a suitcase full of pure cocaine. We walk over to the other pick-up. It is long and wide with low, rather elegant lines. I see the Ford insignia at the centre of the steering wheel. Rodrigo hands me the keys, Caroline's passport and money in pesos and dollars.

He says, 'This passport is good for entering the US, but not for international, as you know. We give you Sarah Collins's passport after the deal's done for you to fly to London with. OK?'

'OK.'

'The tank's full. You have map in cab. You go to Mexico City, then you take the Pereferico Norte ...'

Carmela interrupts him. 'You follow signs to Querétaro then ...'

'I have a map,' I say.

I get into the car, wind down the window and start the engine. Carmela leans too close to me and says, 'You take care now.'

I nod at her, find reverse and back slowly past the other pick up and through the yard outside. I swing the wheel over and come to a halt beside the back door of the house. Rodrigo and Carmela emerge from the outbuilding, shading their eyes from the sun. I glance up and see Juanita looking down from a high window. I engage drive and move off round the side of the house. Guards see me coming and swing the gates open. I accelerate down the drive and turn onto the road.

I drive slowly while I get used to the width and the solid feel of the truck, and keep an eye out for Pilar. She can't have got far since she got over the wall. Just as I am getting worried that she didn't make it, she steps out from behind the yellow flowers of a bush at the roadside. I stop the truck and she hops in, giggling excitedly. She winds the window down as I pull away and I suddenly see how young she is as the wind blows her dark hair back from her innocent face.

'We need to find you some food,' I say.

'In Mexico City.'

'That's about four hours.'

'I want to get away from here.'

Her tone tells me that she means it, and I concentrate on negotiating the bends as we descend towards the highway. When I explained the deal and the plan to her in bed last night, she asked me to take her to Ciudad Juárez, opposite El Paso on the Mexican side of the border. When I asked her what she planned to do, she told me she intended to cross the border and make her way to Los Angeles where her brother lives. When I offered to help her get across the border, she said that she preferred to go alone, and that with the money she had it would be easy.

On a tight bend, I slow down and pull over to allow a donkey cart labouring up the hill to pass us. Pilar looks at the old man holding the reins and turns her head away from him as the cart lumbers past.

'Something wrong?' I ask.

'I thought I knew him, but it's OK.'

I drive on. Pilar looks thoughtful, but stays silent.

We reach the highway and roll northwards with the sun climbing above the hills to the right of us. I remember the old man on the donkey cart and ask, 'Are your family near here?'

'Not any longer.'

'How come?'

'They are dead.'

'I'm sorry, I shouldn't have pried.'

She sits silently, looking out of the window at the mountains. After a while she says, 'We were farmers.'

'It's beautiful country.'

'We grew corn and limes mostly and we sold in the market.' After a pause she continues, 'We were six children, me and five brothers. We were poor, but we were getting by, but then my father's brother starts to grow marijuana on his farm and sell it in the market to men from the city. He is making much more money, so my father starts to grow marijuana and sell it as well. All at once, there is plenty to eat and we have new clothes and everyone is happy, and soon all the farmers in the mountains are growing it and the men from the city are buying it. Then one day, the man my father sells to tells him that the soldiers are coming to burn the fields, but that if he pays money to him, the soldiers will not burn our fields. Some days later, they come and burn all the fields around us but they don't touch ours and my father is accused of informing to the authorities. Then the battles between the farmers start and everyone is making deals and forming gangs and there are guns in the house and these rivalries go on and on and finally Manuel and Rodrigo come with their men and kill my parents and my brothers, except for one who gets away, and then they take me to where you found me.'

Pilar sits back and wipes the tears from her eyes. I slow

the truck and look for a place to stop, but she says, 'No, no, go on please. I do not want to be here.'

I put my foot down and pull out into the fast lane. The drone of the engine, the whine of the wind and the highway sliding beneath the truck eventually bring us into the present. I reach over and cover her hand with mine. Moments later she is asleep.

We cross the great white bridge over the Mezcala River. It can't be more than a week since I crossed it with Lee on the way to the reception, although it seems longer. Cars are parked on the middle of the bridge and people are leaning over the barrier, looking down at the gleaming water hundreds of feet below. Pilar sleeps beside me as we whoosh past them and on through the rugged countryside, which begins to roll more gently as we leave the highlands and approach Mexico City.

I stop at the first gas station I see. It's the middle of the night in London, but I head for the payphone. After a couple of false starts the call connects. Several rings later I'm about to hang up, when a muffled voice answers.

'Graham?' I say.

'Er ... yes?'

'It's Rina.'

'Ah ... hello.'

'How is she?'

'Well ...'

'Is she still in the hospital?'

'Erm ... no.'

'She's back home?'

'Well, no.'

'Then where is she?'

'Well … no one really knows.'

'What?'

'When I went back this morning, they told me she'd discharged herself.'

'Oh, Christ.'

'I don't know what to do.'

I curse myself for being so far away. She could be anywhere, but if I was there, I could at least try to find her.

I say, 'Is there any reason why she wouldn't come back to the house?'

'I don't think so.'

'Did you have a row or anything?'

'No.'

I can think of a couple of places she could be, but I have no phone numbers with me or any way of finding out. My address book's in the safe, but if I let Graham know where it is and give him the combination, he's going to wonder why his girlfriend's sister has so many guns and knives and gold bars.

Graham says, 'I'm not really sure what to do.'

'Just stay where you are and wait, if you can, Graham.'

'Yes, of course.'

'I'm sure she'll come back soon.'

'I hope so. When are you …?'

'I'll be on a flight tomorrow night.' I'm lying. Even if the deal gets done and I get away, it'll be the day after. I say, 'I'll call as soon as I can.'

'Right.'

'Stay where you are.'

'Yes.'

'Goodbye, Graham.'

'Goodbye.'

I put the receiver down and lean against the wall. I try to banish the thought of Georgie wandering the streets of London and wasting away. I need to get this business done and get back as fast as I can. I make myself go to the counter and buy water and burritos.

When I return to the car, Pilar is stretching and yawning. She says, 'Where are we?'

'Almost at Mexico City.'

I hand her a burrito and a bottle of water, reach into the glove compartment, take out the map and say, 'How's your map reading?'

'Not so good, I think.'

While she munches into her burrito, I study the map and locate our position. I can see the Periferico Norte, the ring road and the exit to Querétaro that Rodrigo mentioned. I show the map to Pilar and trace the route from the ring road to the autopista and on to the highway to Querétaro with my finger.

She nods, licks a blob of red sauce off her finger and says, 'OK, yes, I can see how to go.'

I give her the map and drive into the city. It's the height of the morning rush hour. We struggle through the chaos of horns and hysteria and, after several near-death experiences, I manage to find the central square that contains the Palacio Nacional where the reception was held. I remember Adelina's luminous beauty as we pass the building and grieve a moment for her.

I pull over, consult the map and manage to find my way to the ring road. The traffic thins as we head north out of town on a tree-lined boulevard. Pilar seems to have grasped the basics of map reading by the time we reach the Querétaro exit and she directs us from there to the autopista and the highway.

The sun climbs above desiccated hills, scattered with occasional trees and patches of sandy scrubland. I look across at Pilar and she gives me a warm smile of complicity. She slides along the seat and puts her head on my shoulder. A ripple of love for her thrills through me and a hope that she won't suffer any more in her life.

24

The shop looks well protected, with a metal grill over the window and two alarm boxes with flashing lights on the wall above. The clock at the top of the stone arch over the window says half past three. We're parked in Kirby Street in Hatton Garden and the shop lies directly in front of us at the junction with Greville Street. I put my mask and gloves on.

'Are you ready?' I ask Sammy.

He nods, puts on his crash helmet and tightens up his safety harness. I tap Claire on the shoulder. She pulls on her mask, picks up the bag and we get out of the stolen Land Rover and walk the few hundred yards to the shop.

I have a look up and down the street to make sure there's no one about, then I take the rivet gun out of the bag, poke it through the grill and puncture the armoured glass in three places. I put the gun back in the bag and give Sammy a wave. He guns the engine and lets in the clutch. Tires squeal and the Land Rover roars towards the shop, ploughs into the metal grill, smashes the armoured glass window, crunches into the shop counter and stops.

Bells start ringing and sparks are crackling off the metal grill onto the roof of Land Rover. There's a scream of ripping metal as Sammy pulls the Land Rover back onto the road. His door's jammed so he passes a sledgehammer to me through the window and crawls out through the hole where the windscreen was. Me and Sammy head to the back of the shop while Claire makes a sweep of the jewellery from the counter and the broken display cases.

We get to the steel door at the back and I shoot the lock. Sammy gives it three cracks with the sledge hammer and the door flies open. I go in and shine the torch over the shelves until I see a black leather case about the size of a cigar box. I pick it up and go back into the shop. Sammy and Claire are picking jewellery up off the floor. I tell them to leave it and we run to the car we've left outside in Greville Street. There are lights on in windows and people are leaning out watching. I see two figures walking towards us as we get to the car. I fire two shots into the air and they turn and run for it.

The bag and the leather case go in the boot and we jump in and take off. We get to the end of Greville Street and Sammy nearly turns the motor over as we screech into Farringdon Road. I tell him to calm down and he slows to a normal speed. We cross over Clerkenwell Road and Claire and I duck down as two police cars race past us, bells ringing, going towards Greville Street. We pull into a side street where we've left Sammy's car. We wipe over the nicked motor, transfer the gear to Sammy's and head for King's Cross, then west along Marylebone Road. Claire's laughing and Sammy's whooping it up and beating the steering wheel in triumph like he's scored the winning goal.

I get out of the car outside the scrapyard and tell them to wait for me back at the flat. I've got the bag with the leather case and the loose jewellery inside it. I unlock the gate and go to the shed. I can see a crack of light at the edge of the blackout curtain in the window. The door opens as I get there and Dave steps out. He takes the bag off me and I follow him into the shed.

There's a grey-haired man in a black coat and hat sitting at the table. I say, 'What the fuck's this?'

Dave puts the bag on the table, picks up a bottle of whisky and says, 'Calm down and have a drink.'

'What's going on?' I say.

'This is Arne. He's from Amsterdam.'

The grey-haired man looks at me and smiles. He says, 'So young.' He gets up and offers me his hand. 'How do you do?' he says.

I shake his hand. Him being foreign seems to make it less dangerous, but I put one hand on my gun as I sit down and knock back the whisky. Dave takes the leather case out of the bag and empties the loose jewellery onto the table. Arne takes a quick look at it, then picks up the leather case and places it in front of him. He takes out a small metal tool, works it into the keyhole and turns the lock. He opens the case and smiles. There are six diamonds on a black velvet pad. He takes a pair of tweezers out of his pocket, screws a black monocle type of thing in one eye and closes the other. He picks up a diamond with the tweezers and studies it.

When he's had a good look at all six, he closes the case and says, 'Yes. All is good.'

He reaches under the table and takes out two small

suitcases that are exactly the same. He puts the leather case in one and passes the other one across the table. Dave opens it and I can see it's full of bundles of white fivers. He takes one out, licks his fingers and starts counting.

Arne stands up, buttons his coat, and puts on his hat and a pair of black leather gloves. He picks up his suitcase and waits while Dave finishes counting, flicks through the other wads, and snaps the case shut.

He shakes Dave's hand and says, 'Goodbye, David. Give my good wishes to your father.' He turns to me and says, 'Goodbye. I hope I will meet you again.' I shake his hand and he raises his hat and leaves.

I turn to Dave and say, 'How much?'

'Twelve large.'

I feel a tingle up my back and I want to shout out, but I sit down, pour a drink and say, 'Come on then.'

Dave opens the case and takes out eight bundles of notes. He pulls a carrier bag from a drawer behind him, puts the money in and hands it to me. I stuff eight thousand quid inside my jacket and say, 'What about the loose stuff?'

'As soon as I shift it, I'll let you know.'

He picks up a gold necklace and looks at it. I say, 'Suits you.'

There's a flash of anger in his eyes before he gives me his twisted smile. I finish my whisky and head for the door.

'See you, then,' I say.

'Yeah.'

• • •

It's still dark as I walk over the rough stones and the twisted bits of metal to the gates and let myself out. I wait on the pavement while a lorry from the coal yard in Westbourne Park Road rumbles past with clouds of black dust billowing off the back end of it, then I cross the road and head for the cemetery.

Once I've stashed the money in the grave, I'm over the railings and walking through the dark streets towards home. Going down St Mark's Road, I pass the end of Rillington Place and I can see the house at the far end where John Christie did his murders. They reckon he killed seven women and a baby, and he hid the bodies in the house, under the floor boards and buried in the garden. They say he was gassed in the war and it made him like he was. I think about how mad Mum was at the end and I suppose it can happen to anyone.

As I round the corner into Blenheim Crescent, I hear a motor behind me. It's a police car so I slip through a front gate and duck down while it passes, going towards Clarendon Road.

I walk the rest of the way home and, as I get to the flat, I notice that Sammy's car isn't anywhere in the street. When I get in, I check that Georgie's asleep then I go down to the living room. I'm expecting to find Claire and Sammy half-drunk, but they're not there. They aren't in Claire's room either and I'm wondering if they've stopped for a drink at an all-nighter.

I go downstairs to the kitchen. It's almost five o'clock and Georgie will be up for school in a couple of hours. I'm still wound up from the job and I know I won't sleep, so I put the kettle on and pick up a book that she's left on the table. I read slowly down the first page and then I turn over onto the second one.

An hour later I'm still reading about this King Henry and all his doings with women and the Pope and that when I hear Georgie shout from upstairs. I run up to our bedroom and find her sitting up in bed looking frightened. I go to her and put my arms round her.

She says, 'The man was here.'

'What man?' I say.

'The blood man.'

I look round at the window. It's locked shut. 'It's all right, my darling, you were dreaming.'

'He was here. The man with all the blood.'

Maureen comes in and Georgie slips out of my arms and runs crying to her.

'I saw him! I saw him! The horrible man made of blood!' she says.

Maureen picks her up, holds her close and strokes her head.

'It's all right, my little lamb. He's not here and you're safe and sound with me. Just a nasty dream, that's all.'

Georgie clings to her, sobbing and pressing her face into her neck.

'Come to bed with Auntie Maureen, eh? Where there's no horrid dreams and no horrid men.'

Georgie nods her head and clings more tightly.

Maureen says, 'We're all right now, just a nasty dream, but we're all right now.'

I open the door for her and she takes Georgie into her room. I watch while she puts Georgie into her bed, gets in beside her and cuddles her.

'There, there … all safe now … all cosy and safe now, my darling,' she murmurs.

Georgie quietens and Maureen looks up at me and smiles. I close the door and go back down to the kitchen, where I get a knife out of the drawer. I press the blade into the inside of my wrist until I can't feel anything but the pain. When the blood starts oozing, I put down the knife, wrap my wrist in a cloth and squeeze it tight. I sit down and close my eyes.

As my head drops forward onto the table, there's a loud knocking at the front door. I get up quickly and go downstairs, hoping it's just Claire and Sammy who've forgotten their keys. There's another loud knock as I get to the door.

I open it and DCI Davis is there with two coppers. They pull me onto the landing, shove me against the wall, pull my arms behind my back and handcuff me.

Davis says, 'Katherine Walker. I am arresting you for the murder of Nicholas Bailey. You do not have to say anything, but it may harm your defence if you do not mention, when questioned, something which you later rely on in court. Anything you do say may be given in evidence.'

They push me down the stairs and out the front door. There's another copper holding open the back door of a police car. A couple of women walking by with little children cross the road to avoid us. The two coppers put me in the back seat and sit each side of me. I twist my wrists until the cuffs dig into me, and stare straight ahead. Davis gets into the front and nods to the driver. Cars and vans get out of the way of us as we turn into Holland Park Avenue. We go left into the Grove and pull in behind the police station. I'm taken out of the car and marched into the nick. Davis and one of the coppers go to the desk and the other one takes me into an office. A tall sergeant with a bald head and a bushy moustache asks me my name and address and age and writes it on a form. A policewoman comes in and takes my fingerprints. I'm taken to another room, stood against a wall and told to turn round. There's a flash and the policewoman takes a photograph of me. She tells me to turn sideways and takes another, and then I'm taken down to the basement and put in a cell.

It's hours later when the policewoman comes and takes me along the corridor and into the room where Davis questioned me the last time. He's sitting at the table reading a sheet of paper. She points at the chair opposite him and I sit down.

Without looking up, he says, 'That'll be all.'

The policewoman says, 'But I thought …'

'Out,' he says.

He finishes reading the paper, writes something at the

bottom of it, then he holds it up and says, 'Do you know what this is?'

I look at the table and say nothing.

'It's a statement by your best mate, Claire Welch, saying how she saw you shoot Nick Bailey in the head at the back of a drinking club in Walmer Road on the night of the second of March.'

He leans towards me and I can smell his sweat and tobacco breath. 'And she's more than willing to tell it to a judge and jury.' He sits back, puts his hands behind his head and says, 'Which means that you, young Miss Walker, are well and truly fucked.'

My legs and arms feel heavy and my stomach's hurting. He's waiting for me to speak, but I just go on staring at the table. My Dad always said to say nothing if they got you. I think of the old bugger when he got out once and took us all to Southend for a day and then got so drunk that he passed out on the beach and couldn't drive us home.

Davis opens a folder beside him on the desk and takes out another piece of paper. He raises his eyebrows and says, 'And what's this?' He looks at the paper and says, 'Ah yes, that's right. A young man called Samuel Clark says he was at the club with Claire Welch and that he also saw you kill Bailey.'

I look up and see the smug grin on his face as he tips his chair back and taps on the table with his pen. 'Oh, and of course there's your old boyfriend, Dave Preston. He saw you do it as well.'

He leans forward and folds his arms on the table.

'Nothing to say, Rina?'

I look down again and he says, 'They haven't hanged a sixteen- year-old for a while now, but you never know, eh? Come up against the wrong judge and he might just ...'

His chair thumps down on the deck and he hits the table with his fist.

'Twenty-five years! You'll be an old bag with every bone in your body broken by the time you get out.'

He leans forward again and says, 'I can get you off with ten, and you'll do seven if you give me a confession and the reason why you did it.'

I look up into his worn-out grey eyes and say, 'Fuck off.'

He swings at me. I duck down and his hand grazes the back of my head.

The door opens. A copper puts his head round it and says, 'Her duty brief's here.'

Davis stands up, sweeps the papers into his folder and walks out. The copper opens the door wider and a little tubby bloke in a brown overcoat and hat walks in and sits down in the chair Davis has just left. He puts a briefcase down beside the chair, takes his hat off and puts it on the table. He only looks about thirty. He's got a round boyish face with dark brown curly hair and sharp little eyes.

He gives me a quick smile and says to the copper, 'Thank you, officer.'

'Bang on the door when you're finished.'

'I know the form, thank you.'

The copper shuts the door behind him and I hear the

key turn in the lock. The little bloke holds his hand out.

'How do you do? Jeffrey Harker. I'm your solicitor. '

I shake his hand and he opens his briefcase and takes out a notebook and a pen.

'Katherine Irene Walker, known as Rina Walker. Yes?'

'Yes.'

'Arrested and charged with first-degree murder on the second of March at an illegal drinking club at number forty-six, Walmer Road, London West Eleven.'

'Yes.'

'Were you made aware of your rights under the law at the time of the arrest?'

I nod and he says, 'The police have statements from three eyewitnesses who say they saw you shoot Nicholas Bailey on the night in question.'

'They were never there,' I say.

'We'll deal with that at a later stage. How do you intend to plead?'

'Not guilty.'

'Good.' He writes something in his notebook, puts it down and says, 'Now. I only have some initial questions at this stage. We will deal with matters in more detail later.'

'All right,' I say.

'Were you at the club in Walmer Road on the night in question?'

'No.'

'Where were you?'

'At home.'

'Was anyone else present?'

'My Mum and my little sister.'

'Can they testify to that effect?'

'My sister was asleep and my Mum's dead.'

'How old is your sister?'

'Nine.'

'I see.' He looks at his watch, closes his notebook and says, 'You will appear before Bow Street Magistrates Court at nine a.m. tomorrow, where I expect you to be committed for trial at the Old Bailey and placed on remand at Holloway Women's Prison until that time. I shall be in court with you tomorrow and I will visit you at Holloway as soon as I have a trial date and all available information relevant to your case.'

He puts his notebook in his briefcase, goes to the cell door and knocks on it. He looks down at the floor until the copper opens it then he turns to me and says, 'Good day, Miss Walker.'

The door shuts behind him. A few minutes later the policewoman opens it and says, 'Follow me.'

She takes me back to the cell and locks me in. I lie on the bed and close my eyes then I turn onto my stomach and push my face into the mattress.

25

Pilar unfolds the map and studies the network of roads and highways that will takes us north towards El Paso. She slides across the seat and points out her preferred route to me. It looks good, as far as I can tell, and we leave the highway at Querétaro and take a fast two lane road through green hills and valleys.

A few hours later, with the sun beginning to sink in the sky, we stop at a gas station. A glum-looking old man in a pair of oil stained dungarees comes out of a wooden hut and makes his way towards the truck. Pilar speaks to him and he fills the tank. I go to the office and look for a payphone to call London, but don't find one.

An appetising smell comes from a shack next door. We walk over and go in. A tiny old woman in a black overall and headscarf is standing on a box behind a trestle table, stirring a brown gloopy sludge in a large pot. She gives us a beaming smile. Pilar exchanges some words with her and she hands us each a bowl of sludge and a slice of tortilla.

We take it outside and sit at a small table under an awning. It turns out to be a coagulated bean stew with misshapen lumps of meat lurking below which look like chicken, but don't taste like it. I ask Pilar if she knows what kind of meat it is and she nods and says, 'Iguana.'

I'm too hungry to be choosy, so I start eating my first reptile. As we are finishing, the tiny lady appears with succulent slices of water melon and oranges. We thank her and she beams at us and disappears into the shack. I sit back, peel an orange and enjoy the simple delight on Pilar's face as she bites into a slice of water melon.

After she's swallowed the last bit of pink flesh, I say, 'Where did you learn such good English?'

'World Service.'

'The radio?'

'World Service and Voice of America.'

'And school?'

'A little, but mostly radio.'

I'm about to ask her about her favourite programmes when an open-body truck, with a group of men standing in the back holding shovels and forks, pulls in and stops beside the pumps. The glum old man comes out of the hut and walks slowly towards it. The driver gets out and speaks to the pump attendant, who unscrews the filler cap of the fuel tank. The men in the back shout and gesticulate at the driver. He lets down the tailgate and they put down their implements, get down from the truck, walk a short distance away and pee in the dirt. The pump attendant appears unmoved as he fills the tank and grunts at the driver. As the men button up and approach the food shack, we decide it's time to leave. We pay the tiny lady, climb into the pickup and get back on the road.

As I climb into the seat, I catch my back on the edge of the door frame and get a stab of pain from the place where the tracking device was planted. I wince and twist round to try to reach the spot between my shoulder blades.

Pilar sees me, so I tell her about having the device put in at Gatesville and how it enables Lee to track my movements. Last night, when I told her about my trip to Texas and the deal I made with Lee, I didn't mention the tracking device.

'Show me.' she says.

I lift my T-shirt and turn away. I feel her fingers brushing the skin around the incision and pressing against the device itself.

She kisses the spot, then she says, 'You want me to take it out for you?'

'Can you do that?' I ask.

'If I can get a blade and some things.'

I remember Lee saying that the chip is close to my spinal cord and ask, 'Are you sure you know how?'

'It is the same as with the piglets,' she says.

'The piglets?'

'The castration. I did it many times on my uncle's farm. You make a clean cut and then take out.'

The image she conjures up makes me slightly uneasy, but the kiss she just gave me and her calm confidence makes me want to trust her. Lee needs to think I'm still tagged until the bust, so that I can get the passport from him that will get me home, but with the chip in my pocket, instead of under my skin, the chances of my getting away at the end are a great deal better. I decide to risk it. I take the box cutter out of my pocket and hand it to Pilar.

She tests the blade on her finger and says, 'This is good. You want me to do it?'

'Yes.' I say.

'It will hurt.'

'I know.'

She opens the door of the pick-up and says, 'I need something else. Wait here.'

I watch her walk across the forecourt and go into the little old lady's shack. Moments later she comes out holding a half bottle of Tequila and a paper bag.

She gets back into the cab and says, 'I have what I need. Drive and we will find a place.'

I start the truck and pull onto the road. I ask Pilar what she's got in the paper bag and she shows me a needle and some fine thread. After a few miles, we see a rough track winding off to the left. I swing the truck onto it and we bump along it until it curves out of sight of the road.

When we reach an area of level grass, Pilar says, 'Here is good, I think.'

We get out of the truck and Pilar looks round to make sure we are alone. She kneels on the grass and motions me to lie down. I take off my T-shirt and feel the burn of the sun on my skin. I lie on my stomach, turn my head to the side, and watch her pouring Tequila over the blade of the box-cutter.

'Are you ready?' she says.

I nod and she dabs Tequila from her fingertips onto the skin between my shoulder blades.

'You be quite still now.'

She feels for the chip, locates it and then makes a cut. I let the pain hold me while I feel her cut me again and then

I get a sharp jolt along my spine as she locates the chip. She pauses for a moment and then she holds her breath and I feel her taking the chip out with her fingers. Moments later, I feel the needle puncture me and the thread running through my skin. She makes another stitch and ties off. I feel her lips on me as she bites through the thread.

'All done,' she says.

I turn over, sit up and kiss her. She smiles, hands me the Tequila bottle and I take a mouthful.

'Thank you, doctor.'

I take the chip and the box-cutter from her and put them in the pockets of my jeans. While we sit on the grass, sip from the bottle and enjoy a quiet moment, I reflect on the surefooted way she handled things just now and how right I was to trust her.

• • •

Rolling hills give way to flat farmland stretching away for miles on each side of us. The road is dead straight and fast. Pilar switches the radio to a Mexican station and Carlos Santana wrings every last ounce of juice out of Black Magic Woman. The air blowing through the cab smells sweet and the sun sinking over the skyline casts long indolent shadows across the road. We drive on for a couple of hours. A sign tells us that we are approaching Torreon and another one informs us that there is a hotel in five kilometres. I ask Pilar if we have come far enough to stop for the night and still get to El Paso by tomorrow evening. She studies the map and decides that we have.

Another sign directs us to a brown two-storey brick building, set back from the road behind a parking lot. It looks run down and forgotten, among a scattering of warehouses and small factories, on the outer fringe of the town. Neon lettering above the main door flickers in a pathetic attempt to inform us that it is a hotel.

We pull into the parking lot and stop alongside a green van, which is the only vehicle present apart from a couple of mopeds leaning near the front door. Two men are unloading various cases and crates from the van and taking them through the front door of the hotel. We get out of the truck and follow them into a dark hallway. I peer into the gloom and make out a reception desk in a corner. Behind the counter, a small man with a bald head, horn-rimmed glasses with thick lenses and a fishy look, bends over a ledger. As we approach the desk he looks at us with surprise, scans Pilar's body and speaks to us in a pinched, squeaky voice.

Pilar looks at me and suppresses a giggle.

'He wants to know if we want rooms,' she says.

'He's more intelligent than he looks,' I say.

Pilar laughs and says, 'Best to get two.'

'Really?'

'I think so.'

I watch the fish write our names in the register with intense concentration. I look at the wooden crucifix on the wall behind him, and conclude that she is probably right about the rooms. The fish gives us each keys and rings a bell on the counter as Pilar orders some food to be sent up to us. Moments later a bellhop with a smart uniform and a cheeky face appears. After Pilar explains that we have no bags, he takes us upstairs and along a corridor to two adjacent rooms at the far end. He unlocks the rooms and shows them to us, appearing faintly amused by the dilapidated condition of them. He shows us the bathroom next door and lingers for a tip, breaking into a broad grin and skipping off down the stairs when I give him a dollar.

We choose the larger room with its cracked and peeling ochre wallpaper, dark brown upholstery and threadbare, earth coloured carpet. I shake a cloud of dust free from the dark red velvet curtains and open the window to try and clear the fetid air. Pilar flops onto the sagging bed. I go over, lie beside her and put my arms round her. I feel the tension start to drain away as she curls into me and kisses my neck. Just as we are easing into making love, there is a knock at the door. I remember we ordered food and go to the door, pulling up my jeans on the way.

I open the door and find the cheeky bellhop holding a large tray, groaning with tapas, tortillas and bottles and glasses. I step aside and he carries the tray to a table, almost dropping it on the way when he catches sight of the half-naked Pilar pretending to be asleep on the bed. He grins at me and says something I don't understand. I point at Pilar, mime sunstroke and give him another dollar. I open the door for him and he scampers off obediently.

I pour two glasses of whisky and take one to Pilar. I sit on the bed beside her and we sip our drinks. I stroke the silken skin around her navel while the whisky unlocks a few more tight muscles. I lie down with her and we melt into one another.

We wake at midnight, eat ravenously and then sleep again. I dream that I am standing on the saddle of a motorbike, turning circles in a circus ring. I look down and the bike is balanced on top of an elephant. The elephant is standing on top of a hot air balloon and far below in the basket of the balloon I can see a tiny lady in black waving at me. She pulls a string which sends a flame shooting up into the balloon and the balloon takes off. We float up from the circus ring and the audience roars and I look down at the circus ring getting smaller far below us and I overbalance and fall off the bike and plunge past the elephant and the balloon and the tiny lady tries to catch me as I fall past the basket, but she can't hold me and I land in the circus ring with a thump.

Pilar is looking down at me over the side of the bed. 'Are you alright?'

I get to a kneeling position and massage my hip. 'I think so.'

'Did I push you out of the bed?'

'No.'

'Are you OK?'

'Yes.'

I sit on the bed and shake away the dream. There is light around the edge of the curtains. Pilar puts her head on my lap and I stroke her hair. She puts her arms round me and kisses my stomach. We roll across the bed and a balm of pure bliss flows over me as I slide my tongue into her.

• • •

I wake and we're lying beside each other. A breeze is making the velvet curtain stir slightly. The sound of the road, behind a mix of cicadas and birdsong, drifts through the open window.

Pilar lazily traces the muscles of my arm with her finger and says, 'You are so beautiful and so strong. Like a python.'

I laugh, put my arm round her neck and squeeze. When I loosen my grip, she nuzzles my ear.

'Take me to England with you,' she whispers.

I feel a tremor of excitement and I want to squeeze her again until we become one person. I take control of myself and pull back from her a little.

'I'd love to but …'

'You have someone?'

'No.'

'Then why?'

She lays her hand on my cheek and her imploring eyes almost make me give way.

I turn to face her and say, 'I only want good things for you.'

'You are good.'

'No. I'm not.'

'I love you.'

'You deserve better.'

'What can be better than you?'

'A life that is honest and free.'

'We can have that life.'

'No.'

'But why?'

'It's too late.'

Tears moisten the corners of her eyes. I get up from the bed and go along the corridor to the bathroom. The shower shudders and spits and finally allows a weak trickle of tepid water to escape. I push my fists and forehead into the mildewed tiles and curse everything.

I shower and go back to the room. Pilar is lying face down on the bed. I touch her shoulder and say we should go. She gets off the bed and stands before me, looking so lost and sad.

I take her in my arms and say, 'I know you'll be happier in America than you could ever be with me.'

Her face darkens. She pushes me away and says, 'You are the same as the men but with a smile.'

I'm about to speak but she slaps my face and turns away. 'Take me to the border.'

We find our clothes, dress in silence and go downstairs to the desk. I ring the bell and our host appears and looks inquiringly at us for a moment as he tries to recollect who we are. Having done so, he applies himself to painstakingly constructing a hand-written bill which he presents to us, as if it were a vital remnant of some precious manuscript. He accepts payment and we bid him goodbye, which seems to confuse him slightly.

The sun is already baking as I pull the truck onto the highway. Pilar sits at the far end of the seat, leaning her head against the window.

26

The screw who's putting the chains on my legs looks up at me and says, 'I'm looking forward to giving you a good long body search when we get you back.'

'You're so fucking ugly, I bet that's the only way you can get a feel,' I say.

She puts her face next to mine and says, 'I wouldn't touch scum like you with a fucking barge pole.'

She slams the door of my cubicle, shouts to the driver and the van moves off.

I'm on the way to the Old Bailey, where I was committed for trial by the Magistrates Court. Harker asked for bail, but there was no chance and I've spent the past three months on remand in Holloway. I get a glimpse out of the window of the massive old building, looking like a fortress in the morning mist. It was quite rough in there until I'd fought a couple of the women and got a reputation.

You don't work if you're on remand and I had time to get really good at reading. I was doing four books a week after a bit and learning all sorts about history and literature. I got friendly with this older woman who was in for fraud and embezzling; she's really educated and she showed me how to use a dictionary and told me what was good to read. She knew about lots of things and could talk really well and I decided I was going to try to educate myself and be like her.

Lizzie came to see me when I first went in. As soon as I saw her, I wanted to hold her so badly. I went towards her and she put her arms out to me, but as soon as we touched a screw pulled me away and shouted that she was ending the visit, but Lizzie pleaded with her and told her she'd come all the way from Scotland, and the old bitch gave in. Lizzie told me that Maureen was looking after Georgie and that she was fine and I was glad to hear it. I'd written to Georgie a few times, but she never replied.

Lizzie said that a copper who was one of her regulars told her that Claire had tried to sell some jewellery to a bloke in a club who was off-duty CID, and that she grassed me up for the murder in exchange for immunity for the smash and grab we did. He told her they got some forensics off Sammy's car and he did the same.

When Lizzie said how she missed me, I wanted to cry but I couldn't let anyone see my weakness. She looked so soft and beautiful in that horrible ugly place, and I wanted to touch her so much, but then the visit was over and she was saying goodbye and doors were banging and screws were shouting and I was back in my cell and feeling more miserable than ever.

The van stops and the screw opens up and unlocks the chains on my legs. She handcuffs me and I'm taken off the van and into the building. I'm locked in a holding cell, where I can see the screw and the court officers writing forms and such.

• • •

The screw unlocks the door and tells me it's time. There's another screw outside the cell and I walk between them along the corridor to the steps at the end and up one flight to a landing. I can hear a lot of people talking as I go up the second flight and suddenly I'm in the dock of the Old Bailey. The talking stops and every head in the room turns towards me.

I look straight ahead and try to breathe slowly. The judge is dead opposite me on his high-backed chair. He's a little fellow with a pointy chin and a hook nose poking out from under his wig. He looks like an old chicken, peering at me over his round glasses. There's more men in wigs sitting at the tables in the well of the court between me and the judge. I can see the barrister who's defending me. His name's Beevers and I nearly don't recognise him in his wig. He came to see me in Holloway with my brief. He didn't say much while Harker was prattling on, but he seemed all right.

A bloke in a wig, sitting directly below the judge, stands up and says, 'My Lord?'

The judge tells him to proceed and he turns round to me and says, 'You are Katherine Irene Walker of twenty-two Portland Road, London West Eleven?'

'Yes,' I say. My voice is steady, even though my legs are shaking.

He turns to the judge, mumbles something else gets another nod from him and says, 'Call the jury.'

I reckon he's the clerk of the court that Harker told me about. A door over in the far corner of the court opens and the jury come in and take their seats. Half are men and half are women and they look like any bunch of people you might see in a pub or on a bus. The clerk hands a Bible to the one on the end of the first row and swears him in. He does the same with the rest and goes back to his seat. He picks up a folder and comes and stands in front of the dock.

He says, 'Katherine Irene Walker. You stand accused of the murder of Nicholas Bailey on the night of the second of March, nineteen fifty-six. How do you plead?'

'Not guilty.'

The clerk goes and sits at his desk. The judge is bowed over, writing. I look up to the public gallery above where the jury is. It looks almost full. A few in the front are scribbling in notebooks. I can't really see the people in the back row, but they look like the Bailey firm up there all in suits and ties. I look for Lizzie but I can't see her and I wonder why she hasn't come. She never came back after that one visit and I'm worried that she doesn't want to know me anymore. The judge is talking to the jury in a high, flutey sort of voice about how they've got to decide whether I'm guilty or not from the evidence only, or some such, and not have any doubt about it and then he tells the prosecution to open the case.

The prosecuting barrister's tall and thin and his gown swirls about him as he walks towards the jury. He pauses in front of them and then he says, 'Ladies and gentlemen of the jury, you see before you a young woman, Katherine Walker, accused of an act of brutal and cold-blooded murder. It is alleged that she shot the man Nicholas Bailey in the head, at point blank range, and made her escape, leaving him for dead. The burden of proof of the indictment rests with the Crown, which I have the honour to represent, and it is my task, in this court, to prove to you beyond all reasonable doubt that Walker is guilty of the crime of murder with which she is charged. To that end, I shall produce witnesses who will testify, under oath, that they saw Walker kill Bailey, heartlessly and of her own free will, on the night in question. When you have heard these witnesses and all the evidence, you must then weigh all elements of the case that the defence will put before you against the case for the prosecution and draw the necessary conclusions.'

He looks at the jury over for a moment then he turns to the judge and says, 'With your permission, My Lord, I should like to call Claire Welch to give evidence.'

The judge nods and the clerk stands and calls out, 'Call Claire Welch.'

It gets repeated twice by the ushers and Claire comes in and looks around the court. She's wearing a light blue poodle skirt and blouse with a black leather belt. She's got her beehive built up high and she's wearing more make up then Coco the Clown. She steps up into the witness box and the clerk swears her in. She glances round at me, but won't meet my eyes.

The prosecuting barrister says, 'Miss Welch, you were at an illegal drinking club in Walmer Road, Notting Hill, on the night of the second of March, were you not?'

'Yeah, I was.'

'Were you accompanied?'

'I was with my boyfriend.'

'What is your boyfriend's name?'

'Samuel Clark.'

'Did you see the accused at that club on that night?'

'I did.'

'Can you describe what she was wearing?'

'Black skirt and a white V-neck.'

'Did you see the accused in the company of Nicholas Bailey?'

'Yes.'

'Were they in close proximity?'

'What?'

'Were they close to one another?'

'Snogging, yeah.'

People in the gallery laugh. The judge bangs on his desk and says, 'Order!'

'And did you see them leave the club together?'

'They went out the back door into the yard.'

'And did you and your boyfriend follow them?'

'Yes.'

'Perhaps you would be good enough to tell the court what you saw in the back yard of the club?'

'He had her up against the wall, feeling her up. She had her arms round him, kissing him. He pulls her skirt up and she takes a gun out of her knickers and shoots him.'

There's a buzz of whispering in the gallery. A couple of the jurors are writing things down.

The prosecuting counsel waits a moment and says, 'And then?'

'Nick Bailey falls on the floor with blood pouring out of his head and she climbs over the back wall and legs it.'

'She runs away.'

'Yeah.'

'Thank you, Miss Welch.'

The barrister sits down. The judge writes for a bit and then Beevers gets up.

'Permission to cross-examine the witness, My Lord?' he says.

The judge nods and he says to Claire, 'How would you describe the lighting in the club that night?'

Claire looks at him as if she doesn't understand. 'I don't know,' she says.

'Bright, medium, dim?'

'Dim, I suppose.'

'The lighting in the club was dim.'

'Yeah.'

'And what time was it when you went, as you claim you did, into the back yard of the club?'

'Gone midnight.'

'And so it was pitch dark outside?'

'Yeah.'

'Where were Bailey and my client standing?'

'By the back wall.'

'And you were standing where?'

'By the back door.'

'Was the door shut?'

'I don't know.'

'Was there anybody else in the yard at that time?'

'No.'

'How could you be sure there was no one else there if it was pitch dark?'

'I don't think there was.'

'You don't think there was?'

'No.'

'But you're not absolutely sure.'

'No.'

'Then how can you be sure that you saw my client shoot Nicholas Bailey?'

'I did see it.'

'The back yard of number forty-six Walmer Road is sixteen feet wide and eighteen feet long. You are telling the court, under oath, that you were able to identify the accused, with absolute certainty, as the murderer of Nicholas Bailey at a distance of eighteen feet and in complete darkness?'

Claire looks towards the prosecuting counsel, but he's looking down at his desk. She looks at my barrister and says, 'I know it was her.'

'No further questions, My Lord.'

Claire leaves the witness box and Sammy's called. He's in his best grey drape with a bootlace tie and blue brothel creepers. He stands in the box, gets sworn in and gives the prosecution the exact same story as Claire. My man has a go at him about whether he could see it was me in the dark, but Sammy says there was the light coming from the back window of the club and he could see me easily.

Dave's next up and he says he was standing near the back door and he ran out into the yard when he heard the shot and saw Nick lying there and me climbing over the wall. The defence council tries to catch him on if he could be sure it was me because of what I was wearing, but he gets it right.

The judge adjourns the case until tomorrow and I get taken down to the cell. I sit on the bed feeling like I've been kicked in the guts. The screw brings a tray of food in and gives it to me, but I throw it on the floor and lie face down on the bed. I want to smash Claire and Sammy into little pieces and stamp them into the ground. I don't expect much from Dave, who's a cringing little ratbag anyway, but I'd never have thought Claire would do this to me. My best fucking mate! I've known her since we were two! That bastard Davis probably threatened her with half a dozen other charges and twenty years inside.

I'm grinding the heel of my hand into the wall when the door's unlocked and Harker comes in. He sits at the table and says, 'It's looking rather bleak, I'm afraid.'

'Tell me something I don't know.'

He opens his briefcase and takes out his notes.

'The prosecution have you identified at the scene by three witnesses, but ideally they'll want motive as well if they can get it. We have a modicum of doubt over visibility by witnesses, but it's not much.'

'What happens next?' I say.

'The prosecution have just disclosed that they are

calling another witness tomorrow.'

'Who?'

'Maureen Welch.'

• • •

I spend most of the night prowling round the cell and wondering what Maureen's going to say. I'm praying she's going to help me, but the prosecution have called her and I know she won't. When she goes into the witness box the next day, she's dressed in a new dark green coat and hat and she looks nervous. She's gripping her handbag in front of her with both hands as if she's expecting someone to grab it off her at any moment.

She gets sworn in and the prosecuting counsel says, 'You are Maureen Welch, the mother of Claire Welch?'

She opens her mouth but nothing comes out. She coughs a bit, clears her throat and says, 'Yes, sir.'

'You need not address me as sir, Mrs Welch, a simple answer will do.'

'Oh. Sorry.'

'That is perfectly all right, Mrs Welch. Now. You are presently living at the same address as the accused?'

'Yes.'

'But at the time of the murder you were not. Is that correct?'

'Yes.'

'But you were living close by and were in regular contact with the accused?'

'Yes.'

'Did the accused ever talk to you about the murder of Nicholas Bailey, either before or after the murder took place?'

'Yes.'

'Before or after?'

'After.'

'Will you please tell the court what she said?'

'She told me she'd done it.'

'The accused told you that she had murdered Nicholas Bailey.'

'Yes.'

'Thank you, Mrs Welch.'

The prosecutor takes a look at the jury and sits down. Maureen turns and walks down the steps of the witness box.

The judge says, 'Wait please!'

She stops and looks him. Her face is red and she looks like she's going to cry.

He says, 'Kindly remain in the witness box. Defence Counsel may have some questions for you.'

Beevers stands and says, 'Indeed I do, My Lord.'

The judge nods to Beevers and looks down at his papers. Maureen goes back in the witness box.

Beevers smiles at her and says, 'Would you like a glass of water, Mrs Welch?'

Maureen says, 'I would, please.'

Everyone waits while one of the ushers comes forward with a glass of water and I can see her hand shaking as she takes it. She takes a few sips and seems to calm down a bit.

The usher takes the glass from her.

Beevers says, 'Just a few questions, Mrs Welch.'

'I'm sorry,' she says.

Beevers gives her another smile and says, 'How would you describe your relationship with the accused?'

'I don't really …'

'Were you close?'

'I suppose, yes.'

'Did the conversation regarding the murder, which you spoke about to my learned friend, take place before or after the recent death of the accused's younger brother?'

'After.'

'Soon after his death?'

'Yes.'

'Was the accused distressed by her bereavement?

'She was.'

'And were you able to comfort her over her loss?'

Maureen starts to cry and looks away. She reaches into her handbag for a handkerchief. She puts it to her eyes and leans on the edge of the witness box.

Beevers waits a moment and says, 'Was it whilst you were comforting her over the loss of her brother that she told you she had killed Bailey?'

Maureen nods.

Beevers says, 'I'm afraid you have to answer the question, Mrs Welch.'

She's still sobbing but she says, 'Yes.'

Beevers goes close to her and almost whispers, 'Why did she do it?'

'Because …'

She puts her handkerchief to her mouth to stop herself. The court goes quiet.

Beevers waits a moment and says, 'Because what, Mrs Welch?'

'I don't know.'

Beevers stands back and his voice rises as he says, 'I think you do know and I must remind you that you are in a court of law and that you have sworn to tell this court the truth, the whole truth and nothing but the truth and that it is a criminal offence to withhold any information that may have a bearing on the case.'

Maureen's shaking now and she's gone deathly pale. He's up close and glaring up at her.

'I ask you again. Do you know why she did it?'

She holds his look for a few moments. Very quietly, she says, 'He forced her.'

'Who forced her, Mrs Welch?'

'Dave Preston.'

'And why did he force her?'

Maureen buries her face in her handkerchief. Beevers shouts at her, 'Answer the question!'

'Objection!' says the prosecuting counsel.

'Mr Beevers!' says the judge.

Beevers goes close to her again and says quietly, 'Why, Mrs Welch?'

She sways against the side of the witness box and she's breathless and pale.

'Because he was scared to do it himself.' Then her legs

give way and she passes out.

· · ·

After they've brought her round and helped her out of the witness box, the court is adjourned and I'm put back in the cell. After a while, Harker and Beevers come in.

Harker's all excited. He's pacing up and down saying, 'We have duress! We have duress!'

Beevers sits at the table and says, 'Sit down, Jeffrey.'

He turns to me and says, 'If we can prove that Preston forced you to commit the murder or intimidated you in some way, we may be able to get the charge reduced to manslaughter. But we are a long way from doing so, as things stand.'

Harker sits down, takes out his notebook and his pen and says, 'In the light of this development, is there anything you can tell us that could help us to prove that you acted under duress?'

I reckon that anything I tell them could lead back to me killing Johnny, so I don't speak.

Harker's waiting, tapping his fingers on the table.

'You must realise that you are now in a position to help yourself,' he says.

He goes on tapping and looking at me, but I stay quiet.

He says, 'The prosecution will petition the judge to be allowed to recall Preston to give him the opportunity to rebut the allegation. If he does so, and we have no means of corroborating it, then you are looking at a very long prison sentence indeed. Are you sure there is nothing you can tell us that will support the accusation that Preston forced you to commit the murder?'

I look at the floor and shake my head. He snorts in anger, shoves his notebook in his briefcase, snaps it shut, bangs on the door and they leave. A screw comes in and gives me a bowl of soup and a chunk of bread. I sit on the bunk, dip the bread into the soup and chew a bit. It tastes of old socks.

An hour later, I'm taken back into court. There's a lot of talking at the desks below me and in the public gallery. The clerk tells everyone to rise and the judge comes in. The court settles and Dave's called to the witness box.

The clerk swears him in and then the prosecuting barrister says to him, 'Do you know the accused well, Mr Preston?'

'No.'

'Do you know her family?'

'No.'

'And yet when you saw her in the club in Walmer Road you knew who she was, did you not?'

'I've seen her about.'

'You both live in the same neighbourhood and you know her name and who she is, but you do not know her well. Is that correct?'

'Yes.'

'Did you encourage or in any way coerce or force the accused to murder Nicholas Bailey?'

'No.'

There's a shuffling sound up in the public gallery. I look up and see some of the Bailey firm near the door shifting along the back row. George Preston comes in and sits at the end of the row. Dave looks up and sees his father, staring down at him.

The prosecuting counsel says, 'It has been alleged in this court that you forced the accused to kill Bailey because you lacked the courage to do so yourself. Is that true?'

Dave's still looking at his father.

The prosecuting counsel says, 'Is that true, Mr Preston?'

Dave's eyes harden and he straightens his shoulders. He looks at the barrister and says, 'No. I done him myself.'

There's a moment's hush and then everyone's talking at once. The judge bangs on the desk and shouts, 'Silence in court!'

It goes quiet and the judge says to Dave, 'Mr Preston. Are you admitting, before this court, to the murder of Nicholas Bailey?'

'Yes,' says Dave.

The judge writes something down, bangs his hammer down and calls for silence again.

Without looking up, he says, 'Take him down.'

Two ushers escort Dave out of the witness box and through a door at the back of the court.

The judge turns to me and says, 'Miss Walker, you are free to go.'

• • •

Downstairs, they try to take me back to Holloway to get my bits and pieces, but I tell them to get stuffed and walk out. I go along Old Bailey and turn into Newgate Street. The sun's shining and the air's fresh and people are coming and going. I feel like I'm light as a feather and on top of the world and even the cars and the buses look fresh and new. Then I hear my name called and I turn round. Lizzie's standing there and I run to her and throw my arms around her and we're laughing and kissing. People are staring at us and so we quieten down and lean against the wall of a bank and she's smiling her gorgeous smile and squeezing my hands in hers and we don't even need words.

After a while, she looks at her watch.

'I've got to go, love. I'm late for a client at the Dorchester. Will you come to mine later?' she says.

I nod and kiss her again, then I watch her hail a cab and jump in it. I'm so excited I feel like I'm going to fly up in the air, so I go into a pub and order a whisky to calm me down, only then I remember I've got no money.

Just as I'm telling the barmaid to leave it, a voice behind me says, 'I'll get that for you, Rina.'

I turn round. It's George Preston and two of his firm and suddenly I'm back on the ground with a bump. I move back against the bar and they stand round me.

George says to the boys, 'Wait in the car.'

He buys two large whiskies and nods to a table at the back of the pub. He sits down opposite me, takes a drink and looks at me for a bit.

Then he says, 'He was always a stupid little cunt.' I can't help smiling.

He says, 'Still, he done the right thing in the end.'

He leans forward, puts his arms on the table and looks into my eyes like he can see right into me. I know he's as hard as they come, but I don't feel scared. I look into his cruel eyes and say nothing, but I'm starting to get the feeling of how my life's going to be.

He sits back, takes a drink and has a look round the pub, then he smiles at me.

'I've got a bit of work for you.'

27

The road is straight and fast. The truck muscles along through the flat scrublands. After a few hours, I stop at a roadside food stand on the edge of Torreon. I go to Pilar's window with a peace-offering of burrito and coffee. She takes the coffee and allows me the trace of a smile. When we've eaten and started moving, she slides across the seat and sits next to me with her hand on my knee. I feel greatly relieved and able to turn the self-loathing down to a tolerable level. I let the road hypnotise me and we make good time. I switch on the radio hoping for more Santana, but have to settle for Pilar's choice of Ritchie Valen's nasal heartache. Eight hours later, after another fuel stop, we leave the scorched desert and blend into the light traffic on Highway 45 into Ciudad Juárez, the border-crossing town on the Mexican side next to El Paso, where Pilar wants me to leave her.

I have three hours before I have to meet Lee. As we near the centre of town, I turn off the main road into an alleyway between two tall buildings where I can park. I kill the motor, find the piece of paper Rodrigo gave me and check the location of the rendezvous at the filling station on Alameda Avenue and Prado Street, where Lee will be waiting. I need a street guide so that I can find the nearest crossing point. Pilar walks to a shop and comes back with a street guide of Juárez and another of El Paso. Between the guide and the map, I can see that Highway 45 continues through town to the crossing point at the Bridge of the Americas. From there it is probably a half hour drive to Alameda Avenue and the filling station on the corner of Prado.

Pilar is turned away, looking out of the window.

Knowing that it is almost time to part, I say, 'We have some time. Shall we find a bar?'

'They do not allow women in a cantina.'

'A café?'

She turns to me and tears well up in her eyes. She looks so very frail and vulnerable and I know that I love her.

She says, 'I am sorry for what I said.'

'I know.'

After a moment she dries her eyes and smooths down her hair. 'I should go now.'

'Wait.'

I move over to her and put my arm round her. 'Do you know anyone here?'

'No.'

'Will you be OK?'

'I think so.'

I want to speak, but can't find words. She reaches for the door handle. I try to let her go, but I can't. She relaxes and curls into me and we kiss deeply, clinging to each other. I feel her pulling away from me and opening the door. I watch her walk away down the alleyway and then she turns the corner and is gone.

I back the truck onto the main road and drive towards

the border. I stop at traffic lights, punch the steering wheel and batter my fists against the roof of the cab until I notice a military jeep full of soldiers nearby, and content myself with gouging my finger into the spider bite on my ankle to force back the darkness.

In the centre of town I park on a main street and buy a suitcase and some clothes, in case of a search by customs, and a roll of duct tape. I find a quiet street and tape the Colt to the top edge of a chassis member. I follow signs to El Paso and soon I am waiting in the queue for one of the check points at the border. Vendors weave in and out of the cars offering peanuts, corn on the cob and all kinds of fruit. I buy a couple of oranges and peel one as we creep towards the Mexican border post.

Customs men lean out of windows and check papers. Some of the trucks get a cursory search, but mostly people are let through quickly. I get to the window and show Caroline's passport to the official. He glances at it and waves me through. I proceed to the American post and an obese and mean-looking American customs man studies the passport and then casually searches the truck and the suitcase. He comes up empty, stamps the passport, gives me a look of mild revulsion and admits me to the United States of America. I leave the bridge and drive into El Paso feeling very alone.

I consult the street guide and make my way to Alameda Avenue. I stop at an intersection while a girl in a wheelchair is pushed across the road in front of me, and I think of Georgie and wonder where the hell she could have gone.

I drive south east, roughly parallel with the border, on a wide two-lane road, flanked by a mix of lowline blocks of houses, factory yards and container depots, interlaced with trees and patches of open wasteland.

It's just past eight o'clock when I reach the junction with Prado Street. I see the filling station on the corner and a small blue car parked behind a tanker at the back of the forecourt next to a tall wire fence. I can see Lee's blond head leaning against the door pillar. I drive in and park alongside him.

He winds down the window and says, 'Great timing. How are you?'

'Ready to go home.'

'That's what we're here for.'

'Everything cool?'

'Yes.'

He gets out of the car, goes to the boot, takes out a leather briefcase, walks round the back of the truck and gets into the cab beside me. He opens the briefcase, lifts the lid to show me it is full of dollar bills and snaps it shut again.

'Nice briefcase,' I say.

'He appreciates a touch of class.'

'Is that a million?'

'In a way, yes, in another way, no.'

'Lee …'

'It's counterfeit.'

'Oh, Christ.'

'But good. The best in fact. Confiscated from the

master. He'll never know.'

'OK.'

'You only need to show it to him, anyways.'

'Do you know about the truck swap?'

'Yes. Did you see the coke?'

'I saw the containers being welded to the truck.'

'Fenders and false gas tank?'

'Yes.'

'Good.'

He takes a piece of paper from his pocket and hands it to me. 'This is your route from here to the farmhouse. Does it match the location they gave you?'

I take out my piece of paper, look at both and say, 'Yes.'

'OK. It'll take about a half hour. You be there at nine and I'll take care of the rest.'

'Where will you be?'

He gets out of the truck and says, 'Don't worry about it.'

He gets into his car, starts the engine, reverses into a tight turn and accelerates across the forecourt. Horns blast as he cuts into the out-of-town traffic.

I open the briefcase and look at the money. I take a hundred dollar bill from my pocket and compare it with a snide one. I can see no difference. Even when I hold them both up to the light, they appear identical.

I slide the briefcase under the seat and look at my watch. It is eight fifteen and I don't want to be early to the meeting. I go to the filling station office and buy a cup of coffee. I sit in the truck and feel how much I miss Pilar's touch. I know I'll never change the way I live and I offer a hope that she finds happiness.

At eight thirty, I crush the coffee cup, crawl under the truck and retrieve the Colt. I drive off the forecourt, turn right onto Alameda, follow the directions and go south on Interstate 10. Twenty miles later, I reach exit forty-nine and turn east. After five miles on a two lane country road, I am looking for a shack on the right with a dirt track beside it. I find the shack, turn onto the track and bump along through arid scrubland for three or four miles until I see the farmhouse at the end of the track. As I approach the house, I can see that most of the roof has fallen in and one of the two outbuildings has collapsed in a pile of rubble. Rusting oil drums, bails of wire and the skeleton of a dead chicken litter the yard in front of the house. Behind the outbuildings, a derelict yellow mechanical digger stands wrapped in the sinewy limbs of some thorny desert creeper, as if the plant had pounced on it and suffocated it.

I stop the truck, kill the engine and wait. I wind down the window and let the Texas breeze ruffle my hair. A brown snake slithers across the track in front of me and disappears under a bush. A bird trills in the silence. In the mirror, I see a mockingbird, sitting on the tailgate of the truck. It flies off as a white pick-up truck appears out of a dust cloud and draws nearer.

There are two figures in the cab. I reach under the seat for the Colt and put it in my back pocket. The truck pulls past me and stops.

Guido gets out, comes to my window and says, 'You search the house?'

'No,' I say.

'Wait,' he says. He takes an AK from the truck, walks to what remains of the front door, pushes it open and goes inside.

I get out of the truck and look round, expecting Lee to appear, but there's no sign of him. Manuel's body sits in the passenger seat of the other pick up. Seen through the windscreen, he looks OK. If he hadn't been killed before my eyes, I would think he was alive.

I hear a burst of gunfire. I vault into the back of the truck, crouch down and peer round the cab. Guido is lying on the ground in front of the farmhouse. Lee and two armed DEA agents in dark blue overalls step out from behind an outbuilding and run towards the other truck.

Lee pulls open the door, points a gun at Manuel's head and yells, 'You're busted, you slimy son of a ... What the fuck?'

He pulls Manuel's inert body out of the seat and it falls to the ground, still in a sitting position. He turns and sees me.

'You fucking bitch!'

He raises his gun. I vault over the cab and aim both feet at his head. He steps aside, but I get a hold on his neck, pull him to the ground and try to wrestle the gun out of his hand. We roll around in the sand. He gets on top of me, pins me down and puts the gun to my head. I spin sideways, get hold of his balls and twist. As he shrieks in pain, one of the DEA agents grabs the gun, pulls Lee off me, and forces him back against the truck.

'You don't want to do this,' he says.

'Fucking cunt,' says Lee, as he sags against the tailgate holding his crotch.

The other agent points his gun at me and says, 'Stand up slowly.'

I get to my feet. He takes the Colt out of my back pocket, pushes me to the other truck, puts my hands on the bonnet and kicks my legs apart. He searches me, finds the passport and the box-cutter and walks me towards the house. Lee follows us, supported by the other agent.

We enter the house and I am pushed into a room at the back which was once a kitchen. The roof is open to the darkening sky. The agent pulls a deformed kitchen chair away from what the termites have left of a wooden table, places it against a wall next to a rusting stove, sitting under metal shelves, and pushes me towards it. I sit down as Lee and the other agent enter. Lee pushes the agent aside and stands in front of me.

He points his gun at me and says, 'Say goodbye, cunt.'

The agent who was supporting him steps forward and tries to grab his gun. 'This is murder, Lee!'

Lee shrugs him off, aims at my head and says, 'No one's gonna miss this piece of trash.'

The agent tries for his gun again and Lee turns and punches him. While his back is turned, I give my bracelet a twist, then I grab him round the neck, pull his head back and dig the blades into his throat just far enough to draw blood. The agents see the blood and move back. I pull Lee to the wall.

With my bracelet still at his throat, I look at the agents and say, 'Guns on the floor, over here!'

They take their automatics off their belts and lay them and their AKs down beside my feet.

'Now back off,' I say.

They stand by the side wall. The one who was trying to stop Lee killing me spreads his hands and gives me an imploring look.

'There ain't no need for this, lady, we can work this out ...'

'Where's your car?' I ask.

'Out back,' he replies.

'Throw me the keys.'

As he puts his hand in his pocket, a door opens at the far end of the room. Rodrigo enters and fires two shots. The agents fall and I let go of Lee. As he bolts for the door, Carmela appears and swings an iron bar into his stomach. Lee doubles over and goes down. Rodrigo's fist comes at me and the lights go out.

• • •

I feel a violent pain in my shoulders and open my eyes. I am hanging by my wrists, which are handcuffed to a pair of hooks on the wall, and my mouth is gagged. My legs are spread and I can't move them. Lee is tied to the chair. He is slumped forward, whimpering and moaning. Blood drips from his nose and mouth.

Rodrigo stands in front of him holding a pair of bolt cutters. Carmela is next to him, breathing hard and wiping blood off her knuckles. She holds one of Lee's hands out to Rodrigo. He raises the bolt cutters and there's a crunch as he cuts off a finger. Lee screams.

Rodrigo holds the finger up to Lee's face and says, 'You have any more friends in our country you are going to tell us about, or you want to lose your balls as well?'

Lee spits blood and slowly lifts his head. He looks over at me and says, 'Why don't you ask my boss?'

Carmela and Rodrigo turn and look at me. Carmela's stare would bore through metal. I try to speak, but can only make a faint groan behind the gag.

Rodrigo drops Lee's finger, opens the bolt cutters, moves towards me and says, 'We start with a breast?'

Carmela steps in front of him and says, 'Let me soften her up a little first.'

She comes towards me, taking off her singlet and shorts. She unties the gag, then she leans her stinking body into me and rips open my shirt and jeans. She delves into my groin then she holds three fat fingers up in front of my face, licks them and gives me a revolting grin. She forces the fingers into me and I lean against the searing pain and grip it hard. Each thrust grinds my back against the wall and wrenches my wrists against the cuffs. She mashes her mouth against mine and forces her tongue between my lips. I retch into her mouth. She spits, pulls out her fingers, then she backs off and says something to Rodrigo. He throws keys to her. She catches them and unlocks one of my wrists. I try to claw at her eyes with my free hand but she bites my wrist, takes hold of my neck and squeezes until I pass out.

I come round on my back on the floor and she's lying on top of me, thrusting her face at me and laughing maniacally. I go for her eyes again, but she punches me and my head swims. She sits up, turns round to face my feet, pins my arms down with her knees and lowers the part of herself that I least want to get close to onto my face. I fight for breath between her thighs as she bucks up and down on my face. As her massive breasts wallop and slap back and forth between her neck and her stomach, I get a glimpse of Rodrigo crouching down to get a better view. After accelerating her pelvic convulsions until I think my skull is going to fracture, she finally raises her head, spews forth a guttural roar of orgasm and collapses on top of me.

As I'm trying to lift her dead weight off me, an engine roars into life outside and light floods the room. Rodrigo shouts something and tries to pull Carmela off me. I slither out from under her and spit out hair and slime. As she gets to her feet, I stand, grab the hooks I was cuffed to, climb the wall and lie on top of it. I see headlights through the window opposite and hear the crack and snarl of branches breaking.

I make out the yellow digger erupting into life beneath its shroud of thorns. Rodrigo is looking through the window with Carmela beside him. I see the cast iron bucket rearing up outside with a snapping and splintering noise as its steel teeth chew through the spiney web that covers it. The tracks churn and the machine turns towards the house. The headlights blind me as the digger crunches over the wreckage towards us. Rodrigo fires through the window at the headlights and receives a barrage of lead in reply that thumps into the wall below me.

Carmela dives at Rodrigo and throws him to the floor. The digger advances. The bucket rises high into the night sky and then crashes down onto the top of the wall. An avalanche of bricks buries Carmela and Rodrigo. The digger's engine splutters and dies.

The silence is broken by the sound of some creature scurrying away on frightened feet. Through a haze of brick dust, I can see the outline of the digger's cab. The door flaps open and a small, nimble figure climbs down the side of the machine, makes its way over the pile of rubble and stands below me.

'All is safe now,' says Juanita.

Relief floods through me and I climb down the wall, fall into her arms and pass out.

I am diving headlong down a long metal shaft, twisting and turning somersaults. I come round suddenly and Juanita is sitting me on a chair. She strokes my forehead and massages my wrists and ankles. She puts a flask to my lips and I swallow whisky. My head clears and I try to connect the lean, black-clad figure in front of me, with a knife on her belt and an AK slung over her shoulder, with the demure little woman in her maid's uniform I knew at the mansion.

She says, 'I have worked for these beasts for years now

and I know what they do and how they do it. I have seen them destroy themselves with greed and ambition and their foolish rivalries. Now it is my turn to take what they have thrown away.'

'How did you do it?

'I knew that a time would come when I could make my husband take power from Manuel and when he did ...'

'You could take it from him?'

She nods, helps me to my feet and says, 'We must go. Can you walk?'

I stand, pull up my ripped jeans and button them. I take the DEA tracking device out of my pocket and drop it beside Lee's body, still tied to the chair and now with a bullet hole in his chest. There's just enough of my shirt left to tie at the waist. I take a couple of tentative steps and Juanita takes my arm.

'I'm OK,' I say.

'Come.'

She leads me out of the house towards the trucks. Guido is lying where he fell beside the truck he arrived in. Juanita crouches beside him and feels for a pulse in his neck. He moans a little and opens his eyes. He tries to speak, but can only make a faint croaking sound.

Juanita slides the bolt on her AK and points it at her husband. He reaches a hand towards her and opens his mouth to try to speak again. Juanita says something to him in Spanish and puts a single shot in his forehead.

She drops the gun beside her dead husband, turns to

me and says, 'The money is in your truck?'

'Yes.'

'Take it out, please.'

I take the briefcase out of the truck. 'Do you want to take the drugs?'

'I just want to get home.'

'I thought so.'

'It's not my line of work.'

'I understand.'

She reaches into her pocket and hands me my passport. Inside there is a first-class air ticket to London.

'I will take you to the airport.'

Something melts inside me and I feel faint and unsteady for a moment. Juanita puts a hand on the back of my neck and says, 'It is OK.'

I look at her and smile.

She says, 'Do you have the American passport?'

'It's buried in the house with one of those DEA agents.'

'No matter.'

She walks to the truck containing the cocaine, gets into the driving seat and beckons me over. I get in beside her and put the briefcase on my knee. She turns the truck round and we move off down the track towards the road.

'Where did you learn to drive a digger?' I ask.

'My father.'

'Really?'

'When my mother died, he would take me and my brother with him to his work. We would run errands and do odd jobs for the foreman and he would take us in the cab sometimes.'

'Is he still around?'

'No.'

The way she replies does not invite further inquiry and we continue in silence. We reach the main road and turn left.

I tap the briefcase and say, 'This million bucks is counterfeit.'

She looks over at me and says, 'You are sure?'

'That's what Lee told me, although it looks pretty good to me. He said it was printed by a top-class forger.'

She pulls the truck over. I open the briefcase and show her the money. She takes out a bill and examines it and then puts it back.

I shut the briefcase and she says, 'We will use it for bribes, they will not know.'

'We?'

She looks away quickly and I know that I've been taken. I suddenly feel very tired.

She turns to me slowly and says, 'We had to be sure you would be there.'

'She doesn't have a brother in Los Angeles.'

She nods. After a moment she says, 'She feels ...'

'Take me to the airport.'

'She wants you to know ...'

'Take me to the airport.'

I turn away from the woman who has just saved my life, grind my thumbnail into my forearm and wish I hadn't left the box-cutter at the farmhouse.

At the airport, I get out of the truck without a word. I take the suitcase I bought in Ciudad Juárez from the back, walk towards the domed entrance of the passenger terminal and go in through the glass doors, appreciating the slight drop in temperature as I walk across the marble floor. I look at the ticket and see that I fly Continental Airlines to Atlanta and then on to London. The departures board shows a flight to Atlanta leaving at midnight.

I go to the Ladies' room, wash off as much of Carmela's stinking residue as I can and change into fresh jeans and a cotton shirt. I change my remaining dollars for pounds at the currency counter, walk to the Continental desk on the other side of the concourse and put my ticket and passport on the desk. A platinum blonde with a bright smile and very white teeth checks me in. When she's done, she calls a male colleague who escorts me to the first-class lounge. After a club sandwich and several whiskies, I board a Boeing 707 and sink into soft leather. We roll down the runway and then the sudden thrust of the jet engines presses me back into my seat. I look out of the porthole and watch the lights of Texas falling away below me.

• • •

It's a little after six in the morning and getting light as the taxi pulls up in front of the house. I pay the driver, unlock the front door and go in. As I put my case down, I hear movement upstairs and then a door opening. A figure appears on the landing. I switch on the light and see

Graham, in his underpants, struggling to put on a shirt.

'Where is she?' I say.

Managing to get the shirt under control as he walks down the stairs, he says, 'There's a letter.'

'Who from?' I ask.

'I don't know, it just says 'She's at Portland'.'

'Show it to me.'

'It's in the kitchen.'

I follow him along the hall and into the kitchen. He picks up an envelope from the kitchen table and hands it to me. After almost twenty years, I recognise Claire's handwriting. I severed all links with Claire and Maureen after they grassed me for murder and testified against me, but this piece of paper tells me that Georgie didn't. I sit at the table and consider what to do. I need to know she's all right, even if that means confronting two people who were happy to see me hanged. I find my car keys and make for the front door.

Graham says, 'Er, where are you …?'

I open the door and say, 'I know where she is.'

'Shall I come?'

'Probably best if you stay here, just in case.'

'Right.'

'And put some trousers on.'

'Yes.'

'I'll call.'

I shut the door and walk the short distance to the car.

The clock on the dashboard tells me it's seven fifteen as I turn off Holland Park Avenue. I park the car towards the far end of Portland Road. I never went back to the flat after I was acquitted, but as far as I know, Claire and Maureen never left. The flat was in Dave's name, so there wasn't much I could do about it. As I walk past the smart white houses towards the flat, I'm taken back to the days when this end of the street was dirty and dilapidated and home to thieves and chancers before the slum clearances and the new building in the sixties. I get to the front door, ring the middle bell of the three and wait.

The door opens and Claire is there. The beehive is gone and the hair is long and silky and feathered from a centre parting. She looks scared and starts to close the door.

I take a step forward, hold it open and say, 'I just want Georgie.'

'She's with Mum.'

Even though she looks frightened, there's a maturity and a determination in her face that I don't recognise from before.

'Let me in.'

'I can't.'

'Why.'

'Mum's very ill and if she sees you, she ...'

'Then send Georgie down.'

'Hang on,' she says and goes upstairs. A moment later she comes down again.

'She won't.'

'What do you mean?'

'Mum's near the end and she won't leave her.'

I know that unyielding side of Georgie when she's

resolved to do something.

I say, 'Is she eating?'

'Yes.'

'Properly?'

'She's a lot better.'

'Did you get her from the hospital?'

'We didn't even know she was there. She just turned up a couple of nights ago. We hadn't seen her since she went to Cambridge.'

'Tell her I'm back and Graham's waiting for her at home.'

'Yeah.'

'Will your mum be going into hospital?'

'She wants to die in her own bed.'

I look at the tears gathering in Claire's eyes and I know she's not only crying for her mother.

I say, 'Thanks for letting me know where she was.'

'I knew you'd be worried.'

She goes to say something more, but I turn and walk to my car.

As I drive home, I pass the end of our old street. The tenements have been knocked down and replaced with new council flats. I think back on how close Claire and I once were and what dangerous times we grew up in together all those years ago. I want to give my love to Maureen and tell Claire she's forgiven, but I know that we have to leave it in the past and go on. I drive away and turn the corner, and I don't look back.